Also by the Author

The Erin O'Reilly Mysteries

Tequila Sunrise: A James Corcoran Story

Fathers
A Modern Christmas Story

The Clarion Chronicles
Ember of Dreams

Italian Stallion

The Erin O'Reilly Mysteries
Book Nineteen

Steven Henry

Clickworks Press • Baltimore, MD

First publication: Clickworks Press, 2023
Release: CWP-EOR19-INT-P.IS-1.0

Sign up for updates, deals, and exclusive sneak peeks at clickworkspress.com/join.

Ebook ISBN: 979-8-88900-005-1
Paperback ISBN: 979-8-88900-006-8
Hardcover ISBN: 979-8-88900-007-5

For Dave and Marilyn, who made me part of their family.

Italian Stallion

Combine 1 oz. Campari, 2 oz. bourbon, and a dash of Angostura bitters into a mixing glass. Stir and strain into a chilled cocktail glass and serve..

Chapter 1

"You know, normal couples go out dancing," Erin O'Reilly said. "They eat out at fancy restaurants. They buy each other flowers and chocolates."

"That so?" Vic Neshenko replied. "I always wondered what normal people did." He shifted his rifle to his left hand and used his other hand to adjust his Kevlar vest. The vest was black, emblazoned with big white letters that read POLICE.

"Quit squirming around," Zofia Piekarski said. The petite blonde shot Vic an elbow. "We don't have enough room in here."

"I can't help it," Vic grumbled. "This damn thing is chafing me. I'm gonna get blisters."

"Better blisters than bullets," Erin said. "Look at Rolf. He's wearing a vest and he's not complaining."

"He never complains," Vic said. "Because he can't talk."

"Of course he can," Erin said, bending down to give Rolf an affectionate scratch behind the ears. "It's not his fault you don't know how to listen."

The German Shepherd tilted his head sideways to give Erin better access. His tongue was hanging out and he was panting, but it wasn't on account of his K-9 body armor or the crowded, stuffy van. Rolf was excited. He knew action was coming and he couldn't wait to get in on it.

"*Platz,*" Erin told him, giving him his German command to lie down. Rolf obediently laid his head between his paws, but his tail would not be restrained. It was whipping back and forth across the floor.

As Erin sat back and tried to get comfortable, she had to admit Piekarski had a point. The surveillance van was very crowded with Street Narcotics Enforcement Unit cops. Officer Firelli and Sergeant Logan were the lucky ones; they got to ride up front, where there were actual seats and headrests. The others—Erin, Vic, Rolf, Janovich, and Piekarski—were in back, stuffed in among SNEU's snooper equipment, weapons, and other gear.

The van itself was more than a decade old, painted a shade of brown that reminded Erin of clogged toilets in subway restrooms. A few months back, the van had taken some rounds during a shootout. A cheapskate mechanic had slapped sheet metal over the holes without even trying to match the color. If the intention had been to create an inconspicuous vehicle, Erin thought, they'd failed. This was the sort of van you wouldn't just remember. If you liked cars, it would follow you into your nightmares.

"So tell me more, Erin," Vic said, twisting his shoulders awkwardly. He was a big guy and there really wasn't enough room for him. "What else do these normal people do? Do they go to bars?"

"Yeah," Erin said.

"How about strip clubs?" Janovich asked.

"Those, too," Erin said, looking directly at Vic. "Especially for the bachelor party."

"I don't think that's a good idea," Vic said.

"You don't want a bachelor party?" Janovich asked.

"We're not even engaged!" Vic protested.

"Choose your next words very carefully," Piekarski advised.

"I'm not talking about bachelor parties," Vic said. "I'm talking booze. We're sitting here, bored out of our minds, armed to the friggin' teeth. Now imagine if we were all hammered. Next thing you know, we're monkeying with our guns and we've got half the wedding party in the hospital with GSWs. That's if we were getting married."

Everyone shut up for a few moments. Erin tried to avoid looking at Piekarski's midsection. The other woman wasn't showing yet, and it'd be hard to tell under her body armor in any case, but Piekarski and Vic were facing an unavoidable biological deadline.

"I'm still surprised you guys are working the day shift," Erin said at last. "I thought you only did nights."

"Timing of the tip," Piekarski said. "We're cruising on caffeine right now. Believe me, I'd rather be sleeping."

"Bullshit," Vic said. "You'd never want to miss the action."

"Speaking of action…" Piekarski said. She banged on the thin metal wall that separated the front of the van and putting her face up to the little mesh-covered window in it. "Hey, Sarge! Anything going on yet?"

"Not yet," Logan replied. "But don't fall asleep back there. This was a good tip."

"I hope so," Vic muttered.

"Firelli has his ear to the street," Piekarski assured him. "If he says there's a delivery going down, he's right."

"Thanks for bringing us along," Erin said. "Vic was getting bored. So was Rolf."

"Yeah," Piekarski said, patting Vic's cheek. "I know how he gets. All work and no play."

"We haven't taken down a perp since that Mafia jerk," Vic growled. "Another day or two and I was gonna have Erin put on the bite sleeve."

"You help with Rolf's training?" Piekarski asked.

"Sometimes, yeah. But I was gonna be the one chewing on her arm."

"How sweet," Erin said. To tell the truth, she was just as happy as Vic and her K-9 to get out of the office. The last major incident they'd been involved in, a bomb blast which had destroyed a car and apparently killed the only eyewitness to a murder, had resulted in the entire Major Crimes squad being temporarily benched.

Captain Holliday had explained it as a question of optics. Internal Affairs had cleared Erin of any culpability in the explosion, but the result had still been a serious dent in the state's case against the son of a prominent Mafia boss. A slap on the wrist was both inevitable and necessary.

The whole thing was absurd, for three reasons. Erin had been culpable in the bomb; in fact, she'd set it up with her boyfriend's help. Morton "Cars" Carlyle might be retired from the IRA, but he hadn't forgotten how to build a car bomb. However, the bombing had been a fake-out. They'd swapped out their witness at the last moment for an unidentified cadaver. That witness was somewhere safe and warm right now, probably sitting on a beach sipping cocktails with Carlyle's best friend. Erin's only concern for the woman's wellbeing was that Corky Corcoran was bound to be hitting on her, in spite of Erin's specific instructions. That was just Corky being Corky.

Last, but not least, Captain Holliday himself had been in on the scheme and had personally approved it. And Vic hadn't even been involved; he'd shown up at the last minute, just in time to see the fireworks. So for the two of them to be punished by being placed on the dreaded "modified assignment" was deeply unfair. But there was no point whining about it. Sometimes you just had to take your lumps, even when you didn't deserve them.

It was part of the Job.

Even a couple of days was a long time for cops like Erin and Vic to shuffle paperwork, and it was particularly hard on Rolf, who'd been completely innocent. The Shepherd's sad brown eyes had remorselessly tracked Erin every hour of those endless days.

Thus, when Piekarski asked Vic if he wanted to ride along on an SNEU stakeout of a suspected heroin dealer, Erin had seized the opportunity to accompany them. Now they were in the back of SNEU's van in a back alley in Little Italy. They were still bored, but at least there was the promise of action in the near future.

"These guys aren't Lucarellis, are they?" was the only concern Erin had expressed when she'd climbed into the van.

"Nah," Firelli had said. "These are freelancers, just setting up shop. Hell, we're probably doing the Oil Man a favor by taking them off the street. We're eliminating his competition."

Erin didn't like the idea of helping Vinnie "The Oil Man" Moreno, but the head of the Lucarellis thought Erin was a crooked cop, so for now, it suited her purposes. So she'd nodded and kept her mouth shut.

"We should've brought a deck of cards," Janovich said.

"Like you know how to play poker," Piekarski said.

"I'm a great poker player," Janovich said. "I'm just unlucky."

"He blew five grand in Atlantic City once," Piekarski told Vic.

"*Really* unlucky," Janovich said. Like the rest of the SNEU squad, he was in plainclothes, wearing his shield on a chain around his neck. Erin, Vic, and Rolf were the only ones wearing vests openly. The others' armor was concealed under their coats.

"If you've got consistently bad luck, it's not luck," Erin said.

"Hey guys, put a sock in it," Logan said through the screen. "We got company."

The squad immediately quieted down, becoming all business. SNEU had a reputation as reckless cowboys, but they were trained professionals at heart. Vic hefted his rifle. The rest of the team drew their sidearms. Erin press-checked her Glock, racking the slide just far enough to confirm a round was chambered.

"We've got a white panel truck," Firelli reported. "Two guys up front. They're backing into the alley across the street. Looks like they're going to the loading dock."

"Wait until they park," Logan said. "We need to confirm their destination."

"Where do we think they're going?" Erin asked quietly.

"The White Stallion Nightclub," Piekarski said. "Firelli's guy says it's a front. Under new management as of last week."

"How many guys we dealing with?" Vic asked. "Besides the two in the truck."

"Don't know," Janovich said. "At least one, maybe more."

"We should have backup," Erin said.

"Why do you think we brought you folks along?" Piekarski asked. "This is how we roll in SNEU."

"Okay," Logan said. "They stopped. They're getting out of the truck. Showtime."

The van's engine coughed reluctantly to life, sputtering and vibrating unhappily. The smell of exhaust filled the interior.

"You guys gotta get a new ride," Vic groaned.

"Hey, you wanted to be here," Erin reminded him as Firelli put the van in gear. The rustbucket lumbered across the street. Firelli wasn't driving quickly, not yet. The whole point of the van was that it didn't look like a police vehicle. He'd try to get as close as possible without spooking their targets.

In back, Erin clenched her jaw and waited. It was all she could do. She couldn't even see out of the van. She hoped Logan knew what he was doing.

The van lurched to one side as Firelli clipped the curb. Erin's head smacked into the metal paneling and she winced. Then the van swung diagonally and came to an abrupt stop.

"Take 'em at the dock," Logan said. "Go!"

Janovich twisted the handle on the back door of the van, swinging it open. He jumped down and went around the vehicle. Vic and Erin were right behind him, Piekarski bringing up the rear. Rolf scrambled beside Erin, claws scrabbling in his eagerness.

The alley was narrow and Firelli had parked at an angle, blocking it almost completely. The officers squirted through the narrow gap at the van's back corner and rushed toward the dock, weapons ready. Behind them, Logan was getting out of the passenger seat. Firelli stayed behind the wheel, ready to drive if they had to run down an escapee.

Erin saw an unmarked white truck at a concrete loading dock. Two men were standing on the dock, staring at them. One was bent over, gripping the bottom of the sliding door, getting ready to pull it open. He stayed that way, frozen, a comical look of surprise stamped on his face. The other was upright, but also caught totally off guard.

It was a textbook bust, Erin thought. They had these guys cold. Everything was going exactly the way it was supposed to. She felt the old thrill of action, the spike of hot adrenaline. It felt so damn good to be out on the street, making moves.

Then somebody shouted "Gun!" and everything went straight to hell.

A pistol went off, three quick shots, the echoes bouncing off the brickwork on both sides of the alley. Erin couldn't see any muzzle flash, had no idea where the shots were coming from. The guy standing on the dock went down in a heap. The other man screamed and dropped flat on the concrete. More shots were fired.

"Hold fire!" Logan shouted. "God damn it, hold—"

"I didn't shoot!" Janovich shouted back.

"Nobody did!" Piekarski yelled, which made no sense at all.

Then a man in a white shirt came out the back door of the nightclub. He had a pump shotgun in his hands. Two more shots went off. Erin took aim at him and slid her finger inside the trigger guard. She was uncomfortably aware that the alley had very little cover. If the gunman raised the weapon and pointed it at her or any of the other cops, she'd have no choice but to shoot.

"NYPD!" several of the squad shouted, voices overlapping.

The gunman turned, but he turned away. He wasn't even looking at Erin or her comrades. He was staring at something on the far side of the truck, something she couldn't see.

"Drop it!" Logan and Vic shouted in perfect unison.

Several guns fired, the echoes of the shots rolling across Erin's ears in a continuous cacophony. Chips of brick and clouds of dust exploded around the gunman, who convulsed violently as at least one bullet hit home. Erin saw blood blossom on the white fabric over his back. The man fell, twisting with the impact, and the muzzle of his gun swung toward the SNEU squad as he lost his grip with his left hand. The shotgun went off with a roar. The man slumped against the wall and dropped the gun, which clattered to the loading dock.

"Taking fire!" Piekarski yelled.

Erin's head was spinning. There were other shooters behind the truck. A rival gang? Lucarelli muscle, maybe? She had no idea.

"Vic!" she screamed.

Vic had dropped to one knee beside the alley wall, his M4 at his shoulder, looking for targets. He glanced Erin's way. "What?" he called back.

She pointed with her leash hand. "Active shooters!"

He nodded, got his feet under him, and rushed toward her. Rolf, at Erin's side, barked excitedly. His tail whipped back and forth, but he stayed with her, waiting for instructions.

Erin ran to the front of the truck, keeping low. A lot of people thought a car's bodywork would stop bullets. They were wrong. Modern cars were flimsy, made of plastic and thin sheet metal. Even a handgun could punch right through. But the engine block was solid. Erin crouched behind it and got ready. She could hear the SNEU officers all talking and shouting at once. Sirens wailed in the background, punctuated by still more gunfire. Backup would be there in seconds, seconds they didn't have.

Vic joined her, dropping down beside her. "Ready?" he asked.

"Yeah," she said. "Rolf, *platz*. On three?"

Vic nodded. "One... two... three!"

The two detectives came up side by side, bringing their guns in line. Erin didn't know what to expect; a bunch of bad-attitude gunmen seemed the most likely. What she saw was a trio of men with pistols, aiming and firing at the loading dock, holding the guns in two-handed grips. They were wearing ordinary street clothes, but they clearly knew what they were doing with their weapons. The guy in the middle had on a pair of sunglasses.

"Drop your guns!" she shouted, taking aim at the guy in the middle.

The middle guy's head turned her way. With the glasses screening his eyes, she couldn't tell what his expression was. He held up his left hand, palm toward her, but his right was still holding the pistol and it was pointed at her.

A shotgun blast came from Erin's left, followed by a volley of pistol fire at her back. At least, that was what she thought. Her ears were ringing from the echoes and she was having trouble placing the gunfire. But the man in her sights wasn't currently shooting, so she hesitated, finger tight on her trigger.

One of the gunmen behind Sunglasses Man saw Erin and Vic. He swung toward them, drawing a bead with his pistol, and snapped off a shot. The bullet ricocheted off the hood of the truck and tumbled between the two detectives.

Vic fired. The M4 was a powerful, accurate rifle, very similar to the so-called civilian AR-15. Vic was an excellent shot and the range was less than twenty yards. He might as well have been standing right in front of his target. The rifle round struck the man high up on the chest and went straight through, exiting in a fine spray of blood.

The third man cursed and fired twice at Vic, before Vic's target even had time to fall down. Erin, operating on reflex and training, shifted aim and pulled the trigger. Her Glock barked. A brass casing spun out the back. The slide snapped forward, chambering another round, and she fired again. Both rounds slammed home, perfect center-of-mass shots. The man toppled backward as if she'd slugged him with a baseball bat. His gun spun out of his hand.

Sunglasses Man let go of his pistol, letting it clatter to the pavement. He had his hands up now. Both his buddies were on the ground, writhing in pain.

"Cover me," Erin snapped to Vic. Keeping her Glock trained on the unwounded man, she walked quickly around the front fender of the truck. Rolf kept pace, his eyes on Erin in spite of the noise and confusion.

"Get down on the ground!" Erin snapped at the man. "On your stomach!"

"Hold it!" Sunglasses Man said. "You don't understand!"

"On the ground, or I'll put you there!" she shouted. "Now! Or I will shoot you!"

Her absolute sincerity was written on her face. He did the

only smart thing and dropped to his knees, then flat on his belly. He laced his fingers behind his neck in a gesture which showed he knew how this sort of thing went.

Erin looped her leash around her wrist and took out her cuffs, dimly aware that the shooting had stopped. Someone was screaming. It sounded like a woman.

"Vic, we need a bus!" Erin called without taking her eyes from her prisoner. "And a first-aid kit!"

Vic made no reply. Erin stood over her target and got ready to cuff him. Rolf watched the man balefully, hoping he'd try something.

"Officer, you're making a huge mistake," Sunglasses Man said. He started to twist his head toward her.

"Don't look at me!" she ordered. She'd heard it all before, and there was too much going on to take any notice of a criminal's bullshit. They had multiple gunshot casualties in the alley, not to mention an unknown number of living perps and unsecured weapons.

"Vic!" she said again. "Call Dispatch!"

There was still no response. The female voice kept screaming.

A thought penetrated the adrenaline-soaked fog of Erin's brain. As far as she knew, there were only two women in the alley, and she was one of them. If another woman was screaming, that could only be...

"Piekarski," Erin gasped. She glanced toward the truck

Vic was nowhere in sight.

"Shit," she muttered. "Shit, shit, shit." She holstered her gun and quickly cuffed the man at her feet, leaving him on the ground. Then she tried to think.

Backup would be there any minute. The sirens were very close. She couldn't do anything for Piekarski that Vic wouldn't already be doing. Her job was to guard these three shooters and make sure they didn't escape or die before the Patrol units arrived.

"Rolf!" she said. *"Pass auf!"*

That wasn't one of his more usual commands, but Rolf knew what it meant. He immediately went stiff-legged and attentive, staring fixedly at the man on the ground. He'd stand guard until she told him otherwise, and if any of the perps tried anything, he'd make them sorry they had.

"You stupid bitch," Sunglasses Man said.

"Shut up," Erin said absentmindedly. "Stay right there. Don't move an inch." She went toward the man Vic had shot. This guy had been writhing around at first, but now he was lying still, which wasn't a good sign. A pool of blood was spreading out around him.

"You stupid bitch," Sunglasses Man said again. "We're cops, you idiot. You just shot two of your own."

Erin went suddenly very cold inside. She dropped to her knees beside the wounded man and pulled his jacket open. Under the leather coat was a black Kevlar vest. Contrary to popular opinion, it wasn't bulletproof; just bullet-resistant. Against Vic's high-powered rifle at close range, it had been about as useful as tissue paper. On a chain around the man's neck hung a gold NYPD shield.

"Oh my God," she whispered. Erin O'Reilly was a tough woman. She'd seen plenty of violence and death in her twelve years on the street. But now her vision went gray. Nausea curled inside her like a sickening snake. She put out a hand to brace herself on the pavement, or she would've fallen over.

Dimly, as if from the bottom of a very deep hole, she heard Sergeant Logan. He was shouting something, but to her ears it was very faint.

"Officer down! We've got an officer down!"

Chapter 2

Just about the only thing to do with a chest wound was to put pressure on it, so that was what Erin did. Unfortunately, the man under her hands had taken a 5.56-millimeter full metal jacket round straight through, which meant he had both an entrance and an exit wound. She couldn't hold both of them at once. Her hands were already soaked with blood.

"I need help over here!" she shouted. "I need a medic! Right now!"

Sunglasses Man was saying something, but she didn't understand a word. It was literally gibberish to her. Out of the corner of her eye, she saw the other man, the one she'd shot, roll over onto his side. He clutched at his chest and sat up. Then he looked at her.

"It's okay," she said. "I'm a cop." That seemed a little redundant, given the big white POLICE label across her chest, but misidentification was the order of the day and she was taking no chances.

"So'm I," he said. He groaned and winced. "You shot me!"

"Did it go through your vest?" she demanded. She felt blood pulsing under her hands. That was both good and bad. The good news was that it meant the man's heart was still beating. The bad news was that he was losing an awful lot of blood with each beat. As blood pressure dropped, the heart sped up to try to bring it up again, which only made him bleed out faster.

He rubbed his body where the bullets had struck. "Don't think so."

"Then help me!"

Tires squealed. An NYPD blue-and-white screeched into the alley and stopped only a few feet short of Erin. Two uniforms sprang out, guns in hand. They paused, taking in the scene. More squad cars were arriving at both ends of the alley. Men and women were yelling excitedly on all sides. Blue and red lights were flashing all around.

"O'Reilly?" the driver of the first car asked, jogging toward her.

He looked vaguely familiar, but Erin couldn't place his name. That wasn't important right now. "This guy's one of ours," she said. "He took one in the chest, through-and-through."

"Copy that," he said. He keyed his shoulder radio. "Dispatch, we need a bus forthwith. Just off Grand and Elizabeth. Officer down."

"We copy," Dispatch replied. "Bus is en route. We've already got that one."

"No," Erin said. "We've got more than one."

"Dispatch, be advised, we have multiple NYPD casualties," the uniform said, remaining admirably calm.

"We copy," Dispatch said again. "All available EMTs are being routed to your location."

The other uniform got down beside Erin. "Okay, buddy," he said to the downed man. "You're gonna be fine. Help's on the way. What's his name?"

Erin gave him a blank look. "What?"

"His name," the cop said again.

"I don't know!"

"You don't know him?" the cop asked incredulously. "What the hell is going on?"

"His name's Plank," said the guy Erin had shot. He'd gotten shakily to his feet and staggered over to them. "Like the piece of wood. Melvin Plank."

"Okay, talk to him," the uniform said. "Keep him with us."

"I'll take over," the other man told Erin.

"You sure?" she asked. "You got shot. Twice!"

"I'm good. Vest stopped them." But he was breathing shallowly. He probably had at least one cracked rib.

Erin gave him a doubtful look.

He impatiently shouldered her aside, wincing as he did so. "This guy's my friend," he said. "I'll take care of him."

Erin yielded. She slowly stood up and turned. Something was going on over behind the panel truck, but she couldn't see what. The screaming had stopped. She didn't know if that was a good thing or not. Rolf, still guarding Sunglasses Man, cocked his head at her.

She had to see if her friends were okay. Erin glanced down at the wounded man. He was unconscious. His buddy was holding a hand over the bullet hole, talking to him quietly and intently. The thought struck her that only seconds before, these men had been enemies to be stopped, killed if necessary. The snake twisted in her guts again.

"Rolf, *fuss!*" she ordered. The Shepherd bounded immediately to her side. Then she ran back the way she'd come. She wasn't sure she wanted to see what was on the other side, but it was something she had to do.

The SNEU squad was in the middle of a cluster of uniformed officers. A dozen Patrol cops were now on scene. Most of them stood in a tight circle, but three were examining the bodies on the loading dock. Erin saw three men sprawled on the concrete. None of them were moving.

As she drew nearer, she saw Vic put a hand on Piekarski's shoulder. The blonde was on her knees. Piekarski turned toward him. Tears were streaming down the woman's face. Vic went down next to her and wrapped his arms around her. His rifle, forgotten, lay on the pavement behind him.

Sergeant Logan stood a short distance off, a blank look on his face. His eyes were fixed staring into the middle distance at something only he could see. He was very pale. Firelli was kneeling across from Piekarski. He was holding one of Janovich's hands between his own.

Janovich lay flat on his back, eyes wide open. He looked startled, as if he'd suddenly noticed something surprising. His lips were slightly parted. A small, dark hole gaped just above the bridge of his nose. There was only a little blood.

Piekarski was sobbing into Vic's shoulder. The big Russian awkwardly patted her.

"Hell of a thing," one of the uniforms muttered. "Hell of a goddamn thing. At least it was quick."

"Jan," Firelli said quietly. He squeezed Janovich's hand and said it again. "Jan."

Erin just stood there, Rolf's leash dangling from one bloodstained hand. There was nothing for her to do, because there was so obviously nothing to be done. She and Vic weren't even supposed to be there. They'd probably get in trouble. But that was the very last thing she was worried about.

*   *   *

"There's ordinary crap, and then there's shitstorms, and then there's this," Lieutenant Webb said. "What were the two of you thinking?!"

"We were thinking of doing some police work, sir," Erin said.

"Don't answer rhetorical questions," Webb snapped. "And this is no time to be a smartass. Do you have any idea how big a deal this is?"

Erin figured this was another rhetorical question, so she kept her mouth shut. But it was a struggle. A dozen angry retorts tried to climb out of her throat. She swallowed them. She could have reminded Webb that Piekarski was crying her eyes out, that the only reason Janovich wasn't in a body bag yet was because Dr. Levine needed to examine him first, or that she and Vic had shot a pair of undercover cops. It was only by the grace of God that Vic's target hadn't died. The bullet had clipped the man's lung, however, and it'd be touch and go. She didn't need to be reminded this was a big deal. But she said none of it.

Webb had arrived with remarkable speed, but Captain Markos of Precinct 5 had beaten him there, as had Internal Affairs; both the Five's IA squad and Lieutenant Keane from Erin's own Eightball were on the spot. Everywhere Erin looked, she saw serious-looking gray-haired cops wearing expensive suits.

"Did you give your statement and surrender your weapon?" Webb demanded.

"This isn't my first OIS, sir," Erin said. Officer-involved shootings had become way too familiar.

"And they got a blood sample and breathalyzer?"

"Yes, sir." She felt enormously tired, and more sober than she wanted to be. She really wanted a stiff shot of Carlyle's top-shelf whiskey. It might steady her nerves.

"You're on modified assignment, obviously," Webb went on. "Not that you weren't already. Damn it, O'Reilly!"

"I didn't kill anybody, sir. Neither did Vic."

"Yet," Webb said coldly.

Erin winced.

"Sorry," Webb said, his eyes softening ever so slightly. "That was out of line. But you have to understand, this one's going all the way to the top. The Police Commissioner's going to have it on his desk before the end of the day. We're not just talking disciplinary action. Heads are going to roll. Some people are going to lose their jobs over this, and there might even be indictments."

"We didn't do anything wrong, sir," Erin said stiffly. "The PC is going to be on our side. They didn't identify themselves until we had them down and in cuffs. They shot at us, sir!"

Webb sighed and fingered one of his ever-present unlit cigarettes. "And what will you do when their recollections don't match yours? Because I guarantee they won't."

"There might be security camera footage of the incident," she said.

"Security cameras? Overlooking a suspected drug den? That seem likely to you?"

"I guess not," she said.

Webb's tone warmed a little more. "How are you holding up?"

"One of ours got killed," she said. *And I shot a cop,* she wanted to add.

"How well did you know him?"

She swallowed. "Too well."

He laid a hand on her shoulder. "That's rough. How about Neshenko? Where is he, anyway?"

"With Piekarski, I think. I don't know. We haven't talked about it."

Webb nodded. "You understand, as long as you're on modified assignment, this can't be your case."

"Then they'd better clear me for duty soon," she growled. "I'm not riding the bench on this one. Sir, who were those guys?"

"Organized Crime Task Force," Webb said grimly. "And don't mess around with them. They've got political clout from One PP. They've got good contacts with the Feds. They walk on air and their shit doesn't stink. You copy?"

"I copy, sir."

Webb looked her in the eye for a long moment, trying to read her unspoken thoughts. She stared back, not even trying to hide her anger.

He nodded. "All right," he said. "You lucked out. The guy you shot is going to be fine. You just popped him twice in the vest and neither round penetrated. All he's got is bruises. So you're in the clear, or ought to be."

"What about Vic?"

"What about him? If the officer he shot doesn't pull through, he's done. Finished."

"That's not fair, sir!"

"You're not a whiny toddler," Webb said sharply. "And nobody cares if you think it's fair. Think about it. Do you seriously think Neshenko could ever walk into a squad-room again if he kills one of ours? Do you think he'd want to? It doesn't matter whose fault it was. That's just the way the cards fall on this one. I'm not happy about it either. He's a thug, but he's a damn good detective if you dig deep enough. And we're shorthanded as it is. I'll do what I can for him, but right now your brother and his team are Neshenko's best chance of keeping his pension."

Erin nodded. Her brother the trauma surgeon was probably already operating on Officer Plank. There was nobody on Earth she'd rather have holding the scalpel when the chips were down.

"What should I do, sir?" she asked.

"Go home."

"I can help."

"That wasn't a suggestion. It was an order. Go. Now. Before

Keane or one of his flunkies corners you. You've already given your statement. There isn't a thing you can do for Neshenko. IAB may need to talk to you for a follow-up. Don't say another word to them without a Union lawyer beside you. And stay as sober as you can."

"Is that an order, too?"

"No, that was advice." He shook his head. "Don't beat yourself up about this, O'Reilly. None of this was your fault."

She disagreed with that assessment, but he held up a hand and she kept her lip buttoned. She nodded tightly.

"Yes, sir," she said.

"And keep your phone on you."

"Copy that, sir."

* * *

Carlyle took one look at Erin's face when she walked into the Barley Corner. Then, without a word, he stood up from the bar, nodded to her, and led the way to his apartment. He went upstairs to his private liquor cabinet, took out a bottle of Glen D whiskey, poured a double for her and a single for himself, and sat down beside her on the couch. Rolf settled himself on the floor at her feet and rested his chin on her foot.

Erin drank most of the Scotch down at one go, Webb's advice be damned, and for once Carlyle didn't scold her for wasting his expensive liquor. She let the fierce heat work its way through her mouth and the back of her nasal passage, warming her from the inside out. Then she sipped what was left of her drink and shivered.

"Thanks," she said. "I needed that. How'd you know?"

He smiled gently. "It wasn't hard to figure, darling. Here it is, middle of your shift, broad daylight, and you come into my pub, pale as a banshee and with blood on your sleeves and under your nails. How bad was it?"

She grimaced. "Pretty goddamned bad. We got in a gunfight."

"With whom?"

"Freelance drug dealers. And some other guys in the NYPD."

He raised his eyebrows. "Friendly fire?"

"Something like that. We were both hitting the same guys at the same time and nobody knew it. Rotten luck. The wires got crossed somehow, and next thing you know, everybody's shooting everybody else. I shot a cop."

"Sweet Jesus." Carlyle laid a hand on her arm. "Is the poor blighter breathing?"

"Oh, he'll live," she said bitterly. "And maybe the guy Vic shot will, too. But Janovich won't. Caught one right in the face. Bam. He was gone before the ambulance got there. Before he hit the ground, probably."

"I see." Carlyle's composure remained unruffled, but his eyes were deeply concerned. "How can I help you?"

She shrugged. "Beats me. They sent me home. I guess the Lieutenant gets to fly solo on this one. That's assuming IAB lets him so much as tie his own shoes. Internal Affairs will probably take point."

"They're pushing you aside?"

"Yeah. So you might as well pour me another. I've got plenty of reasons to drink and not a one to stay sober. Well, Webb told me not to get drunk. But screw him."

"I think perhaps—" Carlyle began, but was interrupted by Erin's phone.

"Son of a bitch," she growled, fumbling at her pocket. "If it's Lieutenant Keane or another of those IAB bastards, they can kiss my ass, and I'll tell them so."

She was surprised to see Vic's name on the caller ID. Holding up a hand for silence, she thumbed the screen.

"O'Reilly," she said.

"Where are you?" Vic asked. His voice was quiet, calm, controlled. Erin wasn't sure she'd ever heard Vic speak in that tone of voice before. It gave her a chill.

"At home," she said. "I just got here a couple minutes ago."

"How fast can you get to my place?"

"Fifteen, twenty minutes. Vic, what's going on?"

"Do it. And bring your dog." Then he hung up.

Erin stared at the phone. "That was weird," she said.

"More trouble?" Carlyle asked.

"Probably. I'd better get going."

"Erin, darling?"

She paused in the act of getting to her feet. Rolf, feeling her balance shift, was already up, tail wagging, ready for action.

"What?" she asked.

"I love you. Be careful."

"Why'd you say that?"

"I said it because it's true."

"No, not the part about love. The other thing. You don't usually say that."

"The thought's occurred to me that this may not have been an accident."

"You think other cops might be trying to whack me?" she asked in disbelief. "You think this was a setup?"

"I think you should check under your car, just in case."

Chapter 3

Erin wanted to think Carlyle was just being paranoid, but she knew for a fact there was at least one dirty FBI agent in the neighborhood. She also strongly suspected there were dirty cops, both at the Five and the Eightball. So maybe it wasn't paranoia.

Regardless, she'd made a habit of having Rolf sniff around her car before she got into it. The chances of a car bomb were remote, but not zero, and it only took a few moments. Rolf finished his search without alerting, so she loaded him into his compartment and slid behind the wheel.

Vic's apartment was a classic bachelor pad: a studio apartment full of rumpled clothes, scary survivalist literature, a big-screen TV, and the heavy smell she could only define as "essence of Neshenko." It was a mix of vodka, deodorant, and machismo.

When he opened the door in answer to her knock, she saw with some surprise that he'd cleaned up a bit. The *Soldier of Fortune* magazines were neatly stacked next to the couch, only a little laundry was lying around, and he'd even hung an air freshener from the ceiling fan.

But if the room looked better than usual, Vic looked worse. His jaw was set so tight she could see the taut lines of muscle in his cheeks. His eyes were like dark marbles. Behind him, on his ratty little secondhand couch, Piekarski was sitting. The SNEU cop didn't look up. She had her pistol disassembled on Vic's IKEA coffee table and was in the process of putting it back together.

"Hey, Vic," Erin said.

"C'mon in," he said, stepping to one side.

Erin and Rolf entered the room. Erin looked around for a place to sit and didn't find one. The couch was a two-cushion love seat and Erin wasn't sure Piekarski wanted her to take the vacant spot. Vic lacked dining room furniture. He didn't even own an armchair.

"Here," Vic said, grabbing a folding metal chair out of a corner. "Thanks for coming."

Piekarski snapped the slide into place on her Sig-Sauer, shoved the magazine into the grip, chambered a round, and holstered the gun. Then she did look at Erin. Her eyes were red and a little puffy, but dry.

"Sorry about Janovich," Erin said lamely. It was totally inadequate, but so was anything else she might have said.

"Thanks," Piekarski said. Her lips were drawn tight across her teeth.

"Vic?" Erin said. "What am I doing here?"

"We're going to figure out what happened today," Vic said. "And we're going to take down the bastards who made it happen."

"Vic, it was a stray bullet," she said. "It sucks, but that's part of the Job. And what difference does it make? All the perps are dead."

"Not all of them," he said darkly.

"You mean the undercovers?" she asked.

"If that's what they are," Piekarski said.

"Webb told me they were with the Organized Crime Task Force," Erin said. "He specifically ordered me not to screw with them."

"Okay, fine," Vic said. "You want out, go. The door's right behind you."

"That's not what I meant," she said, bristling. "But I want to know what I'm getting into here. This is going to be in the papers, Vic. That means it's going to go political. The PC probably already knows what happened."

"No, he doesn't," Vic said. "Because nobody knows what happened. Not even us, and we were there."

"IAB is investigating," she said.

"And they're so helpful and trustworthy," Vic said. "When I go to bed, I have them come over and tuck me in with a glass of warm milk and a bedtime story."

"Erin, they never said they were cops," Piekarski said. "They never even tried to make an arrest. One of them yelled 'Gun!' and they just started shooting. Did you see a gun?"

"Yeah, the one guy had a shotgun," Erin said.

"He didn't come out until after the shooting started," Piekarski said. "And neither of the other two was holding a weapon at the start."

"They both had pistols," Vic said. "Stuffed in their waistbands. One of them managed to get his out and fire a couple shots before our guys put him down. But like Zofia said, that was after."

"These guys didn't act like cops," Piekarski insisted. "They didn't want to make arrests. They came to kill the perps. And if they hadn't thrown down like that, Jan wouldn't have been hit."

"That's why this is a job for IAB," Erin said. "Keane's an asshole, I agree a hundred percent, but he's a smart, ruthless asshole. He'll figure it out."

"If you're gonna try to convince me of that, try to at least sound like you believe it yourself," Vic said. "Look, are you in or out?"

"I'm in," Erin said. "You've saved my ass plenty of times. Hell, you gave my brother's wife the shirt off your own back. Of course I'm in. I just don't want to see you get burned on this. Face it, Vic, you're not the world's most diplomatic guy."

"Thank you."

"That wasn't a compliment. Listen, you know that frat-boy thing?"

"Yeah." Vic finally cracked a slight smile. "I remember that rapist you Tased in the nuts. That was a good one."

"I haven't heard that story," Piekarski said, and Erin was glad to see both of them taking an interest in something other than payback.

"Some other time," Erin said. "My point is, I stepped outside the lines on that one and if it had gone bad, I might've lost my shield over it."

"For real?" Vic asked.

"Yeah. Holliday told me himself. So I have to ask you, Vic. Is this worth it?"

"I'm pretty sure these assholes executed a couple of guys today," he said. "And when we got in the way, Janovich got nailed. It could just as easily have been you, or me, or Zofia. Hell yes, it's worth it. If these punks are hiding behind the shield, I'm taking them down."

"Okay," Erin said. "But we have to be smart about this."

"Meaning what, exactly?" Piekarski asked.

"I'm guessing you're on admin leave, too?"

"Yeah," the other woman said gloomily. "The whole squad's been benched."

"So we can't work this like a normal case," Erin said. "We need to be discreet."

"I'm discreet," Vic said.

"You're about as discreet as a jackhammer," Erin said. "We have to be really careful nothing leaks. Otherwise, the Organized Crime guys will hear about it and we'll be cooked. That means no official requests to anyone we don't trust a hundred percent. No calling Dispatch for anything unless it's life-or-death. We fly under the radar."

"Like working a deep undercover operation," Piekarski said, nodding. "I'm game."

"The good news is, nobody's expecting much from us until we're cleared for regular duty," Erin said. "So we'll have some time, and not a lot of oversight."

"What's the bad news?" Vic asked.

"I only see three options," she said. "Either we're dealing with a tragic misunderstanding, in which case we'll end up chasing our tails and maybe getting the PC pissed at us; or it's a squad of dirty cops, which is going to really cause a stink that's going to get all over everybody; or it's a conspiracy, in which case we won't know how deep it goes or who to trust."

Vic, Piekarski, and Erin looked at each other. They said a lot with their eyes, though nobody said anything out loud for about fifteen seconds. Then, almost in unison, all three of them nodded.

"Let's do this," Erin said.

*   *   *

"Which way do we want to come at it?" Piekarski asked. They had Vic's laptop on his coffee table. The two women were seated on the couch. Vic was leaning over the back of the sofa between them, looking over their shoulders. Rolf, realizing no bad guys needed to be bitten just then, had curled up on the floor next to Erin and gone to sleep.

"How do you mean?" Vic asked.

"We can start with the cops, or we can start with the dealers," Erin said, seeing what Piekarski was getting at. "Either way, we're looking for motive."

"Have they identified the dealers yet?" Vic asked.

"Not that I know of."

"Then we'd better start with the cops," he said, not unreasonably.

"Melvin Plank," Erin said, entering the name into the NYPD's database. She didn't have access to his full service jacket, but she ought to at least be able to find his current assignment.

A portrait popped up on the screen, accompanied by a page of text. All three of them started scanning the document for relevant information.

"He works out of the Twelve," Piekarski said. "What the hell was he doing in the Five's backyard? That's our turf."

"Organized Crime Task Force," Erin reminded her. "Those guys can go anywhere in the city."

"But they're supposed to clear it with the local precinct if they're running an op," Piekarski said. "I don't think Captain Markos heard a thing. He seemed pretty pissed."

"Yeah," Vic agreed. "I saw him yelling at some suit from One PP."

"He's been on the Job a while," Erin said. "Ten years. Hey, this is interesting. He started out on the Patrol beat at the Five."

"In Little Italy?" Piekarski said. "That's a weird coincidence."

"No it isn't," Vic said. "I mean, it's weird, but no way it's a coincidence."

"In Major Crimes we don't believe in coincidence," Erin explained to Piekarski.

"Who's his current CO?" Vic wondered.

"Conrad Maxwell," Erin said, finding the relevant section of the personnel file. "Detective First Grade."

"Ooh, he outranks both of us," Vic said. "I hate him already."

"You hate everybody," Erin said.

"I do not!"

"Everybody not in this room."

Vic thought about that for a second. "Well, maybe," he said. "So who's this Maxwell punk?"

"Just a second." Erin typed in the name. A new face filled the screen. Even without the sunglasses, she recognized the man immediately.

"Isn't that the guy you arrested?" Vic asked.

"Yeah," Erin said. "Sunglasses Man. Let's see what we've got on him. Okay, he's a twelve-year vet. Looks like he came up from Patrol in Little Italy, too."

"Imagine that," Vic said dryly.

"He's got a commendation for valor," Erin said. "He used to be a Narc. A couple years back, he shot two dealers when a bust went sideways."

"Clean shooting?" Piekarski asked.

"That must be how IAB ruled it," Erin said. "Otherwise there's no way he'd still be on active duty. I'd love to see his fitness reports."

"Unfortunately, we don't have clearance for his report card," Vic said. "So unless you're tight with one of the higher-ups at the Twelve, or maybe the PC... What's on your mind, Erin?"

Erin didn't answer immediately. She was thinking about a Lieutenant she knew who was based at Precinct 12. He could definitely access Maxwell's files.

"She's planning something," Vic said to Piekarski. "You can always tell. She gets real quiet and her eyebrows crinkle up like that."

"Shut up, Vic," Erin said. "I'm trying to think."

"It's hard for her," he added.

"Screw you," Erin said. "I have a guy I can call."

"Is he solid?" Piekarski asked.

"I'd trust him with my life," she said, not mentioning the fact that she already did.

"Who is he?"

"I'd rather not say."

"What the hell is that supposed to mean?" Piekarski demanded.

"Easy, Zofia," Vic said with uncharacteristic tact. "Let it go. She's got her reasons."

"I just need to make a quick call," Erin said. "I'll be right outside."

Chapter 4

"Hello?"

"Hey, Phil," Erin said. "I'm fine."

She started every conversation with Phil Stachowski the same way. He was in charge of her undercover assignment, so every time she called him, there was a chance she was in some sort of trouble.

"Good. What's up?"

"I need a favor," she said, glancing up and down the hallway outside Vic's apartment. It was deserted. *God*, she thought. *I sound more like a mobster every day.*

"What can I do for you?" Phil asked. His voice was calm and reassuring. Erin had trusted him with some of her deepest, darkest secrets. He'd never let her down.

"I need everything you can get on Conrad Maxwell."

"Detective Maxwell?" Phil said in surprise.

"You know him?"

"I know him." Now Phil sounded more guarded. "Erin, what's going on here?"

"It's complicated," she said. "I need to know what's in his file. Not just the stuff I have access to."

There was a short pause. "If I'm hearing you right, you're asking me for the sorts of things only his CO would know," he said carefully. "Not to mention whatever Internal Affairs may have on him."

"That's right," she said.

"You're Major Crimes, Erin. Not IAB. You aren't cleared for this."

"So you're saying no?"

"If I'm going to do this, I need more. What do you suspect him of?"

"That's just the thing, Phil. I don't know until I see his file. Look, he and his squad screwed up a drug bust. Vic and I were riding along with SNEU. The whole thing turned into a real clusterfuck. His guys started shooting, so did the bad guys, and next thing we know, an SNEU cop is dead and one of Maxwell's guys is badly hurt. Not to mention three dead perps."

"And you think he's up to something shady?"

"That's what I'm trying to figure out."

"IAB will go over this with a fine-toothed comb," Phil said. "If he's got any red flags in their system, they'll come down extra-hard on him."

"So you're saying no," she repeated.

He sighed. "I don't want to. I want to give you every bit of support I can. But this limb is too shaky to go out on, for either of us. I'm protecting you, too. There could be all kinds of blowback on this, and the last thing you need right now is attention. We're almost ready to shut down your operation, thanks to our mutual friend. Everything going okay with him?"

"As far as I know." Phil was talking about Corky.

"Keep your eye on the ball, Erin. This is the bottom of the ninth. It's no time to go chasing wild pitches."

She rolled her eyes. "Now you sound just like my dad."

"Is he a baseball fan, too?"

"Of course."

"What would he tell you to do?"

It was her turn to sigh. "He'd tell me to stay in my own dugout and let IAB handle it."

"Your dad's a smart guy."

"Yeah, I know. Sorry to bother you."

"You can call me anytime. For any reason. You know that."

"Copy that. Catch you later."

"I'll be here, Erin."

Erin hung up. "Damn," she muttered, sliding the burner phone into her pocket. So much for having a card up her sleeve. She couldn't really blame Phil. It'd been a big ask. But now what could they do? It wasn't like they could just call up Internal Affairs.

She blinked. Maybe she could do exactly that. And maybe she did have a card to play after all. She pulled out her other phone, her main one, and called up a number she hadn't used in a while. It was a long shot, but she was confident the worst that could happen was another refusal. She took a deep breath and put the call through.

It rang once, twice. Then a woman answered.

"Jones."

"Hey, Kira," Erin said. "Long time no see."

"Erin?" Kira Jones sounded both surprised and pleased. That was promising.

"One and the same. How've you been?"

"Busy. I can't talk long, we've got this thing in Little Italy. It's going to be all over the evening news."

"Yeah, I know about that. It's the reason I'm calling."

"Oh, God. You're involved with that? I thought it was SNEU and Organized Crime."

"Vic and I tagged along with SNEU."

"Vic was there too?"

"Yeah."

"What a mess."

"That's one word for it."

"Did you... I mean, how involved were you?"

"I fired a couple of shots," Erin said. "But none of them did any permanent damage."

Kira's sigh of relief was audible. "Thank God for that. I'm not on scene. Keane left me back at the office. I can't really talk about the investigation, of course, but I'm starting to build background."

"That's why I'm calling."

"Oh?"

"I need to see an IAB file on one of the other officers."

"Erin, you know I can't do that. Not without permission from your Captain. In writing."

"Kira, this is important. I'm not asking an Internal Affairs cop. I'm asking an old friend."

Kira's voice dropped to a near-whisper. "Do you know what could happen if I gave you something like that? I could get demoted. Reassigned. Fired!"

"I swear, this is for the good of the Department," Erin said. "I give you my word, none of this is going to come back on you. No matter what."

"You can't possibly promise that." She paused. "What file did you want, anyway?"

"Conrad Maxwell. He's a Detective First Grade in Organized Crime. I just need to know what IAB had on him before today. If there was anyone else I could ask, I would. I'm sorry to pull you into this."

Kira hesitated. Erin held her breath. Kira Jones was a good cop with a razor-sharp mind, but she didn't have as much in the way of guts as Erin would have liked. Seconds ticked by.

"A cop died today," Erin said. "And this guy's got cover from higher up. If we run this through channels, he'll skate. I'm sure of it."

"I'll see what I can do," Kira said at last. "But if I find anything you shouldn't know, I'm not giving it to you."

"Copy that," Erin said, letting her breath out. "And thank you. I won't forget this."

"I won't let you," Kira said. "You owe me one. A big one. Tell you what. I'll get you what I can tomorrow morning. But we'd better not do this in-house."

"Deal. How about breakfast?"

"Sure thing. I'll come by the Corner. Seven-thirty?"

"See you then."

* * *

"Success?" Vic asked when Erin came back inside.

"I think so," Erin said. "But not with the channel I was planning on using."

"Who do you have to screw to get what we need?"

"Kira Jones. But that name doesn't leave this room. She's risking her job for us."

"That doesn't sound like the Kira Jones I know," Vic snorted. "The one I know doesn't like taking risks. Remember? That's why she transferred out of Major Crimes and started riding a desk."

"That's not fair," Erin said. "Not everybody's cut out for gunfights and explosions."

"They're not?" Piekarski asked. "Who is this you're talking about?"

"Former squadmate," Erin explained. "She ran with us for a few months. We took down some major bad guys together, but we had a few too many close calls and she got shook up and transferred out."

"Lost her nerve," Vic said. "I don't think we can trust her."

"She'd never betray us," Erin said. "Kira may not be a gunfighter, but she's loyal."

"She's IAB," Vic said, as if that settled the debate.

"And IAB is exactly who we need if we want the dirt on Maxwell," Erin shot back. "Or do you have a better plan for getting his files? Hack into the NYPD database, maybe? Break into One PP after hours?"

"No," Vic said sulkily.

"He's cute when he pouts, isn't he?" Erin asked Piekarski.

"He is that," Piekarski agreed.

"When do we get the files?" Vic asked.

"Tomorrow morning. She'll come by the Barley Corner for breakfast."

"What else do we have?"

"My squad's doing a thing for Jan," Piekarski said. "Tonight, at the Final Countdown, eight o'clock. Cops only. You guys are welcome."

"I'll be there," Vic promised.

"Me, too," Erin said.

Vic glanced at his watch. "We've got a few hours to kill before the get-together. Then, after that, you'll want some sleep before you meet with your snitch."

"She's not a snitch," Erin said.

"Oh, sorry. My mistake. You'll be meeting with your contact who's going to feed you sensitive information without official authorization. What would you call her?"

"A friend."

"Right. Anyway, what can we do right now?"

"We need victim IDs," Erin said.

"They're suspects, not victims," Vic said.

"Right now they're both," Erin said. "Piekarski, did your squad know who these guys were?"

"Firelli got the tipoff," Piekarski said. "He said it was independent operators, but word on the street was that they'd gotten their hands on a big shipment of heroin. If he had names, I didn't hear them. You could ask him tonight."

"I'll do that," Erin said.

"I'm wondering how a bunch of no-name freelancers would've ended up with a load of H," Vic said. "They had to either rip off somebody local, or they've got their own supply chain. Either way, we should've heard about it. Where'd the shit come from?"

"Firelli said it was from Turkey," Piekarski said.

"That sounds like a Mafia job," Erin said.

"My thoughts exactly," Vic said. "It'd also explain why Organized Crime would be sniffing around them. But it sounds like these guys aren't that well connected."

"What was in the truck, anyway?" Erin asked. "Did anyone get a look inside?"

"It had to be drugs," Piekarski said. "Two armed men in the truck, another one waiting right inside? What else could it be?"

"Guns, underage hookers, hijacked consumer goods," Vic said immediately.

"The contents of the truck will be in the official reporting," Erin said. "After an incident like this, with a police casualty, the brass will want everyone to know about the big shipment of whatever they got off the street. They'll want people to think it was worth it."

"It wasn't," Piekarski said. She cleared her throat and ran the back of her hand across her eyes. "Shit, these hormones are really screwing with me. I keep leaking."

"You lost a friend today," Erin said. "It's a normal reaction."

"I want to kill those sons of bitches," Piekarski said. "Is that normal, too?"

"Pretty much," Vic said.

"I expect they'll release the names of the guys who got shot," Erin said. "Probably tomorrow. I think our only chance at getting IDs before that is to work through the ME's office."

"Is Levine doing these?" Vic asked. "Or is it someone we don't know?"

"I can find out where they took the bodies," Piekarski said. "It won't raise any suspicions if I ask because..."

"Because you'd want to know about Janovich," Erin said quietly. "Of course."

"I'll call the Five," Piekarski said, taking out her phone and moving to the window, facing away from the other two. As she passed Vic's bed, she grabbed a tissue from the nightstand and blew her nose.

"How's she holding up?" Erin asked Vic in an undertone.

"How do you think?" he whispered back. "How would you be if I caught one in the face? Or Webb?"

Erin bit off her usual witty comeback. This was no time for jokes. "Do we know who shot Janovich?" she asked instead.

"No idea," he said. "They'll run ballistics. I don't think any of the Organized Crime guys had a direct line of fire, but that doesn't mean anything. It could've been a ricochet."

Erin nodded again. A lot of people didn't know that bullets really could go around corners. They just had to hit a hard surface at the right angle. Gunfights involved a lot of bizarre physics. That was why police had used shotguns instead of rifles for so many years; shotgun pellets didn't have nearly as much power and tended to stop when they hit things. High-powered bullets overpenetrated and bounced all over the place. They could end up almost anywhere.

"There was a lot of shooting," she said. "I don't know if we'll ever know which rounds went where. Vic? Vic!"

Vic was a tough guy, a hard-headed street cop who loved a good fight. He had a softer side, but he hid it so well most folks never even suspected it. But now, with startling suddenness, his face crumpled. His shoulders shook and he made a sound halfway between a cough and a gasp.

"Vic!" she said again, grabbing his shoulder. "What's the matter? Are you hurt?"

Piekarski had just hung up the phone and turned back toward them. The blonde rushed across the room.

"Vic!" she said sharply.

Vic waved a hand at them, motioning them back, and shook off Erin's hand. He took in a slow, shuddering breath, held it, and let it out again. His eyes were closed.

"Any chest pains?" Piekarski asked. "Numbness in your arm?"

"No, I'm fine," Vic muttered. He opened his eyes and looked at the two women. "What?"

"Shit," Piekarski said. "I thought you were having a heart attack."

"It kind of looked like it," Erin agreed. She was genuinely alarmed. "What happened?"

"Nothing," Vic said.

"It didn't look like nothing," Piekarski pressed. "What was that?"

"It just hit me," he said. "Out of nowhere. I shot a cop! You understand that? I shot a goddamn cop!"

"So did I," Erin said. "I get it."

"No," he said. "You don't. Our vests aren't rated to stop rifle rounds, not without trauma plates. I could've killed him. I should've killed him! The only reasons he's not dead right now are I made a lousy shot and only fired once. Don't know why, either. I should've given him at least three."

"Maybe you had an angel looking over your shoulder," Erin said.

"And maybe he'll still die," Vic said. "Hell, maybe he's dead right now."

"My brother's saved guys who were hurt worse," she said. "And the rest of the docs at Bellevue are almost as good as he is. It's okay, Vic."

"Don't," he said. "Don't tell me that. None of this is okay. Not one damn thing."

"That's why we're here," Erin said gently. "To help make this right."

"What if we can't?" Vic asked.

"Then we'll find some bad guys and kick their asses anyway," Piekarski said.

Chapter 5

"They've got Jan at the Eightball," Piekarski reported. She'd just gotten off the phone with the Medical Examiner. "So that's where they'll have the rest of them, too."

"Good," Erin said. "We can work with Levine."

"She's weird, but she knows us," Vic said.

"All coroners are weird," Erin said. "Let's go."

"Hold on a sec," Vic said. "What're you carrying?"

"My backup piece," Erin said, pulling up her pants leg to show her ankle holster with its snub-nosed .38.

"That's no good," he said. "Not in a real gunfight. That little toy doesn't have any kind of range. Don't you have an off-duty gun? Something serious?"

"Not at the moment."

"Okay, you'd better take one of mine." Vic walked to his bedside. A large gun safe was bolted to the floor. He knelt and punched in the combination. "What're you looking for?" he asked over his shoulder.

"You got a Glock?" Erin asked.

"Boring," he said. "And no, I don't. Plastic-frame piece of shit."

"It's accurate, tough, and reliable," Erin replied. "Sorry it's not glamorous enough for you."

"Oh, here we go," Vic said. He came up with a hefty-looking automatic. "Oh yeah, this is perfect."

"What the hell is that?" Erin asked.

"Colt Delta Elite," he said proudly. "2009 model, blued steel, diamond texture wrap-around grip. Eight-round capacity, ten-millimeter Auto. Based on the classic 1911 Colt .45. Recoil spring's a little stiffer on account of the heavy recoil of the ten-mil round."

"That's something you got out of one of your gun-porn magazines, isn't it," she said.

"Maybe," he said. "But it's a damn good gun. It may not have the capacity of your nine-mil, but you want stopping power, it'll knock a bad guy right into next week. Here, see how it feels."

Erin took the pistol, pulled back the slide to ensure it was empty, and tried bringing it up in both hands. "It's heavy," she said.

"That's because it's a real gun, made with real metal," he said. "Almost a pound heavier than that squirt gun you carry."

"I don't know," she said. "I kind of feel like I'm carrying your dick around with me. You think Zofia's okay with that?"

"As long as you keep it well-oiled and give it back when you're done with it," Piekarski said, somehow managing to keep a straight face as she said it.

"I've got two spare mags for it," Vic said. "Just remember, it's got a bigger kick than you're used to and it only holds eight shots." He collected the weapon's accoutrements and handed them to her.

"We're going to the morgue," Erin reminded him, buckling the holster to her belt, loading the Colt, and sliding it into its temporary resting place. "All the bad guys there are already dead."

"You never know," he said.

"What about you?" Erin asked.

"What about me? I've got my Sig." He patted the Sig-Sauer at his hip.

"IAB didn't take it away?"

"I was using your rifle, remember? Never pulled my sidearm. IAB's got a bunch of your guns, none of mine."

"And I never fired mine," Piekarski said gloomily. "I should've, but I didn't."

"And I shouldn't have, but I did," Erin said. "So here we are."

*   *   *

"I never thought I'd be sneaking into my own precinct house," Vic said, glancing over his shoulder as he reached for the door leading out of the Eightball's garage.

"We're not sneaking in," Erin said. "Or if we are, we're doing a piss-poor job. They've got our cars entering the garage, plus we're on camera right now."

"Yeah, but we're not telling our boss we're here," he said. "And we're not supposed to be."

"I think that was more advice than orders," Erin said.

"And we're not going past the front desk," Vic went on. "The morgue's downstairs. Besides, if we run into an officer we know, what're you going to tell him?"

"As little as possible," Erin said.

"Like I said," Vic said. "Sneaking."

The three cops and one K-9 made their way down to the Precinct 8 morgue. As luck would have it, they didn't run into anyone unexpected. All they found was Sarah Levine with one of her favorite companions: a dead man.

Levine didn't look up when they came through the swinging doors. It was likely she hadn't even noticed them. She was doing an autopsy on a naked male body. Erin noted, with some thankfulness, that it wasn't Janovich. It was bad enough knowing he was in a refrigerated drawer nearby. Seeing him get cut open by Levine's clinical, impersonal scalpel might have been too much.

"Hey, doc," Erin said.

Levine didn't react. Idle chitchat was something she neither participated in nor understood.

"Do you have an ID on the bodies from the shooting yet?" Erin asked.

"Yes," Levine said. "Keep the dog back. We need to avoid foreign contaminants. It shouldn't be here."

"Rolf, *platz*," Erin said. Rolf immediately lay down on the tile floor and planted his snout between his paws.

"Who were they?" Vic asked, bending over the body Levine was working on. Death held no horror for him.

"Dental records were unnecessary," Levine said, continuing her work without interruption. "All four had fingerprints on file, clear matches. Casper Janovich, Gianni Manzano, Carlo Manzano, and Luca Frazetti."

Erin had her notepad in hand and was frantically scribbling names. Piekarski was standing back, trying not to look too closely at Levine or her subject.

"COD?" Erin asked.

"Preliminary cause of death is gunshot wounds for all four subjects," Levine said. "Janovich was killed by a single penetrating wound to the cranium. In the absence of an exit wound, I presume the bullet is still lodged in the cranial cavity. Judging from the diameter of the entrance wound, the bullet was either .38 caliber or nine-millimeter. It likely struck the inside of the back of the skull and ricocheted and tumbled, traumatically destroying brain tissue. Death was instantaneous."

Piekarski made a miserable, liquid retching sound. Erin turned toward her just in time to see the other woman double over and empty her stomach onto the floor of the morgue.

"Shit," Vic said, seeing what was happening a moment too late. He hurried to Piekarski's side and put a hand on her back.

"Sorry," Piekarski mumbled, wiping her mouth with the back of her hand.

"Jesus," Vic said, glaring at Levine. "What's your problem?"

"My current problem is completing four autopsies on short notice," Levine said. "Compounded by pointless interruptions and biological contamination."

Erin shook her head at Vic. It was useless trying to point out Levine's lack of social awareness. "What about the other three?" she asked the Medical Examiner.

"All three suffered multiple gunshot wounds," Levine said. "I haven't yet determined which wounds directly led to death, but all were struck by at least two bullets which would have proved fatal. All wounds were inflicted by pistols, outside contact range, probably between ten and fifty meters."

"Anything else you can tell us?" Erin asked.

"The two Manzanos are brothers," Levine said. "I estimate their ages as between twenty-five and thirty. Frazetti is older, probably mid-thirties. Janovich is—"

"We know about Janovich," Erin interrupted, trying to prevent another *faux pas*. "And if the other three are on file, we can get their info from there."

"Then why did you ask?" Levine asked, irritated.

"Sorry," Erin said. "We'll get out of your way and let you work."

"That's a good idea," Levine said. "There's a hose next to the door."

"A hose?" Erin repeated blankly.

"To wash the vomit down the drain," Levine said, pointing to a steel drain in the floor.

"Oh," Erin said. "Yeah, we'll do that. Thanks, doc."

"All of this will be in my report," Levine said. Then she paused. "Not the vomit. Only information pertinent to the post-mortem examinations. My report will be thorough, accurate, and honest."

* * *

"Sorry about that," Piekarski said. "That was such a rookie move."

"Forget about it," Erin said, glancing up and down the corridor outside the morgue. "Everyone repaints the floor sometimes."

"The doc was out of line," Vic said.

"It's not really her fault," Erin said. "She's not used to talking to live people."

"It's these damn hormones," Piekarski said. "God, I feel like such a cliché. I'm pregnant, so I must be puking my guts out every morning. I swear, I'm not. Not usually. But in there…"

"We get it," Vic said. "It's fine."

"So now what?" Piekarski asked.

"Now we find out about these Italians," Erin said, holding up her notepad. "But we'd better stay out of Major Crimes."

"We can use our onboard computers," Vic said. "So now we can camp out in our cars, like a couple losers cruising for free wi-fi. I love this job."

"Nothing I'd rather be doing," Erin said.

Rolf wagged his tail and stared up at her with adoration. He had no sense of irony or sarcasm whatsoever. He was living his best life.

They split up in the garage, Vic and Piekarski going to Vic's Taurus and Erin taking Rolf to her Charger. Then it was time to gather some data.

As Erin worked on her computer, Vic's car crept over next to hers. Piekarski rolled down the passenger window so they could talk. Rolf poked his head through the porthole between the front seats and rested his chin on Erin's shoulder.

"I don't get it," Erin said after a few minutes. "I thought you said these guys were freelancers."

"That's what Firelli told me," Piekarski said. "Why?"

"The Manzano brothers were Lucarellis," Erin said. "Plenty of known associates in the Family. They've got jackets an inch thick, chock-full of narcotics violations. These guys were hardcore dealers for the Oil Man."

"Looks like it," Vic said. "I got the same with Frazetti. These bastards worked for Vinnie, all right. What the hell was going on there?"

"Maybe they peeled off to form their own operation when the Lucarellis had their shakeup," Erin suggested. "They've got records going back years. That means they would've come up under old man Acerbo and Material Mattie."

The other two nodded. Erin was referring to Vittorio Acerbo, former head of the Lucarellis, and his longtime narcotics chief, Matthew Madonna. Both men had been permanently retired earlier that autumn when Acerbo's treacherous right-hand man Vincenzo Moreno had made his move to seize control of the Family. Those assassinations had sent shockwaves through the New York underworld that were still making ripples.

"You saying Vinnie the Oil Man doesn't foster loyalty in his henchmen?" Vic asked, raising an eyebrow.

"I'm saying he'd throw his own mom under the bus without batting an eye, and everybody else knows it," Erin said. "If we don't get him, one of his own guys is going to blow him away one of these days, just out of self-preservation instinct."

"But in the meantime, he's our problem," Vic said. "What do you think, Zofia?"

"I think I'd better pump Firelli tonight," Piekarski said without much enthusiasm. "We need to know who else knew about today's shipment. Somehow, it got leaked to Organized Crime. So we need Firelli's source."

"Maxwell knew to be there," Erin agreed. "But he could've gotten the info from a different source than Firelli."

"Won't know until we ask," Piekarski said.

Chapter 6

Erin stared into her glass of Guinness. You took a drink to toast success, she thought morosely. You drank to drown your sorrows, at home alone or in sad, dirty little dive bars. You drank when you hung out with friends, or to wash away the stress of another long day pounding pavement. And you drank when one of those friends got killed. No wonder it was so easy to be an alcoholic.

The motley assortment of men and women around her raised their glasses. They were in a side room at the Final Countdown, specially reserved for the occasion. Everyone in the place carried a shield. Most of them were on the Street Narcotics Enforcement Unit or the Five's Patrol roster, but a few, like Erin and Vic, hailed from other precincts. All of them had known Janovich.

Sergeant Logan stood at the front of the room, flanked by Firelli and Piekarski. Logan had on the ragged leather jacket he always wore when working the street. He held up his glass and waited for silence. As the others watching him, he cleared his throat awkwardly.

"Jan would be sorry to miss this," he said. "He never wanted to pass up a good party."

"Especially one where he wasn't buying," Firelli added, drawing a laugh.

Logan nodded and gave Firelli half a smile. "That's right," he said. "We've got a tradition in SNEU. Some of you know it. At the end of a long one, we come back here. If we bust mostly Italians overnight, Firelli gets the first round. You remember him. Roberto Firelli. On the street they call him Bobby the Blade. A real tough guy. When he joined the Force, they had to frisk him before they'd let him into the Academy."

Firelli ducked his head and raised a hand in acknowledgment. "They never gave me back my knife, either," he said. There were more chuckles.

"If we get more Irish, that means it's my tab," Logan continued. "On account of my rich ethnic heritage."

"Wopstat and Mickstat," Erin muttered, remembering what the SNEU folks had told her. They claimed it wasn't racist, since they had wops and micks on the squad.

"Janovich was a Polack," Logan said. "Like Piekarski, here. And unfortunately, the Poles just don't have the imagination or ambition to be criminals. They've got to settle for being working stiff civilians. Or the really slow ones end up as cops."

"Poor bastards," somebody said from the back of the room.

"I worked SNEU with Jan for almost five years," Logan said. "And let me tell you, that guy was as dumb as a box of doorknobs, but he was as solid as they come. You could run vertical patrols all night with him. We'd get done, quads killing us from all those stairs, sweat soaking through our shirts, stinking like hell from rolling around in some junkie's puke while we were slapping the cuffs on him, and Jan would still be smiling, ready to go out and do it all over again."

Logan raised his glass all the way over his head. The amber liquid caught the lights and sparkled. "I don't know if you're watching us, Jan, but if you are, here's to you, you crazy illiterate son of a bitch. This is it, buddy. Last shift's over. End of watch, man. We'll miss you."

Every glass in the room went up. Erin blinked away sudden tears and slugged back a gulp of stout, taking what comfort she could in the familiar dark, bitter flavor. On her right, Vic coughed and pretended he had something caught in his eye. Between them, Rolf leaned against her leg. The Shepherd knew Erin was emotional, but didn't know why. He did what he always did; stayed close and let her know he was there for whatever she needed.

After the toast, the officers mingled, forming little groups. They were sharing anecdotes, all the odd, funny, awful, strange things that happened on the Job. There weren't many tears now. Everybody was almost desperately upbeat and cheerful about the whole thing, as if getting murdered in a stupid, pointless shootout was nothing more than a minor inconvenience.

Erin and Vic drifted over to where Piekarski and Firelli stood against the far wall. Firelli was already on his second drink and looked like he'd be needing a refill soon. Erin wouldn't be surprised if he was actively trying to get drunk as fast as possible.

"Hey, Firelli," Erin said, clapping him on the shoulder.

"O'Reilly," he said. "Thanks for coming."

"Wouldn't miss it," she said.

"You know what they say," Vic said. "If you miss a guy's funeral, he won't come to yours."

"You heard anything about the arrangements?" Erin asked.

"Not yet," Firelli said. "Logan got in touch with Jan's dad. He's flying up from Fort Myers tomorrow. I guess they'll sort things out when he gets here."

Erin nodded. "He have any other family?"

"An ex-wife," Piekarski said. "No kids."

"Thank God for that," Firelli murmured, earning him a sidelong look from Piekarski and confirming for Erin that Piekarski's condition wasn't common knowledge.

"Look," Erin said. "I don't want to rehash what happened out there, and I know you already went over the whole thing for IAB and your captain, but I have to ask you something. Who told you about the heroin shipment?"

Firelli gave her an unhappy look. His scraggly little mustache was never impressive, but this evening it looked particularly sad and bedraggled.

"We know this wasn't your fault," Piekarski said, slipping her hand into his and giving it an encouraging squeeze. "This doesn't have anything to do with you."

"I got it from a CI," Firelli said. "A guy I know who lives on the street."

"Homeless?" Erin asked.

"Yeah. Army vet, got hooked on the bad shit while he was in rehab, couldn't hold down a job. Same old story, you know how it goes. Good guy, but screwed up in the head. He's got his ear to the street, knows what's going on in Little Italy."

"Any idea where he got the info?" Vic asked.

"Junkies hear stuff like that," Firelli said, shrugging. "He heard it from a guy he knows who's got connections with this importer, a guy who goes by Stallone."

"As in, Sylvester?" Vic asked, raising his eyebrows.

"As in, the Italian word for a male horse," Firelli said. "You know, stallion."

"So that's not his name?" Vic asked.

"It's a street name," Firelli said patiently. "I don't know his real name. He's a guy who can get horse for you."

"Horse is a street name for heroin," Erin added.

"Yes, Erin, I know that," Vic said. "I'm not a rookie. You can call it dope, smack, tar, dragon, China white, Mexican brown, junk, skag, mud, brown sugar, snow, or whatever, I'll know what you mean. It's all the same shit."

"What'd your guy hear from this Stallone mope?" Erin asked.

"My guy said there was a new player in town," Firelli said. "Somebody waving lots of cash around and looking to buy into the narco game in a big way. Stallone was moving a lot of product to these new kids. My guy got the word on one of the main deliveries and passed it to me. I told Logan and he figured we had a chance to nip off this new gang before they really got going."

"Why would the dealer give up his connection like that?" Erin wondered.

"He wasn't telling the cops," Piekarski said. "He was telling a customer where he could get his next fix."

"So how'd that get back to Organized Crime?" Vic asked.

"Same way it got to us, I expect," Firelli said. "What's it matter? The bad guys are dead. Now, if you'll excuse me, I'm planning to drink till I can't remember any of this."

"Just a second," Erin said. "How would we talk to this Stallone guy?"

"What for?" Firelli asked.

"So we can find out why Jan died," Piekarski said.

"Jan died because of a stray fucking bullet!" Firelli snapped. "Let it go! You're trying to find some reason in this? There isn't any reason! I got hit last time things went sideways, and this time it was Jan's turn. I got lucky, he didn't. That's all there is to it. You try to go any deeper, you'll go nuts. It's just luck of the goddamn draw. This is a cosmic damn casino and the house always wins in the end."

Piekarski backed away from Firelli. "Jesus, man," she said quietly. "I didn't mean—"

"Neither did I," Firelli said more softly. "I'm sorry. I just... God, I was standing right next to him when he got hit. It was one of the guys on the dock. The son of a bitch was lying flat on his belly. He wasn't even aiming at us, just firing blind. Unbelievable. Million to one chance. One second everything's fine, next thing you know, bam! Out of nowhere."

"Crazy world," Vic agreed.

"It's senseless," Erin said. "I get what you're saying. But just because there wasn't any meaning doesn't mean we can't find some. Let's make this mean something."

"How do you plan on doing that?" Firelli asked.

"By finding the truth, for starters," she said.

"And for that, we need to talk to this importer," Piekarski said. "Can you set it up?"

"I don't know," Firelli said. "Maybe. I'll have to talk to my guy on the street again, see if he can put me in touch. I... shit, I really did want to get drunk tonight."

"I know the feeling," Erin said. "But the times I most want it are the times it's the worst idea."

"You're right about that," Firelli said ruefully. "You sound like my wife. Okay, I'll take a walk in the old neighborhood after this. If I can set something up, I'll let you know. But no guarantees."

"Thanks," Piekarski said.

"Say," Vic said. "How come they call you Bobby the Blade?"

"I used to be a ganger," Firelli said. "Had one hell of a juvie record. They probably shouldn't have let me into the NYPD at all. I was pretty good with a knife. Hung out with this one guy, Gino the Fish."

"Let me guess," Erin said. "He sold fish?"

"Yeah," Firelli said. "And other stuff, under the ice in his trucks. He had these filleting knives, beautiful ones. Made out of that fancy swirly steel; Damascus, they call it. Anyway, one day they found Gino in back of one of his trucks, on ice. Frozen solid. They never solved that one. I always figured he just pissed off the wrong guy. I didn't care at the time; I was just a dumb teenager. I got my hands on one of his knives and it became sort of my signature."

"You still have it?" Vic asked.

"Yeah, I do," Firelli said. "I keep it sharp. It usually hangs out in my knife block in my kitchen these days. Good steel. Hey, it's a fish knife, not a fighting knife. Totally legal."

"Every knife is a fighting knife when the chips are down," Vic said.

"True," Firelli said. "Look, guys. I don't know what you're doing. This isn't exactly by the book, is it?"

"Does that bother you?" Erin asked. "Bobby the Blade?"

"If it'll do right by Janovich, I'm in," he said. "They took me off the street. They didn't take the street out of me."

*   *   *

Erin and Rolf returned to the Barley Corner a little before midnight. Erin had been drinking steadily, swapping beers, shots, and stories with other cops. If not for Rolf's guidance, she would have had trouble walking a straight line. Vic had given her a lift. Strangely, he'd stayed stone-cold sober. Erin guessed he wasn't done working for the night, but he'd evaded her questions along those lines and she hadn't pressed him.

Carlyle was sitting at the bar on his usual stool, surveying his domain. The pub was busy. It looked like the Teamsters were well-represented; Erin saw lots of broad shoulders, pot bellies, tattoos, and beards. She wormed between enormous men, making her unsteady way toward the bar.

"Hey, Erin!"

It took her a second to place the voice. Then she saw the bearded, gap-toothed grin of Wayne McClernand. He was a trucker and small-time smuggler for the O'Malleys, a man who'd done time upstate but who really wasn't a bad guy once you got to know him.

"Evening, Wayne," she said, forcing herself to focus on his face. The room had a swimming, shimmering quality. "How's the Beast?"

"Purring like a cat," Wayne said happily. The Beast was his semi-truck, his pride and joy. "You ever need anything moved, you call me."

"I'll do that," she said. "You have a good night."

"Say," Wayne said as she started to turn away. "You haven't seen Corky lately, have you?"

"Can't say I have," she replied. Little alarm bells went off in her beer-soaked brain. "How come?"

"Well, seems to me he blew town in a hurry," Wayne said. "Just dropped off the map. Some of the guys need to talk to him about stuff. I've been asking around. I wanted to make sure he was okay. Thought you might've heard something. Y'know, in case he's..."

"You kidding?" Erin said. "Nothing's going to happen to Corky. He's too damn lucky. If he wasn't, he'd have been dead years ago."

Wayne guffawed. "Yeah, guess you're right. He'll turn up. Your people didn't snatch him, did they?"

"No, he's not under arrest." She paused. "At least, not as far as I know. I guess it's possible."

"If you do see him, tell him I said hi," Wayne said.

"I'll do that," Erin said. She almost added that Corky was out of town, but remembered in time; that was supposed to be secret, which meant she shouldn't be spilling it to random guys in bars, no matter how drunk she was.

Erin joined Carlyle at the bar. He got to his feet to greet her, dropping a hand for Rolf to sniff.

"Evening, darling," he said. "And how about yourself? I know it's been a hard one."

"You could say that," she said.

"Get you anything, Erin?" the bartender asked, sliding along the far side of the bar toward her.

"No thanks, Danny," she said. "I'm pretty well sloshed already."

"I've never been to a gathering when a copper's been cut down," Carlyle said quietly. "Obviously. But I'd imagine it's not too different from when a lad in the Life gets retired."

"I guess so," Erin said. She looked down to make sure the stool was where she thought it was. Then, with great deliberation, she sat down. She didn't fall off the stool, so it was a success.

"Anything I can do?" he asked.

"For Janovich? No. If you sent flowers, people would take it the wrong way."

"For you, then?"

"You can find out about the Manzano brothers and Luca Frazetti."

"Those names aren't ringing a bell, darling. What sort of business might these lads be in?"

"They used to run drugs for the Lucarellis, but I heard they might've gone independent recently. If you could just see what you can pick up, I'd appreciate it." Erin noticed her eyes were moving erratically. She was having trouble focusing. She hadn't realized she was quite that drunk.

"I'll do that, darling. Anything I should know about them in the meantime?"

"All three of them are on slabs in the Eightball's morgue," she said. "Along with Janovich." Then, unexpectedly, she teared up. She blinked angrily.

Carlyle's hand, high on her shoulder, was warm. He massaged the base of her neck. "It's all right, darling," he said softly.

She leaned against him. This was a bad idea. The bar stool rotated and she started to fall. Carlyle caught her before she could take a header to the floor.

"Oops," she said.

"I've been a publican for a great many years," Carlyle said. "So I've some notion what I'm talking about when I say you've had enough for one night. Let's get you upstairs and into bed."

"You're just trying to get me in bed," she said as he steered her toward the apartment.

"Aye, that's what I just said," Carlyle said. "I assure you, my intentions are nothing but honorable."

"There was a bunch of drugs coming in," Erin said. "Heroin. From Turkey. Guy called Sylvester. No, that's not right. Stallone. That's it. Heard of him?"

"I don't traffic in narcotics, Erin. You know that." Carlyle punched in the combination and got them through the door. Rolf, at Erin's side, watched her with concern. He could smell the alcohol fumes coming off her in waves, and he could tell her balance was off.

"Yeah, but you know people," she said. She climbed the stairs one careful step at a time. Carlyle was beside her, an arm around her back. "Shit. I got hammered."

"It's understandable," he said. "You're toasting a fallen comrade. What better time for an Irishman to drink? Or an Irishwoman?"

"Wayne," she said. "McClernand."

"I saw Wayne downstairs aye," Carlyle said. "What about him?"

"Asked about Corky. People are talking. About him."

They made it to the top of the stairs. Carlyle went with Erin to the bathroom and stood in the doorway. She fumbled out her toothbrush and made a decent effort at scrubbing her teeth.

"That doesn't surprise me," he said. "Corky's a noticeable presence. He's left a void by his absence."

"He'd better come back soon," she said. "And he'd better not be screwing around with that witness. I said I'd cut his nuts off if he tried anything."

"Then I'd best hide the kitchen knives," Carlyle said with a smile.

"Kitchen knives," Erin repeated. "Heard something about those tonight. Bobby the Blade."

"Another Lucarelli?"

She laughed weakly. "No. One of ours. Getting harder to tell the difference. I'm not making any sense, am I?"

"It's possible I'm not understanding you fully," Carlyle said diplomatically. "You'll be wanting some water. Two glasses, or you'll regret it come morning."

"Don't tell me about hangovers," she said. "I know all about them. We're old friends, hangovers and me."

"I don't doubt it."

"Bed," Erin said. "I'll deal with all this crap in the morning."

"That's a grand plan, darling. Are you wanting me to stay with you?"

She thought about this longer than she really needed to. "No," she decided. "I'll be fine. I think I'll just pass out for a while. Besides, I've got Rolf."

Rolf gave her a long-suffering look and nosed her hand.

Chapter 7

Carlyle's advice about water had been good, but it hadn't been enough. Erin woke up with her brain feeling about three sizes too large for her skull. The bedroom's curtains had been installed by a man who lived by night and slept late, so at least it was dark, but her pulse was like a sledgehammer trying to break out of her head.

She sat up gingerly, managing not to disturb Carlyle. He was fast asleep. He'd get up sometime around ten-thirty or eleven, no doubt feeling comfortable and well-rested. She resisted the urge to smack him in the face with a pillow.

Rolf was already wide awake, up on his paws, dancing with eagerness. It was morning, and that meant it was time for their run. Running was one of the best things in the world. It came in slightly behind getting to bite a bad guy, and definitely behind his favorite rubber Kong ball, but it was up there.

Erin groaned quietly and shuffled into the bathroom. The face that greeted her in the mirror reminded her of people she'd busted in her Patrol days. Her eyes were bloodshot, her hair was a mess, and her skin was paler than usual. The only good news was, she didn't think she was going to throw up.

"You did this to yourself, kiddo," she muttered, splashing cold water on her face. There was something she needed to remember, but she hadn't quite gotten her thoughts in gear yet. It occurred to her that she wasn't wearing any pants; just her underwear and an old NYPD T-shirt. She went back to the bedroom to get dressed. Rolf pranced alongside her, annoyingly perky.

The bedside clock read 7:23. She'd overslept. She usually got up around six, but she hadn't remembered to set an alarm. Something was supposed to happen this morning. But what?

"Kira," she groaned. She had seven—no, six minutes now. Fortunately, the meeting would be taking place only one flight of stairs below her. She could make it, but she needed to move.

Erin tossed her sleep shirt into the corner and grabbed a pair of socks, some slacks, a bra, and a blouse, not even trying to match colors in the dark. She threw on the clothes and hurried back to the bathroom to untangle her hair.

Rolf followed, but his tail was wagging more uncertainly now. Erin wasn't wearing her running clothes. This was all wrong. He didn't understand, but he was starting to suspect his morning run might not be happening. This was shaping up to be a disaster. The Shepherd decided to take independent action.

As Erin finished combing her hair and tying it back in a ponytail, she heard a metallic jingling from the bathroom doorway. She turned to see Rolf standing there, his leash and collar clamped between his jaws, hope shining in his big brown eyes.

"Sorry, partner," she said, ruffling his fur. "No time. It's my fault. Maybe we'll squeeze in a run later."

Rolf flattened his ears and ducked his head. She was not forgiven; not yet. But he knew his duty. He stuck close beside her, consenting to let her buckle on the collar. He sulked his way down the stairs at Erin's hip, snout pointed toward the floor, tail dragging.

The Barley Corner was a nighttime hot spot, but it had a decent breakfast crowd. Most of these guys were truckers, fueling up for a long day behind the wheel. The breakfast menu was big on eggs, bacon, steak, oatmeal, and—oddly enough— cornflakes. Carlyle had explained to Erin that Ireland was the world's number-one per capita consumer of cornflakes. Nobody seemed to know why this was the case, but the Irish loved them, so Carlyle's pub provided them.

It wasn't hard to spot her visitor. Kira Jones, sitting in a booth by the front wall, stood out amid the crowd of big, hairy blue-collar guys. Kira worked for Internal Affairs these days, so she dressed professionally. From the neck down she looked like a businesswoman: black blazer and slacks, white button-down blouse, stylish ankle boots. But she'd managed to retain her individuality in her hair. It was cut very short on one side, nearly shaved down to the skull, and the other side was kept long, flopping over. That hair was dyed electric blue at the base and crimson at the tips. In her ears were three studs and two silver earrings, shaped like something Erin couldn't identify. She also had a diamond stud in her left nostril.

"Morning," Erin said, sliding into the seat across from her.

"Hey," Kira said. "How're you doing? You don't look so good."

"We had that thing for Janovich last night," Erin explained. She didn't think Kira looked great, either, but didn't say so. The other woman was visibly nervous. She was fiddling with the rings on her right hand and was having trouble meeting Erin's eye.

"And there's Rolf," Kira said, smiling more genuinely. "We ought to get a dog for our office."

"You've already got the Bloodhound," Erin said, using Lieutenant Keane's nickname.

Kira made a face. "I was thinking more like a golden retriever."

"You don't think that would be a little off-brand for IAB?" Erin couldn't resist asking.

"Look, Erin, I know you think we're the bad guys," Kira said. "But if that was true, would I be here now?"

"No," Erin said. "I'm sorry. And I do appreciate it."

One of the waitresses came to take their order. Kira asked for V8 and a fruit salad. Erin's stomach was doing flip-flops, so she settled for oatmeal and coffee.

Once the waitress had gone, Kira glanced around. Then she reached into a shoulder bag lying next to her on the seat. She eased a folder out of it and held it out under the table.

"Seriously?" Erin said.

"Go on, take it," Kira said. "I already feel like an idiot. You're the one who wants to do this secret agent bullshit."

Erin took the folder. She looked down and started to open it.

"Not here!" Kira hissed. "Geez!"

"Kira, there's nobody from IAB here except you," Erin said. "I know these guys, and they're the furthest thing in the world from cops. You're safe here."

"The way you say that, I don't feel safe," Kira said. "I can't believe you're living here! I bet there's half a dozen outstanding warrants in this room right now."

"That's probably a low estimate," Erin said. "But they're really not so bad, once you get to know them."

"I used to work the Gang Task Force," Kira said. "Remember? I've been around guys like this. They're exactly as bad as I think."

"Yeah," Erin said. "That's where you got that hair. I'm surprised Keane lets you keep it."

"He tried to get me to change it. I convinced him it was fine, that it'd put the rank and file at ease."

"How do you like it? Working IAB?"

Kira looked down at her hands again. "It's fine, I guess. I don't miss that crazy shit we used to get into, don't get me wrong. But sometimes..."

"You miss Major Crimes?"

"A little, yeah. Mostly I miss you guys. Working for Keane, it's... it's different."

"What's he like?"

"You know that feeling you get sometimes, like somebody's following you? That prickle on the back of your neck when you're walking alone down a dark alley?"

"Yeah?"

"He's kind of like that, all the time," Kira said. "He's smart. Like, scary smart. And he notices *everything*. But he doesn't always say so. He likes to store things up. I feel like he's always planning, always making moves, like he's playing five or ten games of chess in his head. And I don't..."

Erin waited. Kira didn't finish the sentence.

"You don't trust him," Erin said quietly.

Kira shook her head. "You know that famous Roman quote? *Quis custodiet ipsos custodes?*"

"'Who watches the watchmen?'" Erin translated. She didn't know Latin, but she knew that line.

"Yeah. Lately I've been wondering who watches the guys who watch the watchmen."

"That sounds like a good way to go crazy," Erin said. "Think that way and you'll go straight down the rabbit hole."

"I'm already there," Kira said. "That's why I'm sitting here with you, outside the rules. I'm watching the watchman-watchers. Because I've got this feeling if I don't, nobody's going to do anything about Maxwell."

Erin felt a thrill. "There's something in his file," she said. "How bad is it?"

"You'll see," Kira said. "And be careful with that. Those are photocopies, not originals. I had to go to the archives to get them. They weren't scanned into the database. Don't leave them lying around, and try not to show them to anyone. You should probably destroy them, once you've read them."

"Jesus," Erin said. "You're saying the NYPD has a file on Maxwell and they buried it?"

"Somebody did," Kira said. "Look, I've said more than I should have already. You're my friend, Erin, and I want to help, but this is all I can do right now."

"Thank you," Erin said. "This means a lot."

"Maybe," Kira said. "But I was thinking about something my mom said to me, back when I was about twelve. I wanted to watch this scary movie with my friends. It was about this spaceship that goes to Hell, and then it comes back, and everybody goes crazy and they all start killing each other. She said, 'Kira, be careful what you see, because once you see it, you can't unsee it.' Which was what the movie was about, come to think of it."

Erin nodded. She gripped the folder more tightly. "I have to look," she said. "I'm a detective."

* * *

Despite what she'd said to Kira, Erin wasn't at all sure she wanted to see what was in the folder. After they'd had breakfast, eaten in near-complete silence, and the other woman had left, Erin went back upstairs. Now she was sitting in the living room, staring at the folder as it lay in front of her. Rolf laid his chin on the table and gave her a soulful look.

What was she afraid of? She was working undercover to dismantle a major criminal organization. She'd been in gunfights and fistfights. She'd been shot, stabbed, and nearly blown up. She'd killed men and held men who were dying. Sean O'Reilly's daughter was plenty tough.

"Morning, darling," Carlyle said. He was standing in the doorway, somehow managing to look more put-together in his silk dressing gown than most men did in three-piece suits.

"What are you doing up?" she asked. "You can't have gotten more than five or six hours of sleep."

"I've been worrying about you," he said, going to the kitchen and turning on the coffee machine. "If you want to know, I dreamed you were in a spot of trouble, so I got up to see if it was true."

"I'm not some damsel in distress," she said. "I get in trouble all the time, but I'm pretty good at getting myself out. And if I can't, that's what I've got Rolf for."

She ruffled the Shepherd's fur. He submitted to it with good grace.

"Nonetheless, I find you here with a face full of worry and a folder filled with the good Lord only knows what dark secrets," Carlyle said, coming in to sit beside her. "Is this something to do with yesterday's unpleasantness?"

"Yeah," she said. "And this is top-secret stuff. Eyes-only, need-to-know shit."

"You're saying I oughtn't to be looking at it?"

"I'm saying even I shouldn't be looking at it," she said.

"Is that why you're hesitating?"

She stared at the plain manila folder. "No. I'm hesitating because I'm scared."

"Erin O'Reilly? Frightened of a few bits of paper? Perish the thought!"

"I'm serious," Erin said.

"I can see that, aye," he said. "What is it you're afraid of?"

"We're looking into another officer," she said carefully. "I was told there's something bad in here."

"And you're afraid you'll find he's a villain?"

"I'm afraid I'll find out he's a lot like me," she said.

"Ah," he said. "There but for the grace of God, you're saying?"

"Something like that."

Erin hadn't told Carlyle just how close she'd come to committing cold-blooded murder herself, not that long ago. She'd gotten as far as laying plans before sanity had returned, in the form of Rolf's cold nose in her face. The experience had left her badly shaken and with more than a few worries about her own righteousness.

He studied her face. "I'm thinking this will be on your mind, no matter what's written on those papers," he said. "What did you have to do to obtain them?"

"I asked a friend to break some rules."

"Then you'd best ensure her risks weren't taken in vain."

"There's something else."

"Aye?"

"If this is what I think it might be, then it means something worse than one bad apple."

"Are you thinking it might mean the rot's gotten into the apple tree itself?" he asked.

She nodded.

"All the more reason to know," he said. "I've spent too many years in thrall to evil men, darling. You need to know who you're working for."

He bent over and kissed her cheek. Then he stood up. "Coffee will be ready soon," he said. "I'll be in the kitchen. No fear, I'll not be looking over your shoulder."

After he'd gone, Erin sucked in a deep breath and flipped open the folder.

She wasn't sure what she'd been expecting. The NYPD Narcotics unit had a checkered history, but it had been pretty well cleaned up after some infamous events back in the Seventies. The documents she was looking at were, as Kira had said, photocopies of Internal Affairs files. They were written in dry bureaucratese and it took her some time to sift through it.

The guy who'd written the reports could have made Armageddon sound boring. Her headache was still pounding away behind her eyes. This was the sort of thing Kira herself excelled at, Erin thought sourly. Why couldn't Kira have just told her what she'd found?

The first bombshell blew up in her face on page three with an oblique reference to substance abuse. Erin sat up straighter and opened her eyes wider. She quickly shuffled through the documents until she found the attached fitness report from Maxwell's CO. Then she pulled out her pen and started circling words like "methamphetamines" and "habitual usage."

"Shit," she said under her breath. Policing was hard, stressful work. There was always the temptation to use chemical assistance to get through the tough days. Erin was lucky her drug of choice—alcohol—was legal. Even so, it could be a mean monkey on her back, and she'd been bitten by that monkey more than once. Her residual hangover was a reminder of that. Narcotics cops, with a ready supply of hard drugs at their fingertips, had to be particularly careful.

She scribbled some quick notes in the margin. Then she grabbed her phone and called Vic. It rang four times, then connected.

"Hrmmmph," Vic mumbled, or sounds to that effect.

"Did I wake you up?" Erin asked.

Her answer was another unintelligible mumble.

"I'll take that as a yes," she said. "You at home?"

This time the answer was decipherable as "Yeah."

"Good. I'm coming over."

"Huh?"

"I'll be there in twenty," she said, standing up and shoving the papers back into their folder with her free hand. "That'll give you time to get moving. I've got something you need to see. Call Piekarski and Firelli, too."

She hung up before he could wake up enough to start swearing at her. Rolf, picking up on her energy, was prancing excitedly. Maybe the morning run was going to happen after all. Or maybe there'd be bad guys to chase. That would be even better.

Carlyle came to the kitchen doorway with a Styrofoam cup in his hand. Steam and a lovely smell rose from it. He extended the cup.

"For the road, darling," he said. "I'd a feeling you'd be off soon. Stern call of duty, aye?"

"Yeah," she said. "Ask around about the Manzanos, okay?"

"I'll do that," he promised.

Chapter 8

Erin and Rolf found Vic and Piekarski in Vic's apartment. Vic was a little more coherent now, but his eyes had shadows under them and he needed a shave. Piekarski's eyes were puffy and bloodshot.

"C'mon in," Vic said. "There's Mountain Dew in the fridge and pop tarts by the toaster."

"I already ate," Erin was glad to be able to say. "Jesus, Vic, how are you not diabetic yet?"

"Firelli's on his way," Piekarski said. "He'll be here as soon as he can. We're not used to getting up this early. We mostly work nights."

"Thanks for coming on such short notice," Erin said.

"I was already here," Piekarski said.

"Oh," Erin said, realizing she'd put her foot right in her mouth. "That makes sense."

"Firelli said he'd be pretty hungover," Piekarski added.

"So am I," Erin said.

"Yeah, thanks, rub it in," Piekarski said. "Brag to the pregnant lady about all the booze you drank. I ought to kick both your asses. You're the reason I'm in this mess, Neshenko."

"It takes two to tango," Vic said. "As I recall, you came after me."

Piekarski backhanded him on the shoulder. "And as I recall, you weren't complaining."

There was a knock at the door. Erin did a quick check through the peep-hole.

"It's Firelli," she reported. "Thank God. I don't want to hear any more about your love lives."

Firelli was reasonably chipper, considering. He had a paper bag in hand, which he extended to them.

"Bagels," he said. "These are the good stuff. Fresh-baked, from a kosher place just down the block from me. Cream cheese, too."

"I'll have one," Erin said.

"You said you already ate," Vic said.

"That was when you were offering me stale pop tarts," Erin retorted.

"They're not stale!" he protested.

"They're pop tarts, babe," Piekarski said. "They come that way."

Firelli drifted over to the kitchen. He glanced at the box of pop tarts, shuddered, and examined Vic's knife block.

"Not bad steel," he said, turning a steak knife over in his hands. "But you really ought to sharpen these."

"I'm a gun guy, not a knife guy," Vic said.

"You ever heard the saying, 'Guns for show, knives for a pro?'"

"You ever seen what happens when you bring a knife to a gunfight?"

"Yeah, I did see that once," Erin said. "But I've seen more than enough dick-measuring contests. Zip up and let's get to work."

"So, what're we doing here?" Firelli asked.

Erin laid the folder on the coffee table. "Guys, before you see this, you need to understand something," she said. "This is from a sensitive source. Nobody takes these papers out of this room but me. And nobody says a single word about them to anybody without clearing it with me. We clear?"

"Copy that," Firelli said. The other two nodded.

"Okay," Erin said. "Have a look."

The other three cops dove in. After a brief scramble, they sorted themselves out and started reading.

"These are Internal Affairs reports," Firelli said. "How the hell did you get your hands on them?"

"You don't need to know that," Erin said.

"I need to know if it was legal," he said.

"I'm not a damn criminal," Erin said. "And no, I didn't steal them, if that's what you're asking."

"Maxwell's a drug addict," Vic said, finding Erin's notes.

"Recovering addict," Piekarski corrected. "Looks like he's got to prove he's clean. He's been getting screened monthly."

"That's in addition to our normal whiz quiz?" Firelli asked, referring to the random urine-sample testing all NYPD officers were required to undergo.

"Yeah," Piekarski said. "He kept his job, but somebody's got him on a short leash."

"Who?" Vic asked.

"Doesn't say," Piekarski said sourly. "But it's got to be somebody in Internal Affairs."

"He should've been fired," Vic said. "Just the possession of meth should've been enough to burn his ass. This guy's got serious protection."

"That's not all he's got," Erin said, looking at another sheet. "This wasn't his first shooting incident."

"Yeah," Vic said. "I've got the rest of that report here. Looks like he nailed three goons in a narcotics bust that went sideways. Report says the bad guys pulled first. It was judged justifiable. All the mopes had long records and they found guns on two of them."

"Got another here," Firelli announced. "Sheesh, this file is riddled. I can't believe this guy. This one's an off-duty shooting. His statement claims a guy pulled a knife on him on the street, close range. He drew and blew the guy away with his personal gun."

Erin nodded. "Do you notice anything about these four victims?" she asked.

"Just a sec." Piekarski had Vic's laptop open and was typing rapidly. "Let's see... All four of them were known Mafia associates."

"Lucarellis?" Vic asked.

"Nope," Piekarski said. "Competitors. Costa family."

"I know the Costas," Firelli said. "Used to know them, that is. They were in the dope business. Good contacts in the Mediterranean. The Lucarellis wiped them out a few years back. I met some of those guys when I was a kid, and later on when I was working Patrol in Little Italy. Tough sons of bitches."

"Not tough enough," Vic said. "How about that? The same guy's been in three fatal shootings, and all of them just happen to be enemies of the Lucarellis."

"What are the chances?" Erin asked rhetorically.

"This isn't proof," Firelli said. "It's circumstantial."

Everyone else looked at him.

"It's not proof!" he insisted. "It looks pretty bad, I agree, but this isn't something we can take to a judge. They'd laugh us out of the courtroom."

"He's right," Piekarski sighed. "The other two shootings were righteous."

"So IAB says," Vic said darkly.

"Exactly," Piekarski said. "So this doesn't represent a pattern of misconduct. Officially."

"But with the drug use, it's an awful lot," Erin said. "There's a pattern here, absolutely."

"This guy's dirty," Vic said.

"I agree," Firelli said. "So how do we prove it?"

"And who's covering for him?" Erin asked.

It was her turn to have all eyes turned her way.

"There's no way Maxwell could still be wearing a shield unless somebody else is protecting him," she said. "Like you said, Vic, he's got serious juice backing him up; probably somebody in IAB. If not them, it's even worse."

"The PC's office," Firelli said. "Shit. This is bad. What is he, married to the PC's daughter?"

"We need to find out who investigated his previous shootings," Erin said. "If it was the same IAB officer every time, that's probably our guy."

"And then what?" Firelli asked.

"Then we take his ass down," Vic said, as if that was the dumbest question he'd heard in a long time.

"Really? You think it's that simple?" Firelli retorted. "That's why we have Internal Affairs, Neshenko. So they can handle this. We don't arrest IAB. That's not how it works. You know what happens to cops who bust other cops?"

"I did it once," Erin said quietly. She and Kira Jones had intervened to stop a compromised officer from committing suicide. They'd saved his life, but cuffed him and dragged him downtown.

"And if you do it again, you'll never be able to keep wearing the shield," Firelli said. "You might as well put on a shirt that says you're a traitor. The rest of the boys in blue will never trust you."

"If we move on this, we'd better have something really solid," Piekarski said. "We need to prove Maxwell got Jan killed. That's the only way this won't blow back on us."

"Damn it, stop making so much sense," Vic growled. "What're you suggesting? That we give up? Walk away?"

"No," Firelli said. "I'm just saying we need to be careful."

"We need to dig into Maxwell's life," Erin said. "Find out who he hangs around with, what he does with his money and whether he's got too much of it, all that jazz."

"You're saying we need to act like detectives," Vic said.

"Yeah," Erin said.

"Fortunately, we are detectives," he said.

"Not all of us," Piekarski said.

"Maybe someday," Firelli said. "I wouldn't mind a gold shield."

"Tell you what," Vic said. "If they throw me off the Force for this, you can have mine. I won't be using it anymore."

"I don't think it works that way," Erin said. "Did you hear from your CI, Firelli?"

"Oh," Firelli said. "Yeah. I was going to get to that. He said he'd vouch for me with a dealer he knows. That guy can put me in touch with Stallone. I'm meeting him at noon."

"Great!" Erin said.

"What should we wear?" Piekarski asked.

"We can't all be there," Firelli said. "He'll spook. I can have one, maybe two people with me. And not you, Neshenko."

"Why not?" Vic looked hurt.

"Because you're big and scary," Firelli said. "When you were in ESU, and they needed to knock down a door, did they just point you at it and have you ram it open with your head?"

"The two of us, then?" Erin said, indicating Piekarski and herself.

Firelli nodded. "You don't look as dangerous," he said. "But the dog stays home. He's way too conspicuous."

Rolf cocked his head at Erin.

"Fine," she said, trying not to meet the K-9's eyes.

* * *

"So, who is this guy?" Erin asked Firelli. They were squeezed into Piekarski's beat-up Mini Cooper, on their way to Little Italy. Firelli's T-bird would have been a nicer ride, but it only seated two, so they'd left it at Vic's place. Rolf was riding with Vic, who'd borrowed Erin's Charger for the purpose. Vic had only agreed to sit this one out on the condition he and Rolf were close by, in case backup was required.

"His name's Benito Argent," Firelli said. "Goes by Benny Silvers. He was a tank driver, US Army. Got blown up in Iraq a couple years back. Then he got hooked on his pain meds, couldn't hold down a job, and ended up on the street."

"That sucks," Piekarski said.

"Yeah," Firelli said. "The lousy thing about working Narcotics is, most of the customers aren't bad guys. Hell, even some of the dealers aren't. But the money they bring in goes to the really shitty guys up the food chain. Those are the ones we really want, but we can't usually get to them, so we end up just scooping up the little fish while the big ones swim away."

"And it's a great big ocean," Piekarski said. "I like to think of it as job security. It's better not to think too hard about what happens to the ordinary schmucks once we hand them off to the DA."

"That's his problem, not ours," Firelli said. "All we do is play cops and robbers and chase them round the block."

"Anything else I should know about Benny?" Erin asked.

"He's a little messed up," Firelli said. "And sometimes he's kind of rude, especially toward women. Don't take it personal."

At Firelli's direction, Piekarski finagled her little car into a space too small for anything longer than the Mini Cooper and they got out. They found themselves looking at a fairly clean, landscaped park just south of Little Italy.

"Columbus Park," Firelli said. "Benny moves around, but he said he'd meet me here with his contact."

"What do you know about this contact?" Erin asked, scanning the area. She felt awfully exposed and vulnerable without Rolf by her side.

"Not much," Firelli said. "All Benny told me is, this guy can put us in touch with Stallone."

"Where's the meet?" Erin asked.

"Those benches over there," he said, nodding toward a trio of wooden benches under the spreading arch of a tree's branches. A low iron fence ran behind the benches, separating them from the park for some unaccountable reason.

"We're a little early," Piekarski said, checking her watch. "Do you think—"

"There he is," Firelli interrupted.

Erin followed his gaze and saw a shaggy-haired man in a wheelchair. He was rolling toward them down the sidewalk, working the wheels with his arms.

"Look, Forrest," Piekarski said. "Now that's Lieutenant Dan."

Firelli shot her a dirty look. "I bet you think that's funny," he said. "You try learning to get around with no legs, see how much you want to laugh about it. And if you think you're being clever and original, you're not. He's heard it all before."

Erin had to admit Benny Silvers did look a little like Gary Sinise's famous *Forrest Gump* character. She buried the thought. Firelli was right; Benny wouldn't appreciate the comparison.

"Benny!" Firelli said, walking toward the man with his arms open in greeting.

"Hey, Bobby," Benny said. "You got a smoke?"

The two men shook hands with apparent warmth. Up close, Erin saw that Benny Silvers couldn't be more than thirty years old, and was probably younger. Combat and street life put a lot of mileage on a man. He would probably be handsome, given a bath, a haircut, a shave, and maybe a little plastic surgery. His cheeks had the stretched, slightly puckered look of burn scars under his scraggly beard. And then there were the legs; or rather, there weren't. His pants were pinned up under a pair of stumps that ended just above the knees. Erin tried not to look at them.

"Sorry," Firelli said. "No smokes. The old lady made me quit."

"That's okay," Benny said. He reached into his army surplus jacket and pulled out a pack of Marlboros. "Here, have one on me."

Firelli held up a hand. "Like I said, I quit. If Sandy smells one on me, I gotta sleep on the couch."

"How long since your last cig?" Benny asked.

Firelli did some quick calculations. "Six months, give or take."

"It'd be worth it," Benny said, cackling. "A nicotine hit is worth not getting laid. Forget about it. You got a light?"

"Sure thing." Firelli took a lighter out of his hip pocket, flicked it to life, and held it out. Benny lit up and took a long drag.

"Not as good as crank, but better than nothing," Benny said. "Hey, how come you don't smoke, but you still carry a lighter?"

"Force of habit," Firelli said. "Hell, I still carry a knife, but I haven't pulled it on anybody in years. Having something that cuts and something that burns can be handy."

"You never know," Benny said, cackling again. His voice had a cracked quality better suited to a man twice his age. "Your old lady know you're hanging out with these two *bambinos*? Aren't you gonna introduce me? Where's your manners?"

"This is Erin and Zofia," Firelli said, sticking to first names.

"Good to meet you," Erin said, offering her hand.

Benny's grip was surprisingly firm and strong, but his nails were ragged and dirty. He had an unpleasant smell about him, one that Erin had long ago learned to associate with meth-heads. His breath was foul and when he grinned at her, she saw he was missing several teeth.

"Pleasure's mine," he said. "Y'know, everything above my knees still works just fine."

"I'll keep that in mind," Erin said in a very neutral tone.

"And a blonde, too!" he said, turning to Piekarski. "You got a nice glow to you. I bet you use some kinda moisturizer. You got great skin. Just looking at you, I can tell you'd taste great. Like a big scoop of vanilla ice cream."

To Piekarski's credit, she didn't blink or flinch. "I've already got a boyfriend, pal," she said. "One that showers regularly."

"Story of my life," Benny said. "All the good ones are taken."

"Where's this guy you want me to meet?" Firelli asked.

"He'll be here. Relax. Don't worry, he'll be glad to see you, especially these two babes. He likes the ladies. Could be a couple minutes, though. You want to sit down while you wait?" He winked at Erin and patted his lap.

Erin took a seat on the middle bench, resisting the urge to scoot as far away from Benny as possible. She thought of Ian Thompson. That man had also come back from war bearing scars and trauma, but he could hardly be more different. What determined which path you ended up walking? Was it a choice, or just sheer dumb luck? She was surprised at the pity she felt toward Benny. He was repulsive, but was that really his fault? And who was she to judge?

Firelli chatted with Benny about life on the street, which was no worse than usual. With autumn wearing on, and winter just around the corner, Benny was starting to think about cold weather.

"You got a place to sleep?" Firelli asked.

Benny laughed. "I got a dozen! I alternate. Don't want to wear out my welcome. Don't worry about me. Things get too bad, I can always find a spot at the shelter. I'm a war hero, remember. I got medals. They wouldn't turn me out."

A man in a black trench coat approached the benches. He was short and heavily built, with very broad shoulders and wavy black hair. He was obviously Italian.

"Hey, here's my man!" Benny said, waving to him. "Cristo, my own personal Jesus! What flavor salvation you got for me today?"

Cristo paused. His eyes darted to the other three.

"Hey, man, they're cool," Benny said. "This here's Bobby the Blade. We go way back, him and me. And these two fine fillies are his associates." He said the word in a way that suggested something that went well beyond a business relationship, tasting each syllable.

"That so?" Cristo said. He eyed Piekarski appreciatively, then shifted his gaze to Erin, starting with her legs and working his way up. "Listen, Benny, I don't know these three. The way things been going, we gotta be careful."

"I know, I know," Benny said, making calming motions with his hands. "But I'm telling you, they're okay. Me and Bobby, we talk all the time. He's always been straight-up."

"What about the other two?"

"The babes? Hey, they ain't no trouble. This here's, uh... Zofia. Am I saying that right? With a Z?"

"Yeah," Piekarski said.

"And this is Erin," Benny went on.

Cristo's face froze. His jaw hung slightly open and a look of absolute terror flooded his eyes.

"Junkyard O'Reilly," he whispered.

"What?" Benny said, not understanding.

"Hold on," Erin said. "I don't know what you heard about me, but—"

She was talking to Cristo's back. The man had recovered his wits enough to make a run for it. Before anyone else could say or do anything, he'd jumped the fence and was running for his life into the park.

"Shit," Erin said under her breath. Then she and Piekarski were off after him.

Chapter 9

The iron fence around the park was only three feet high. Erin braced one hand on the top rail and vaulted it easily, Piekarski right on her heels. Piekarski had her phone at her ear as she ran, and she was shouting something into it. Erin caught the words "south," "park," and "foot," but didn't pay much attention. Cristo's sudden movement had given him a head start and the Italian was really moving. He barged through a line of trees and shrubbery onto a path, scattering startled New Yorkers.

Erin skidded sideways, coming within a whisker of bowling over a gray-bearded old gentleman. She kept running, tracking the fleeing Cristo, who cast a frightened glance over his shoulder. It was a mistake; Cristo ran smack into another pedestrian. He hit the ground rolling, came up, and continued his panicked flight, but the accident had cost him half his lead.

Erin pumped her arms, inwardly blessing all those early-morning runs, and cursing the fact that Rolf wasn't with her. The K-9 would have already ended the pursuit. Rolf could do thirty miles an hour over flat ground.

Cristo broke from the trees into an open clearing, ten yards ahead of Erin. He sprinted toward the basketball courts at the southern end of the park. He risked another backward glance and Erin saw blood streaming down his forehead from his collision with the pavement. His eyes were very wide.

What was the matter with this guy? She hadn't made a single aggressive move, hadn't even had a visible weapon, let alone one in her hand. He'd used her Mob nickname, which meant he'd recognized her, but he wasn't reacting like a career criminal who'd just seen a police officer. Hell, he hadn't even been doing anything illegal at their meeting. The smart thing to do would've been for him to play it cool and walk away. She couldn't have done a thing about it.

Maybe she shouldn't be chasing him. This might spoil Firelli's plan to work up the chain to the mysterious Stallone. The pursuit had been ninety percent reflexes and instinct. When a bad guy ran, you chased him. It was just one of those things. Cops and K-9s understood this.

"Stop!" Erin barked, but it was wasted breath. Nothing short of death or physical impossibility would keep Cristo from running. He charged onto the middle basketball court, where a handful of young men were playing a pickup game. One of them was just going up for a jump shot when Cristo's shoulder caught him in the hip. The player went off balance and tumbled to the court with a yelp. The ball bounced out of his hands and over the sideline.

"Hey! What's the matter with you?" another player shouted. His teammates added their own questions in much ruder language. Cristo ignored them, flinging open the gate in the chain-link fence that bordered the southern edge of the courts. He tried to slam the gate, but it didn't latch. Erin hit it only a second or two behind him and plowed through. Piekarski was right there with her.

They were on a grid of concrete sidewalks now, passing the public restrooms and closing on a playground. Erin saw little kids on the jungle gym, their moms and nannies watching them, and her heart jumped into her throat. Cristo was headed straight into the middle of them. He was obviously terrified and desperate, and he might very well be armed. There was no telling what he might do.

The thought of her gun flitted through Erin's mind and she immediately dismissed it. Drawing a weapon in a crowd of innocent bystanders would only make things worse. She poured on more speed, closing the distance.

A little girl, about the age of Erin's niece, stood squarely in Cristo's path, staring at the onrushing man with wide eyes. Cristo paid no attention to the kid. He was looking back again, straight at Erin, and didn't see the girl.

He also didn't see the very large man running toward him on a diagonal collision course. The man was broad-shouldered, bulky, and had the face of a thug. He was also holding an unusually big and strong German Shepherd's leash, and his face, though alarming, was one Erin was very glad to see.

Vic clotheslined Cristo with one muscular arm. The smaller man's forward motion stopped as abruptly as if he'd run headlong into a brick wall. His feet kept going two strides further than the rest of him, flying up as he fell flat on his back.

Rolf, barking excitedly, pounced on the downed man, planting his front paws on Cristo's chest. The ninety-pound dog barked in his face, daring him to move. Rolf hadn't been ordered to bite, so he didn't, but he wanted his quarry to know that biting was still an option that was very much on the table.

Erin was there a second later, followed closely by Piekarski. Both women were breathing hard. Vic looked at them, then back at the downed man.

"Somebody want to tell me what the hell's going on?" he asked. "I thought we were trying to be inconspicuous."

"Thanks, Vic," Erin said. "Where'd you come from?"

"I was parked down on Worth Street," he said, pointing a thumb back the way he'd come. "Then I get a call from my girl saying you're chasing some chump south, and could I do something about it. So I got your mutt, I saw this idiot running away from you, and here we are."

"Jesus Christ!" Cristo whimpered. "Get him off me! I won't tell nobody! I won't say nothing! Don't let him eat me!"

Rolf barked at him again. It was a good thing he didn't understand. His professionalism would've been offended by the suggestion that he might eat a criminal.

Erin knelt down beside the terrified man. She put her face beside Rolf's. "What's the matter with you?" she demanded. "Why'd you run?"

Cristo's eyes shifted to the other two cops. "Get her away from me!" he begged. "She's gonna kill me!"

Piekarski and Vic exchanged quizzical looks. "Zofia, who *is* this guy?" Vic asked. "What'd he do?"

"I didn't do nothing!" Cristo said.

"I didn't ask you, dickwad," Vic said.

"Why'd you run?" Erin asked again.

"Because you were gonna kill me!" Cristo said.

Erin was baffled. "I wanted to talk to you," she said. "Why would I want to kill you?"

"You're Junkyard O'Reilly! You kill guys all the time!"

"Wait a second," Piekarski said. "Hold on just a minute. What's this guy talking about, Erin?"

"Later," Vic said.

"Your other guys got Luca and the Manzanos!" Cristo babbled. "Now you're coming for me! I swear, I didn't know! You gotta tell Vinnie I didn't know!"

"Vinnie?" Erin repeated, trying not to sound as surprised as she felt. You didn't want the subject of an interrogation to know when you were confused. "The Oil Man?" she guessed.

"I was just moving the stuff!" Cristo went on. "I didn't set up the deal! It was just a job, that's all!"

Erin's mind was racing. "You were moving the drugs for the Manzanos and Frazetti," she guessed. "And you got them from Stallone."

"Yeah! It was him! It was all his idea! He's the one you want! Not me! Get your dog off me! He's gonna bite my face off!"

Rolf wagged his tail and continued standing on Cristo. Now that the humans were talking, it seemed unlikely he'd get to do any biting, but Erin seemed glad he was where he was, so he stayed right there, awaiting instructions. He was pretty sure he'd done the right thing. Maybe he'd even been a good enough boy to get his rubber Kong ball.

"He won't unless I tell him to," Erin said. "Keep talking. You move product for Stallone. That means you know where he is and how to find him."

Cristo nodded frantically. "You gotta promise you're not gonna kill me!" he begged. "You can't! Not with all these people around!"

"I'm not going to kill you," Erin said. "Not without a really good reason. Who was the buyer? Was it Frazetti?"

"No. I got the shit to the Manzanos. They were taking it to Frazetti. But Frazetti was working for someone else."

"Who?"

"I don't know. I don't know! I swear! Stallone set it up! He knows. Talk to him!"

"And where can I find him?"

"He hangs out at Original Vincent's."

"The Italian place at Mott and Hester?" Piekarski asked.

"Yeah! You can find him there! Can I go now?" Cristo asked with pathetic hopefulness.

"No," Erin said. "But I think Rolf can stop stepping on you now. Rolf, *fuss!*"

Rolf hopped off Cristo and pranced to Erin's side, looking up at her expectantly.

"*Sei brav,*" she said, reaching into the pocket of her coat and extracting Rolf's favorite rubber ball. He stared raptly at it. She dropped it into his waiting mouth. He immediately began happily working his jaws. The rubber made wet squeaking sounds.

"What do we do with this mope?" Vic asked, grabbing Cristo's shoulder and yanking him to his feet.

"We'd better take him in," Erin said. "We don't want him tipping off his boss. Do you guys want to stash him back at the Five?"

"Can do," Piekarski said. "What're we charging him with?"

"Nothing at the moment," Erin said. "You can hold him overnight without charges."

Firelli jogged up to them. "Hey, guys, what gives?" he demanded. "You scared the crap out of Benny. Last I saw of him, he was rolling north as fast as his arms could move him. Is this your idea of a low-key operation?"

"Sorry about that," Erin said. "I swear, it wasn't our fault."

"I thought you were okay," Cristo said to Firelli in sulky tones. "You nearly got me killed!"

"Nobody was going to kill you," Erin said wearily. "We're just going to keep you off the streets for a day or so. If you're in as much danger as you say, you should thank us."

"What now?" Firelli asked.

"Now we're going to Original Vincent's restaurant," Erin said.

"I love Italian food," Vic said.

"Who doesn't?" Erin said. "Italian food is like Irish whiskey. Everybody loves it."

*   *   *

"Why can't I go?" Cristo whined.

"Because you're going to ID Stallone for us," Erin said. "Once you do that, you can go sit in a nice comfy holding cell."

They were sitting at a side table in Vincent's restaurant. Vic had Cristo pinned between him and the wall and was keeping a close eye on him. Erin was seated across from them. Piekarski and Firelli had taken another table, next to the door. Rolf was in Erin's Charger, enjoying a pleasant early-afternoon nap. Erin had left him his rubber ball, so he ought to be happy enough when he woke up.

"Stallone ain't here," Cristo said.

"You told us he would be," Erin reminded him.

"Yeah, well, maybe he stepped out for a while."

"Then we'll wait."

"Can I get you folks anything?" the waiter asked. He looked very dapper and old-school in his black vest and bow tie.

"Just coffee for me, thanks," Erin said.

Vic took his eyes off their prisoner long enough to give the menu a quick once-over. "I'll have some of your famous shrimp balls," he said. "And coffee."

"Excellent choice, sir," the waiter said. He shifted his attention to Cristo. "And for you, sir?"

"I'm not hungry," Cristo said sullenly.

"C'mon," Vic said. "The Department's buying."

"They are?" Erin said.

"Hell yes," Vic said. "We can expense this. We're on official business. This is a stakeout. Only without the steak."

"Just veal, chicken, seafood, and pasta, sir," the waiter said with an artificial smile. "But we're always glad to cater to New York's finest."

"Maybe a salad," Erin said. "I'll have the Caesar."

"Very good, ma'am," the waiter said.

"And you?" Vic said, elbowing Cristo.

"Gnocchi," Cristo said. He rubbed his side and glared at Vic, who just grinned at him.

"You ever eat here before?" Vic asked Erin.

"No," she said. "You?"

"Nah. There's gotta be, like, a thousand restaurants in New York."

"At least," she agreed. "You like shrimp?"

"It's okay," he said. "My rule of thumb is, if a place says one of their dishes is world-famous, you'd better order it. If a cook does something well, he's proud of it. They say their shrimp balls are famous, that's good enough for me. I'll try anything once." He frowned. "I didn't know shrimp even *had* balls."

"I don't think that's what they meant," Erin said, making a face.

"Just so we're clear," Vic said to Cristo. "When this punk comes in, you tap my foot with yours. I don't want you to say anything, and I sure as hell don't want you staring at him. Just two taps, that's it. You got that?"

"Yeah," Cristo muttered.

"Or I could just take a walk and leave you here with Junkyard O'Reilly," Vic added with a nasty smile. "Just the two of you. She'll take real good care of you."

Cristo blanched and clamped his mouth shut.

Their food arrived after a wait that seemed longer than it was. Stakeouts were like that. When you didn't know how long you'd be waiting for something, or whether it would happen at all, time crawled. On the plus side, Erin reflected, there were plenty of worse places to hang out than a nice little Italian restaurant.

"Hey, Erin, you gotta try one of these," Vic said, pushing his plate toward her. "I've got no idea what's in them, but they're fantastic."

"Shrimp, I expect," she said, poking a shrimp ball with her fork and taking a bite. "You're right. These are really good!"

Vic stiffened slightly. Erin looked at his carefully neutral expression, very uncharacteristic of Vic, and knew he'd gotten Cristo's signal. She wanted to turn around and have a look. Instead, she turned her head toward the wall, which was covered with framed photographs. The pictures were behind glass. In the glass, she could see a faint reflection of the room. She saw a man walking to a corner table.

"That's him?" she asked quietly.

"Yeah," Cristo said.

"You sure?"

He nodded.

"You're gonna just stay right there," Vic told him. "We'll be back for you in a minute."

"He'll run the second our backs are turned," Erin predicted.

"No, he won't," Vic said. In one smooth movement, before Erin or Cristo knew what he was doing, he whipped out his handcuffs, snapped one bracelet around Cristo's right wrist, and closed the other one around the back of the drug dealer's chair. "Just hang tight, buddy," he said.

Erin nodded to Vic. They stood up in unison and started toward the corner of the room. Erin got her first good look at Stallone. He was a square-jawed, darkly handsome man with thick, wavy hair and a scar at one corner of his mouth. The scar pulled his lip into a sardonic sneer that did remind her a little of the famous actor. He was wearing a black leather jacket over a turtleneck sweater. His hands, resting on the tabletop, had rings on four of the fingers.

Drug dealers didn't last long on the street without developing an extremely good danger sense. Stallone was no exception. Erin and Vic hadn't gone more than two steps toward him when he was up and moving for the door. He wasn't running; the motion had no panic about it. He was walking quickly and purposefully.

Firelli and Piekarski stepped in front of the door. Firelli made eye contact with Stallone and shook his head. Piekarski pulled back her jacket to show her shield and her holstered pistol.

Stallone's shoulders slumped for a second. Then he recovered himself and turned to face Vic and Erin. He reached under his jacket.

"Don't!" Erin snapped. She and the other three cops all went for their guns. Vic, who hadn't been worrying about concealment, got his Sig-Sauer out first. Erin was a half-second later, hampered by the unfamiliar weight of Vic's ridiculous hand cannon.

"Whoa," Stallone said, holding up his other hand. He slowly drew out his hand, making no sudden movements. He held a snub-nosed revolver between his thumb and index finger, the muzzle dangling to point at the floor.

"Drop it!" Vic and Erin ordered in unison.

"Okay, okay," the man said, laying the pistol on a nearby table. "Relax, guys. I don't want trouble."

"Says the guy carrying a concealed weapon," Vic snorted. "You know the drill, buddy. Face the wall and spread 'em."

"Care to tell me what I've done?" Stallone asked, obeying their instructions. He'd obviously been frisked and arrested before, probably more than once.

"Besides packing that pistol?" Erin replied. "I don't suppose you've got a permit for that."

"Before that," he said. "You didn't know I was strapped till just now."

The other restaurant patrons were chattering excitedly. Several of them had their phones out and were taking pictures and video. Erin handed Vic her handcuffs, since his were already spoken for. As he started cuffing Stallone, Erin noticed that several of the bystanders weren't looking at the arrest. That was unusual enough that she followed their gaze to see what was more interesting than an ongoing bust.

She was just in time to see the side exit swing shut behind a dining-room chair which was, presumably, still shackled to a frightened Italian.

"Oh, you have got to be kidding me," she said, spinning on her heel and taking off after him.

Chasing the same perp twice in less than two hours was embarrassing. Chasing the same perp when he was trying to run and dragging a piece of furniture by one wrist was downright silly. If Cristo had been thinking clearly, he would have picked up the chair and carried it in his arms. Then again, if he'd been thinking clearly, he wouldn't be making a break for it while handcuffed to a chair in the first place. It clattered and rattled behind him, bouncing off the sidewalk and dragging at him like a ball and chain.

Erin caught up to him before he'd gotten fifty yards. The chair smacked against a newsstand. The chair caromed into Cristo, tangling his legs, and he went down in a heap. By the time he'd gotten himself sorted out, Erin was standing over him, arms crossed.

"Didn't we already do this?" she said. "Now I've got you on resisting arrest and misdemeanor theft, too."

"What're you talking about?" Cristo asked. "I didn't steal anything!"

She tapped the chair with her foot.

"I couldn't help that! You guys chained me to it!"

"Which is why we've got you for resisting arrest," she said. "Come on, get up. Let's go return the chair. Good thing it isn't broken, or we'd have you on vandalism, too. That thing's sturdier than it looks."

Chapter 10

"So, now what?" Piekarski asked.

The four of them were standing outside the restaurant. Stallone was stuffed in the back of Piekarski's Mini Cooper. Cristo was sharing Rolf's compartment in Erin's Charger, which made the Italian very nervous. Rolf was watching the man closely, daring him to try anything.

"Now we lean on Stallone," Erin said.

"That easy, huh?" Firelli asked. "And just where were you planning on doing that?"

"In an interrogation room," she said.

He raised his eyebrows. "Won't that put us on the radar?"

"Shit, he's right," Vic said. "We have to be careful. If we take these mopes back to the Eightball, Keane's gonna hear about it. And if we go to the Five..."

"Then our IAB guys will know," Piekarski finished. "But we can't just shove them in some dark basement. We're not the CIA. We're cops. We have to follow the rules, and the rules are, we need to process them. They get their phone call, they get their lawyer, the whole deal."

The officers looked at one another for a long moment.

"She's right," Erin said. "But we haven't Mirandized them yet. They're technically not under arrest."

"Better not tell them that," Vic said. "What if they ask to leave?"

"Then we put them under arrest. But the moment we do, Stallone's going to lawyer up."

"What about the other guy?" Vic asked. "Cristo?"

"He's kind of an idiot," Firelli said. "So he might not know any better. Did you see that crap with the chair?"

"Yeah, why did you cuff him to the chair?" Erin asked Vic. "We don't really need him anymore anyway. We could just turn him loose. We can't pin any real crime on him."

"If you feel that way, why'd you chase him?" Vic shot back.

"He still had the restaurant's chair, thanks to you. They were going to want it back."

Vic shook his head. "I guess I was remembering that magician. You remember? The guy I left in the back of my car?"

"And he vanished," Erin said, smiling at the memory. "That's what you get for leaving an escape artist unsupervised."

"Exactly. I like my perps to stay where I left them. So I locked the punk down."

"Can somebody explain one thing to me, please?" Piekarski said.

All heads turned toward her.

"Why did he think you were going to kill him?" Piekarski asked Erin. "He was scared half to death. And he recognized you. We didn't ID ourselves as cops. Do you know him?"

"Never saw him before today," Erin said.

"He called you Junkyard O'Reilly," Piekarski went on. "You've got a Mob nickname?"

"So do I," Firelli said mildly.

"That's different," Piekarski said. "You used to be a street hood. Erin didn't. Her dad was a cop. What'd your dad do, Firelli?"

He sighed. "My old man held up delivery trucks," he said. "He'd get tipped off about shipments and he'd jack them. His gang had an arrangement with the delivery guys. They'd hand over the merchandise, nice and easy, and nobody ever got hurt. It was civilized, as far as armed robberies go."

"And you didn't look surprised," Piekarski went on, turning to Vic. "What do you know about this?"

"You ever think of going for your gold shield, Zofia?" Vic asked. "You got detective instincts."

"Someday, maybe," she said. "Stop dodging the question."

"Everyone here has their secrets," Vic said, giving her a pointed look. "Maybe we all better stop digging before we uncover something nobody wants out in the open."

"What's he talking about?" Firelli asked.

Piekarski's cheeks flushed. "None of your goddamn business," she snapped. "I'm not stupid! You got a witness blown up, Erin. And you were there, Vic. What happened that night? That was a serious screw-up. There should've been a big departmental investigation. How come IAB only gave you a slap on the wrist and temporary desk duty? And what was it, a car bomb? Isn't that a crazy coincidence?"

"Piekarski, you want to stop talking right now," Erin said quietly.

The other woman stared at her. "Who are you protecting?" she demanded.

"Zofia," Vic said, laying a hand on her shoulder.

Piekarski shook him off. "When is somebody going to tell me what the hell's happening?"

Vic said nothing and gave Erin a look that held a lot of unspoken thoughts. Piekarski turned from him to Erin, who also stayed silent.

"Don't you trust me?" Piekarski asked.

"You need to trust us," Erin said.

"I don't deserve this," Piekarski said bitterly.

"You think that's what this is about?" Erin shot back. "Janovich didn't deserve to catch a bullet."

Piekarski's jaw tightened. "Just promise me you'll tell me the truth one of these days."

"Absolutely," Erin said. "But right now, we need to figure out what we're doing with those two bozos we caught."

"Like you said," Vic said. "We only really need one. That's half our problem solved right there."

Erin nodded. She walked the ten feet to her Charger and opened the back door. Rolf cocked his head at her.

"Let me out of here!" Cristo begged. "He's gonna bite me!"

Rolf opened his jaws and let his tongue hang out. He looked smug.

"Stand up," Erin said, pulling Cristo out. "Turn around."

She unlocked his cuffs. "There you are," she said. "You're free to go."

"That's it?" he asked in disbelief. "You're not charging me?"

"Do you want us to?" Vic asked. "Because if you're still standing there by the time I count to three, I bet I could think of something. One..."

They watched the frightened man scamper away. He kept looking back as he ran, as if he expected to see them taking aim at his retreating form. Then he made it around the corner and vanished from view.

"The way I see it," Vic said, "we don't really want Stallone either. We only want what he can tell us."

"He's a drug dealer," Piekarski said. "And we took a gun off him."

"And if we were street cops, that'd be good enough for a felony collar," Erin said.

"I *am* a street cop," Piekarski said.

"And this is an unofficial investigation," Erin reminded her.

"Fine! What do you suggest?"

"Let's just have a quiet talk with him, somewhere private."

"So you *do* want to stick him in a dark basement?"

Vic snickered. "I'll get the rubber hose," he volunteered.

Erin didn't laugh, didn't even crack a smile. She was very aware of just how close to the line they were walking. "None of that," she said. "Not even as a joke. Let's go for a little drive. I'll ride in back with him. Vic, you can tail us in the Charger."

"Again?" he said. "Rolf and me, we're gonna be good buddies by the time this whole thing is over."

Rolf gave Vic a dubious look. Then he looked back at Erin and cocked his head again.

"It's okay, kiddo," she told the K-9. "I need you to keep an eye on this big goon for me."

Piekarski got behind the wheel of her Mini Cooper. Firelli took the shotgun seat and Erin slid in back beside Stallone. The little car started rolling.

"Finally," Stallone said. "Let's get this over with."

"What's your real name?" Erin asked.

He blinked. "You're busting me and you don't even know my name?"

"They call you Stallone on the street," she said. "What's it say on your birth certificate?"

"And your arrest reports," Firelli added over his shoulder.

"Dom Silvestri," Stallone said.

"And Dom is short for...?" Erin prompted.

"Dominic. Mom thought I should be a monk when I grew up."

"Really?"

His scarred mouth twisted a little tighter. "Of course not. My mom's an Italian Catholic. She wants something like twenty-three grandkids. That'd be tough to get with a celibate son."

"How long have you been in the heroin business, Dom?" Erin asked.

"Wow, you get right to it," Silvestri said. "Say, you look kind of familiar. Do I know you?"

"We haven't met," Erin said.

"No, I swear, you look so familiar," he said. "What do they call you?"

"Detective O'Reilly," she said. "Major Crimes."

"Junkyard O'Reilly?" he said, starting in surprise.

"Some guys call me that," she said.

Silvestri looked out the window. "Hey," he said to Piekarski. "We're headed east."

"What about it?" Piekarski asked without turning her head.

"The police station is west," he said. He was trying to keep his tone conversational, but Erin heard the uneasiness just below the surface.

"We're not going there just yet," Erin said. Not many civilians knew the exact location of the nearest precinct house.

"Where are we going?" Silvestri asked.

"Just for a little drive," Erin said.

Silvestri swallowed. Then he straightened his shoulders and looked her in the eye.

"I'm not going to beg," he said.

Erin was surprised by the wave of self-disgust that swept through her. "I don't want you to," she said. She couldn't help being a little impressed by the man. She knew she wasn't going to murder him, but he apparently didn't know that, so his courage, though unnecessary, was genuine.

"I know the Oil Man sent you," he went on.

"How do you know that?" Erin asked.

"You're here, aren't you?"

"Dom, I'm here because of what went down at the White Stallion," Erin said. "All I want from you is information. You play straight with me, I swear, you'll walk out of this car alive."

"I've never been to the White Stallion," he said.

"But you sold a big shipment to the Manzano brothers," she said. "And Luca Frazetti."

"You've got no proof that was me," Silvestri said. It was the sort of thing only a guilty man would say and they both knew it, but neither of them cared much. All it did was confirm for Erin that she was on the right track.

"Who did the Manzanos and Frazetti work for?" she asked.

"The Lucarellis," Silvestri said. "They were with them for years. You know that."

"And you know they weren't working for him anymore," she retorted. "Don't bullshit me. They went freelance. And they had too much product for you not to know who you were selling to."

He looked surprised. "You didn't know?" he asked.

"Know what?" Erin asked.

"The Manzanos were tight with Material Mattie," Silvestri said, referring to the late Matthew Madonna, former narcotics chief of the Lucarellis. "They couldn't stand the Oil Man. When Mattie got capped, they cut loose. They took Frazetti with them."

"Where did they go?" she pressed.

He gave her a funny look. "They don't tell you anything, do they," he said. "They just point you at your target and turn you loose. I'm not the guy you should be asking these questions."

"Who should I ask, then?" she asked. A worm of uncertainty was wriggling around in her midsection.

"Your boss," Silvestri said.

For an insane instant, Erin thought he was talking about Lieutenant Webb, or Captain Holliday, or maybe even the Police Commissioner. But that was nonsense. Silvestri was talking about crime, so he was referring to her underworld boss. And he didn't mean Vincenzo Moreno. That only left one person it could be.

"The O'Malleys are out of the drug business," she said, shaking her head.

"You sure about that?" Silvestri asked. He'd recovered from his earlier fear and his smile had a mocking, pitying cast to it.

Confirmation died on Erin's lips. *But Evan O'Malley said so!* Her inner voice protested, only to be met with the sardonic answer, *Yeah, and Evan O'Malley's never lied about anything, especially not to a cop.*

"I'm not saying I sold anything to the Manzanos," Silvestri said, with the caginess of a man who'd had too many brushes with the legal system. "I'm just saying, whatever they had in that club, it was bought by the Irish."

* * *

"Pull over," Erin said.

Piekarski swung the Mini Cooper out of the traffic lane, coming to rest against the curb. Vic brought the Charger in behind them. Erin unlocked Silvestri's cuffs.

"Get lost," she told him.

He stared at her for a long moment.

"Go on," she said.

"You're not what they say," he said.

"Oh, I'm exactly what they say," Erin said. "You're just not on my shit list. But you will be if I see you again. Now beat it."

"The least you could've done was drop me closer to home," he said with a faint smile.

"Are you complaining?" Erin asked.

"He sounds like he's complaining to me," Firelli said.

"Don't push it," Erin said.

Silvestri got out of the car, rubbing his wrists. Almost everybody did that after the handcuffs came off. They hadn't even been that tight. The bracelets had left no mark on his skin. It was just one of those things. The drug dealer watched them drive away. Then he started walking toward the nearest subway station.

"Let's get a cup of coffee," Erin suggested, pointing to a café half a block ahead.

Vic parked as close to them as he could and joined them. He had Rolf in hand and he didn't look happy. He met them at an outside table. The weather was cool enough that the rest of the patrons were inside, so they had the curbside seating all to themselves.

"You let that bastard walk?" he demanded. "Along with that other punk? This is the NYPD, not a fishing club. Catch-and-release isn't our style."

"They're not who we're after," Erin said. "We can pick those losers up any time we want. Remember, the dealers didn't tip Maxwell and his buddies off."

"Not a chance," Firelli agreed. "They lost their clients."

"But we don't know who else they talked to," Vic said. "I thought that was the point of the whole thing. Or did he spill when you had him in the car?"

"He said who his customers were," Piekarski said. She glanced at Erin. "Sort of. You want to tell him?"

"He said it was the Irish," Erin said. "The O'Malleys."

"I thought they were out of the heroin business," Vic said.

"That's what I said," Erin replied. "But he seemed pretty sure of it."

"You've got contacts in the O'Malleys," Firelli said. "You want to lean on them? Maybe something will shake loose."

"Oh, I'm going to talk to them," Erin said grimly.

"What should we do in the meantime?" Firelli asked. "Now that we're done burning my street contacts, that is."

"Someone needs to run Maxwell's financials," Erin said.

"Can't Ki—our IAB contact do that?" Vic asked, catching himself at the last moment.

"That contact's already stuck their neck way out for us," she said, shaking her head. "We can't ask for more."

"Of course we can," Vic said. "This is Major Crimes, not the bush league. We leave it all on the field. For Christ's sake, Erin, people are *dead!* Including one of our friends!"

"I know that!" she snapped. "Why do you think I'm doing this?"

"Fine," Vic sighed. "I'll run his financials."

"Discreetly," Erin reminded him.

He rolled his eyes. "It's not like I'm gonna put on a ski mask and rob his bank."

"That could be discreet," Piekarski said. "Assuming you leave the mask on."

* * *

Erin called Carlyle from her car. She tried to ignore Rolf's reproachful eyes, but she could feel them drilling into the back of her skull. The K-9 was having some concerns about the current direction of their partnership. He kept getting left in the car with Vic and he didn't like it. She'd have to do some training with Rolf. That ought to earn his forgiveness. Vic sulked in the passenger section. He hated accounting busywork.

"Afternoon, darling," Carlyle said.

"I need to see Evan," she said without preliminaries.

"What about?" he asked, immediately cautious.

"The drug trade in Little Italy."

"You're in luck," he said. "I didn't want to mention this earlier, on account of your current troubles, but Evan's wanting a wee get-together at his flat in the city. You weren't precisely invited, but you'd be more than welcome."

"Who's going to be there?"

"Finnegan, Miss Blackburn, the Snake, Maggie, and myself. But Erin, I don't know that Evan can be of much assistance in the matter of narcotics. He's out of that particular trade, and good riddance."

"That's not what I've been hearing."

Carlyle was silent for a few seconds. "I think you'd best accompany me tonight," he said at last. "From the sound of things, the two of you will be needing a clarification session. It's scheduled for eight o'clock sharp, so we ought to be leaving at half past seven. Are you coming back to the Corner now?"

"No. I owe Rolf some outside time. He's been very patient. I'll be at Central Park."

"Grand. Ta, darling."

"Dog training?" Vic said. "I'm in."

"You'll need to wear the bite sleeve," she said.

"I'll take that over running some loser's financials any day," Vic said.

Rolf's cold, wet nose poked Erin in the ear. She looked at him out of the corner of her eye.

"Okay, okay, kiddo," she told him. "We're going."

He licked her face. All was forgiven.

Chapter 11

"Rolf! *Fass!*"

Rolf launched himself across twenty yards of open ground. His target scarcely had time to brace for the impact. Then ninety pounds of fur, fangs, and fury piled into Vic. Rolf's teeth clamped down on the man's arm. Even with the protection of the heavy bite sleeve, those teeth could leave bruises.

Vic staggered back a step but managed not to go down. He clenched his jaw and held his arm suspended. Rolf's paws lost their purchase and he dangled in midair, but he didn't let go.

"Stop fighting my dog!" Erin shouted, using the proper script for the encounter.

"I'm not fighting him," Vic replied. His voice was tight with strain. "I'm trying to keep him from tearing my arm off."

"Rolf doesn't tear arms off," she said, closing on the man and dog. "Break them, yeah, but he's never dismembered anybody. Yet."

"I don't want to be the first," Vic said. "So how about getting this mutt off me?"

"*Pust!*" she ordered. Rolf immediately let go and dropped to the grass. He barked excitedly, tail lashing back and forth. He loved bite work more than just about anything. Maybe, if he was extra eager, he'd get to do it again.

Erin fished out Rolf's Kong toy and tossed it to him. "*Sei brav,*" she told him.

Rolf's world shrank to the size of the black rubber chew-toy. He snatched it out of the air faster than the human eye could follow. Then he went down on his belly, paws wrapped around his treasure, gnawing away for all he was worth.

"You ever think maybe he's a little *too* keen on his job?" Vic asked, pulling off the bulky bite sleeve. He spoke lightly, but he had worry lines on his forehead.

"Yeah, but I think the same thing about you," Erin said. "What's eating you?"

"Besides that mangy furball?"

"Yeah, besides that."

Vic took a look around. A few bystanders had noticed the K-9, but were prudently keeping a safe distance, so they had this little corner of Central Park to themselves.

"This is getting dangerous, Erin," he said.

"As long as you wear the sleeve, Rolf won't really hurt you," she assured him. "He knows his work and he'll always go for the arm."

"I remember one guy he bit on the ass."

"That was because he couldn't reach the arm. And if you recall, that bite on the backside just might have saved your life."

"Whatever. I wasn't talking about that. I'm talking about this case."

"We've dealt with worse guys before."

"I know. I'm worried about your cover. This could get you blown."

"How do you think?"

"Suppose that loser was right and the O'Malleys are behind the drug operation," he said. "What're you going to do? Arrest them? That'll look just great to your buddy Evan and his goons. They're supposed to think you're on their side."

"I've got no intention of arresting anybody tonight," she said. "Remember, if anybody tipped Maxwell off, it was the Lucarellis, not the O'Malleys."

"Yeah, I remember that," Vic growled. "I also remember what Vinnie the goddamn Oil Man thinks you did for him. Erin, there's no way you can win this game. If you burn the O'Malleys, you wreck your undercover op. If you stick it to the Lucarellis, same thing. And if you don't nail either of them, this whole thing is a waste of time."

"Vic..."

"Tell me I'm wrong."

"Maybe I should just tell Rolf to bite you some more," she muttered. "Okay, smartass, what do you think I should do?"

He shrugged. "I'm just a dumb meathead. What the hell do I know?"

"What are you hoping to get out of this?" she asked.

"Me? I'm just trying to help my girl out. I didn't know Janovich that well, but he meant a lot to Zofia, so I'm gonna help her out. Plus, if it *was* a botched hit, then that means Maxwell and his buddies are crooked, and I friggin' hate crooked cops. Hell, I hated you for a while, when I thought you were dirty."

"That's sweet, Vic."

"What do you mean it's sweet?"

"You're saying you don't hate me now."

"Oh, I still hate you," he said with a grin. "Just for different reasons."

"That's okay then," she said. "And don't worry. Evan O'Malley believes I'm in his corner. The bombing convinced him and Vinnie which side I was on. As long as I don't do anything directly against them, I can make this work. But I think I'd better talk to my handler before I go see Evan."

"Will I ever get to meet this handler of yours?"

"I hope not. If you do, it means things have probably gone pretty seriously wrong. Do you want me to drop you anywhere?"

"Nah, I'll take the subway. You sure you don't want backup?"

"Tonight? Don't you think it might be a little hard to explain the big, scary Russian?"

"Fine. Have all the fun without me. As usual."

*   *   *

Phil Stachowski always answered Erin's calls, no matter when, no matter where. He'd promised she could contact him any time, and he'd always been as good as his word. Even over the phone, Phil radiated a calm, comforting energy. Erin wondered how he did it. She didn't think she was as calm on her best day as he was on his worst. Maybe he was on some sort of meds.

He picked up on the second ring of her special phone. "Hello," he said.

"Hey, Phil," she said. "I'm fine. But you need to know what's about to go down."

"I don't suppose this is about that officer who was shot?"

"Yeah. I wasn't supposed to be there, but I was. The whole thing was a huge mess. It should've been a routine drug bust, but the Organized Crime Task Force showed up. Phil, they just started shooting, no warning. Next thing I knew, everybody was shooting everybody else. Here's the thing; I heard from a guy on the street that the mopes running the drugs were fronting for the O'Malleys."

"You told me the O'Malleys weren't dealing heroin anymore," Phil said. "Was this some other drug?"

"No, it was H," she said. "Lots of the stuff. We're talking kilograms."

"Is your source credible?"

"Iffy. But I think he believed what he was telling me."

Phil thought about that for a moment. "If it's true," he said, "it's a violation of Evan's agreement with Vincenzo Moreno."

"Yeah," Erin said.

"When countries break treaties, they go to war," Phil went on. "When mob bosses break agreements, it's the same thing."

"They go to the mattresses," she said grimly. "I've got a sit-down with Evan tonight at eight. I'll try to figure out what's going on. Maybe we can head this off before it gets ugly."

"Be careful, Erin. Don't jeopardize your cover. It's not worth it."

"Copy that."

"Where will you be?"

"Evan's penthouse. The O'Malley senior leadership will all be there. Except Corky, of course."

"Right." Phil knew about Corky's little jaunt off the edge of the map. "That means Carlyle will be the only ally you'll have in that room. And he's no fighter."

"It won't come to a fight," she said with more confidence than was really warranted. "Besides, I think I'll bring Rolf this time."

"Won't Evan think that's an aggressive move?"

"If anybody asks, I'll just tell them I'm worried about cops getting targeted. We think Janovich's shooting was just bad luck, really, but I won't tell the O'Malleys that. With one cop dead and another in the hospital, they'll understand a little paranoia."

"This isn't paranoia. It's healthy caution."

"It's getting harder to tell the difference," she said. "I'll call you after."

"Copy that," he said. "I'll wait up for you. And remember, for tonight, you can't be a cop."

"Right."

"I'm serious. They need to see what they want to see when they look at you."

"I've got this, Phil."

"I know. But still..."

"Yeah, I know. Be careful."

*   *   *

"Be careful," Erin said again.

"I'll try, darling," Carlyle said. "But have you heard the proverb, 'The safest place to hide is in the mouth of the wolf?'"

"I was talking to myself," she said. "We're going into a dangerous situation without backup or protection." She reached behind herself and fastened the hooks on her bra. It was a special one. In place of the underwire was a recording wire and miniature thumb drive. She made sure no funny bulges were showing through the fabric, then pulled a blouse over her shoulders and began buttoning it.

"I've heard it said that the suit is modern man's armor," he said. He was on the other side of the bedroom, knotting his necktie. It was deep crimson, nicely contrasting with his customary charcoal-gray suit.

"I'd rather have Kevlar with ballistic plates," she said. She'd considered wearing a skirt, knowing it would make her less visibly threatening, but that would make it harder to conceal her ankle holster, so she stuck to her usual black slacks. The little .38 revolver nestled against her right leg, just above the shoe.

"I trust you've a plan?" he asked.

"That depends," she said.

"On what?"

"On whether Evan really is dealing drugs in Little Italy."

"Are you planning on teaching him the error of his ways?"

"No, he's a lost cause. I'm just trying to figure out the truth."

He smiled. "You say that like it's a simple thing."

"I'm not planning a confrontation," she assured him. "This is all about gathering information, nothing more. Nobody's going to get hurt tonight."

"Are you ready?" Carlyle asked.

"Just about. Give me a couple minutes to do something with my hair and dab on a little makeup."

"You look lovely already."

She kissed him on the cheek. "That's sweet of you. But you were talking about armor a minute ago. If a man has his suit, a woman has her cosmetics kit. I may be a tough street bitch, but I'm feminine enough to know that."

"I never forget you're a woman," he said with a wink worthy of Corky Corcoran.

Chapter 12

Erin had only visited Evan O'Malley's penthouse once before. It was in Tribeca, one of the most expensive neighborhoods in Manhattan. The doorman, resplendent in his dark green uniform with polished brass buttons, bowed slightly and opened the door for her, Carlyle, and Rolf.

"Ms. O'Reilly, Mr. Carlyle," he said in tones of professional respect.

"Should I have tipped him?" Erin asked Carlyle as they waited for the elevator.

"No need," he replied. "Evan compensates the lad quite well. He's not precisely a typical doorman."

"I noticed the shoulder holster," she said. The man's uniform was well-tailored, but not quite well enough to conceal the telltale bulge from a veteran cop's eye. Erin thought of Carlyle's own bodyguard. Ian had driven them to the meeting, but he wasn't coming in. He'd wait in the car. She wasn't worried about him; Ian was a former sniper and could be very patient. But she would have felt better having him watching her back. At least they had Rolf.

They got out of the elevator and were immediately accosted by a pair of Evan's goons. The men relaxed when they recognized Carlyle, but they looked at Rolf with wary eyes.

"What's with the dog?" one of them asked.

"He's mine," Erin said, taking the conversational offensive. That was usually a good idea when dealing with street thugs. Let them think you were scared and they'd be all over you. "You got a problem with him?"

The other goon nudged his buddy. "Hey, that's Junkyard O'Reilly," he said in a low voice. "Don't you know about her and her dog? Anyway, she's been here before. The dog's okay."

Comprehension dawned on the first guy's face. "Hey, no problem," he said hastily. "I didn't mean nothing, ma'am. Go on in."

Erin nodded to him, concealing a smile. There were definite upsides to having a scary street rep. She led Rolf past the guards and into Evan's apartment.

Yet another of Evan's guys met them at the door. Erin knew this one.

"Hey, PR," she said. "How's things?"

"Going good," Paddy Ryan said. He was Evan's personal assistant, and though his smile seemed harmless, even friendly, Erin didn't trust him an inch. "Haven't seen you in a while. I hope you're well."

"I'm fine," she said, giving him the lie that most often fell from her lips.

"You still got your dog, I see," he said, offering Rolf his hand. Rolf sniffed it, keeping his eyes on Erin. "He's a good lookin' animal, for sure. The others just got here; you're right on time. They're in the den. Remember where that is?"

"We do, lad," Carlyle said.

"Good to see you, too, Cars," Ryan said. "How's business? Booming?"

Carlyle favored the weak pun with the slight smile that was all it deserved. He helped Erin with her coat and handed both it and his own to Ryan, who hung them in the closet. Then they walked into Evan's den.

It was a dark room, finished in wood paneling. Erin's shoes sank into expensive, thick-pile carpet. The room was dominated by the card table in the center, around which sat Evan O'Malley and most of his lieutenants. Evan was facing the door, looking straight at Erin with his cold blue eyes. To his right sat his chief enforcer, Gordon Pritchard, AKA the Snake. Pritchard was a small, slender man, the right side of his face horribly scarred by old burns. He raised a single black-gloved finger in acknowledgment. He remained perfectly still otherwise, giving a sense of coiled, dangerous energy.

The other three at the table were less intimidating. Little mousy Maggie Callahan was on Evan's left, shuffling a deck of cards. If Erin hadn't known Maggie was Evan's bookkeeper, she would have thought the woman incredibly out of place. But Maggie had a near-perfect memory for numbers. She didn't just keep Evan's ledger; she *was* his ledger.

The final two members of the gathering, seated across from Evan, were Kyle Finnegan and Veronica Blackburn. Finnegan looked disheveled as ever, with an expression of mild, vacant concern wandering across his face. Veronica was dressed to kill, wearing a little too much makeup and too little clothing. She was practically popping out of her tight-fitting, low-cut top, her skirt was just barely long enough to be decent, and her heels were so tall Erin had trouble believing the other woman could walk in them.

Erin knew all these men and women, so she didn't pay much attention to the outer trappings. She was trying to gauge their current emotional state. Evan was impossible to read. Pritchard was cool and calculating. Maggie seemed a little twitchier than usual. Finnegan was... Finnegan. He didn't play by the same rules as most people.

Veronica smiled at Erin and Carlyle. "Hi," she said. "Glad you could come. You look good, Cars. You working out these days?"

"When I can, Ms. Blackburn," Carlyle said.

"Well, it shows," Veronica said. "You're looking fine too, Erin. I hope they're not running you too ragged on the job."

"I manage," Erin said. She thought Veronica was nervous. The other woman normally spoke in a husky, too-seductive voice, coming on strong, enjoying making the men and women around her as uncomfortable as possible. Now she seemed brittle, eager to please but off her game.

"Thank you for coming, both of you," Evan said, getting to his feet. "I see you've brought your dog again, Miss O'Reilly."

"Seemed like a good idea," Erin said.

"Oh?" Evan raised an eyebrow a fraction of an inch. "Why might that be?"

"I don't know if you'd recall this, sir," she said. "But last time I was here, I got jumped on the sidewalk outside. I don't want that happening again."

"It won't," Evan said. She was talking about the late Mickey Connor and he knew it. "Please, take your seats. Mr. Ryan will take your orders if you want any refreshment."

"Whiskey, neat, if you please, lad," Carlyle said.

"You too, ma'am?" Ryan asked Erin.

"I'm actually in the mood for a cocktail," Erin said.

"Okay," Ryan said uneasily. "What do you want?" He was a good gangster and aide, but not a particularly skilled bartender.

Erin pretended to think, tapping a finger against her chin. "Isn't there a drink called an Italian Stallion?" she asked innocently.

"Maybe," Ryan said helplessly, but Erin didn't care. She wasn't even looking at him. She was watching the reactions of the others at the table.

Maggie didn't seem to be paying attention and might not have even heard what she'd said. Pritchard appeared bored. Evan's mouth tightened slightly but he didn't otherwise react. Veronica flinched visibly. And Finnegan cleared his throat.

"A horse, a horse, my kingdom for a horse," he quoted.

"I know that one," Erin said. "Shakespeare, right?"

"*Richard III*," Carlyle said. "His last words, unless I'm mistaken."

"Um... what's in an Italian Stallion, ma'am?" Ryan asked.

Erin had no idea. She hadn't even known for sure that there was such a drink. Maybe there wasn't. She wracked her brain for a recipe, any recipe.

Carlyle, the publican, came to her rescue. "An ounce, I think, of Campari," he said. "Two ounces of bourbon and a wee dash of bitters."

"Yeah, that's it," Erin said. It wasn't what she wanted to drink, but now she was stuck with it. If it had bourbon in it, she thought, it couldn't be that bad.

"On the way," Ryan said and made himself scarce.

"It appears some of us have things on our minds," Evan said, staring at Erin. "But there's no rush. We have all evening. Maggie, deal the cards. If you'd care to purchase your chips, ladies and gentlemen?"

"Let's to it pell-mell," Finnegan said to no one in particular. "If not to heaven, then hand in hand to hell."

*　*　*

Erin was no better than decent at Texas hold 'em. Fortunately, she was playing with Carlyle's money, so dropping a thousand dollars was something she could shrug off. It would have given her mother fits to know Erin was gambling for real money, in the company of gangsters. That the money itself was incidental would have only made things worse for Mary O'Reilly, who had raised four children, three of whom had gone to college, on a Patrol cop's none-too-generous salary.

Tonight, for a pleasant change, Erin's luck was good. She was assisted by the fact that Veronica was playing terribly, as was Finnegan. Erin's stack of chips gradually grew, at the expense of everyone else at the table.

"Luck's your lady tonight, darling," Carlyle said as Erin laid down a full house, eights over fours, beating Evan's three eights, both of them making use of a pair of eights in the river. She raked in the biggest pot of the night.

"So it seems," Evan said quietly. He showed as much emotion at the loss of three hundred dollars as he would have over misplacing a handful of pocket change.

"I don't trust the cards," Erin said. "Atlantic City is full of people who think they're lucky."

"Uncertain way of gain," Finnegan said. "But sin will pluck on sin."

"That's how casinos make their money, aye," Carlyle said.

"I guess I'm glad I'm lucky in something, anyway," Erin said.

"Had a run of bad luck in other things?" Veronica said. "Join the club."

"Do I detect a hint of bitterness, Ms. Blackburn?" Carlyle said. "On the basis of a few turns of the cards? I should think we've all ample funds to cover a wee bit of misfortune at games of chance."

"It's easy for you to talk," Veronica said. "You've got the cash rolling in. What about the rest of us?"

"I was under the impression our finances were in a grand condition," Carlyle said. Erin forced herself to look at him and not so much as glance Maggie's direction. Carlyle was watching Evan as he spoke. He didn't bat an eye at Maggie.

"They are," Evan said. "Is there something about which you're dissatisfied, Ms. Blackburn?"

Veronica's lip curled. "What do you think?" she shot back. "I lost better than half my income."

"If you're referring to recent business decisions that happened at the topmost level of this organization, I'm sorry you're displeased," Evan said in clipped, formal tones. "Perhaps I should remind you that your controlling interest in the late Mr. McIntyre's affairs was a temporary expedient and was never intended to replace your previous and present function."

"So I should be a good girl and scurry back to my street corner?" Veronica said. "I did good work for you, Evan."

"For which you've been compensated," Evan said coolly.

"I can do more," she persisted. "Didn't I prove that?"

"We've had this conversation," Evan said. "If I change my mind, you'll be the first to know."

"How about you, Cars?" Veronica said abruptly, turning to Carlyle. "You got anything going that needs someone to help make it happen?"

Carlyle's eyes went from her to Evan and back again. "I don't think this is something we ought to be discussing," he said.

"Things are a little unstable to be talking about big organizational changes, if you ask me," Erin said.

"What do you mean, Ms. O'Reilly?" Evan asked.

"I mean there's a reason you got out of the drug trade, sir," she said. "Between the Lucarellis and the Colombian cartels, it's gotten a lot more dangerous lately. You remember what happened to Liam McIntyre."

"None of us are likely to forget," Carlyle said.

"Bloody he was, and bloody was his end," Finnegan said.

"Kyle, why do you always talk funny?" Veronica demanded.

"I clothe my naked villainy with odd ends stolen out of holy writ," Finnegan said. He took a sip of his drink, shuddered and cleared his throat. "Is it Wednesday?" he asked.

"It's Friday," Erin said.

"Really?" Finnegan scratched his head. "Alcohol only affects me on Wednesdays. Or at least, it used to. Did anybody notice the phase of the moon?"

Erin decided to ignore Finnegan and turned back to Evan. "The Oil Man's been having some housekeeping troubles," she said. "A few of his guys weren't happy with how things shook out after Mattie Madonna went down, so they struck out on their own."

"Not smart," Pritchard rasped.

"They found that out the hard way," Erin said. "All three of them got clipped."

"I heard about that," Evan said. "What's your point?"

"They were shot by police," Erin said.

"It's a hazard in that business," Evan said. "One more reason I'm glad I don't participate in it."

"It was a setup," Erin said. "Those cops went there planning to kill those guys."

She saw a flicker of interest in Evan's eyes. "Is that so? And did you hear anything along those lines, Ms. O'Reilly?" he asked.

Erin suppressed a wave of revulsion at his implication. She reminded herself that here and now, she wasn't Erin O'Reilly, straight-arrow detective. She was Erin O'Reilly, gun for hire. Evan was asking if she'd been offered the job. How would a woman who'd killed for the mob handle this situation?

"Nobody thought to ask me," she said, trying to put a little petulance into her voice, but not too much. It wouldn't do to overact. She wished she'd taken theater classes in college, back when she'd been so focused on preparing for the police academy. Nobody had told her she'd need to lie so much.

"Who passed the order?" Evan asked.

"I'm not sure," she said truthfully. "The Oil Man had the most motive. He'd be taking out his competition at the same time as he was getting revenge on some traitors. But I've been asking around, and word on the street is that the Italians were working for someone else."

Evan raised an eyebrow. "Really? And who might that be?"

Erin looked at him steadily. "I was hoping to discuss that with you, sir."

There were several seconds of complete silence. Veronica uncrossed and re-crossed her legs. Maggie bridged the cards and shuffled them twice. Finnegan hummed a tune that Erin found faintly familiar but couldn't place.

"We'll take a few minutes' break," Evan said, getting to his feet. "I need to attend to some brief business. If you'd be so kind as to step into my office, Ms. O'Reilly?"

Erin stood up. "I'd be glad to, sir," she said. Rolf scrambled to his paws when Erin got up, ready for action.

Evan paid no attention to the dog, leading Erin down a short hallway to a door. He fished a ring of keys from his pocket and unlocked the door, which was also protected by a keypad. He stepped in front of the pad as he entered the code, so there was no way Erin could see it. Then he opened the door and ushered her in.

The first thing Erin noticed about the office was that it was windowless, which struck her as very odd. Its walls were lined with soundproofing material, making it look like a weird cross between a corporate executive office and a musician's recording studio. A new-looking computer sat on an antique wooden desk. Erin wondered what was on the hard drive. Probably nothing too incriminating; Evan was too smart to keep anything truly awful on his personal devices. He had Maggie's remarkable brain for that.

"Close the door, please," Evan said. Erin did so. He didn't sit down, nor did he offer her a seat. There was only one chair in the room, a black leather swivel chair in front of the desk. Evan opened one of the left-hand desk drawers and brought out a bottle and a pair of shot glasses.

He poured her a shot of Glen Docherty-Kinlochewe whiskey, then poured another for himself. Erin wanted to keep a clear head, but it was more important not to insult him or put him on his guard by refusing, so she accepted it and took a sip. It was better than the cocktail had been.

"If you were implying I had anything to do with the unpleasantness in Little Italy," he said, "you're very much mistaken."

Erin nodded and waited. He hadn't brought her into his inner sanctum just to give her a boilerplate denial.

"Why does your street source think I was involved?" Evan asked.

"He didn't say why," Erin said. "But he was sure it was your people."

"It wasn't," Evan said flatly.

"Sir," she said, choosing her words carefully, "I know you can't go against the agreement you made with Vinnie Moreno, not without restarting the war you guys just finished. So I thought maybe there was a loophole. If someone under you was to come to an arrangement with, say, a few discontented Lucarellis, you could truthfully tell Vinnie you weren't going back on your deal. You'd have a couple of layers of insulation, but you'd still be in a position to benefit. It'd be a smart play if you wanted to be in on the action."

"That's a very interesting theory, Ms. O'Reilly," Evan said. "You continually impress me with your perception and resourcefulness. Mr. Carlyle has been proven right about you at every step. You've been very valuable on several occasions, and I appreciate it. Who would you say has been performing this extracurricular activity for me, in order to provide plausible deniability?"

"I don't know that, sir."

"Humor me. Venture a guess."

"Veronica's the obvious one," Erin said. "She ran a narcotics operation for several months, so she knows how it's done. She's ambitious and pissed off about getting demoted, so she'd be pretty motivated to carve out a big piece of the pie."

"Yes, Ms. Blackburn does seem rather upset about the fallout from recent events," Evan said. His eyes reminded Erin of the deep, cold Arctic Ocean. "I can see how she might have considered such an action."

Erin's heart lurched. *Oh, shit,* she thought, steeling herself not to show her thoughts on her face. *This wasn't about deniability. You really didn't know!*

"As I said, you've proven yourself a valuable asset," Evan said. "You don't need to say anything further. Thank you for your insight. We should return to the others now."

Mechanically, Erin followed him back to the den. Rolf, at her hip, nosed her hand. She absently rubbed his head between the ears. Her thoughts were racing. She needed to get away from these gangsters, to talk this over with Carlyle, and maybe Phil. But the evening was far from over.

Game face, kiddo, she silently told herself. She was skating around the edge of the truth. She just hoped the ice wasn't too thin.

Chapter 13

Every head in the room turned toward Erin and Evan when they walked in. More specifically, they were all looking at Erin. She felt the pressure of those eyes and knew they were wondering what she and Evan had been discussing. She tried not to give anything away.

"If you'd deal, please, Maggie?" was all Evan said.

"Anyone want anything else?" Ryan asked from the doorway.

"Guinness," Erin said. She'd had plenty of hard liquor and needed to stay sharp.

The others ordered more drinks and the game continued. Erin's luck stayed good. Carlyle gracefully folded when Erin had a spade flush. Veronica went all in, bluffing on a pair of sixes.

"Just not your night, I guess," Erin said as she scooped the other woman's remaining chips into her own pile.

"I'm out," Veronica said, pushing her chair back and starting to stand. "Guess I'll call it a night. I've got some stuff—"

"Sit down," Evan said, his voice pure ice.

Veronica blanched under her heavy layer of makeup. "Evan—" she began.

He nodded to her chair. "Sit," he repeated. "We're not done yet."

Pritchard, on Evan's right, stirred slightly in his chair. One of his hands dropped below the tabletop. It was a smooth, nonchalant movement, but to Erin's street-smart eyes, it was as threatening a gesture as if he'd hauled out a shotgun. Every instinct in Erin screamed at her to go for her own gun, or to dive for cover. She made herself stay where she was.

Veronica licked her lips. "I don't know what that bitch told you," she said. "But it's got nothing to do with me."

Carlyle shifted. "Miss Blackburn, I'll not have you speaking that way of Erin," he said. Nobody, not even Erin, paid any mind to him. Their attention was riveted on Veronica and Evan.

Veronica slowly, reluctantly sank back into her chair. She gripped the edge of the table with both hands. Her long, scarlet-painted nails dug into the woodwork.

"Thank you," Evan said. "Now, Maggie?"

"The girls don't bring in nearly enough these days," Veronica said. Her voice had a brittle edge to it. This was no longer the sultry, seductive purr Erin had come to expect from her. It was the voice of a frightened, angry, desperate woman on the wrong side of forty rough years.

Evan said nothing.

"That's not where the money is," Veronica went on. "It's in drugs, and you know it, and you pissed it away. Why? Because of me? I told you, I didn't know what Mickey was planning! I had nothing to do with it! I thought you believed that!"

"If I didn't believe that, do you think you'd be sitting here now?" Evan replied quietly. "And are you really asking me to explain my business decisions to you?"

"I was earning money," Veronica said. "Real money, and you took that away from me! What did I ever do to you?"

"Lass, you're embarrassing yourself," Carlyle said gently. "Let it be."

Veronica turned on him with angry words on her lips, but she gulped them back. "Cars, you get it," she said. "Tell him! I know what you think of me, I know you don't like drugs or girls, but you've always had a good head for business. The labor rackets aren't what they were twenty years ago. Ten, even. There's millions of dollars in Little Italy. *Millions!*"

"And you thought you'd get your hands on a few of those millions," Evan said. "Behind my back. What did you think would happen? How did you imagine this would end? Did you really believe I wouldn't find out?"

"I just wanted what was mine," Veronica said. "I've had to fight for every single thing in this world, every day, every step of the way. You haven't had to fight for anything, not for a long time. I think maybe you forgot what it's like."

Erin clenched her jaw to keep it from dropping open. *Nobody* talked to Evan O'Malley that way. Maybe Veronica figured she had nothing left to lose. Maybe she thought Evan would be impressed if she showed some spine. If so, it was a very risky play.

Evan's face didn't change. "I think we've had enough for one night after all," he said calmly. "Maggie, if you'd cash everyone out? You've had a good night, Miss O'Reilly."

Erin managed a nod.

Maggie took a stack of bills from a cigar box next to her. She counted them out swiftly and accurately, distributing them to those players who still had chips.

"Thank you all for coming," Evan said. "You can be on your way."

Veronica's hands released their death-grip on the table. She let out a breath.

"Mr. Pritchard, Miss Blackburn, I'll need the two of you to stay a short while," Evan added, almost as an afterthought. "We have a small bit of business to attend to. It won't take long. I'll say goodnight to the rest of you."

Erin didn't budge. Carlyle gently took hold of her shoulder.

"Come along, darling," he said in an undertone. "We've places to go."

Erin's head was spinning. Her gut told her this was a very dangerous situation. The right thing to do, the thing she'd been trained to do, was intervene. But what would that do to her undercover assignment? What would she tell Phil? Captain Holliday? Carlyle?

She got slowly up from her chair. She felt like lead weights were hanging off all her limbs. Veronica was staring at her and Carlyle with a mute, desperate appeal.

"We can take care of it tomorrow," Veronica said to Evan. "I'll come by early. I'll just go with Cars now. If you're worried about me, he can keep an eye on me."

"We'll handle this now," Evan said.

Pritchard was on his feet. Erin didn't recall seeing him move. Snake was a good nickname for him; he had a curious, slithering way of moving. He was calm, eerily fast, and completely silent. He was standing just behind Veronica's chair now, his black-gloved hand resting on the chair less than an inch from her bare shoulder. His other hand was in his coat pocket.

"Goodnight, Miss Blackburn," Carlyle said. His voice was steady. He steered Erin toward the door. Maggie had already left the room. Finnegan paused in the doorway, watching the others with a curious, vacant smile.

Rolf nudged Erin. He looked at her with his intent, soulful brown eyes. He knew she was upset, but not what was happening. He nudged her again, trying to make her smile, to soften. It wasn't working and he didn't know why.

Erin was good at quick, life-or-death decisions. You couldn't survive twelve years as an indecisive cop. But she didn't know what to do here. So she let Carlyle guide her out of Evan's den. For the first time, she thought of his den in the other sense of the word, the lair of a predatory animal.

Ryan handed Erin her coat. Carlyle, ever the gentleman, helped her put it on. Then, before Erin quite knew it, Ryan had opened the door and they were outside Evan's penthouse, standing in front of the elevator under the eyes of Evan's guards.

"Quite a night, I'm impressed," Finnegan said. He and Maggie were a few feet apart. Finnegan was looking at Erin now.

"Impressed?" she echoed.

"Well, one does one's best," Finnegan went on. His eyes gleamed with sudden, mischievous amusement. "Here's to us!"

"I don't understand you," Erin told him. She was in no mood for Finnegan's weird ramblings. If the doors had opened early, she might have shoved him down the elevator shaft just to shut him up.

"*Schadenfreude* is such a wonderful word," Finnegan said. "Untranslatable. Leave it to the Germans to come up with such a precise term. Almost clinical. Is it any wonder the first psychoanalyst spoke German? So does your dog, doesn't he? And dogs understand human emotion, perhaps even better than humans do. And then, 'dog' is 'God' backwards, come to think of it."

He extended a hand toward Rolf. The K-9's ears flattened back against his skull. His hackles bristled and he gave a brief, warning rumble in his chest.

"Better not," Erin told Finnegan.

The elevator bell dinged and the doors slid apart. Finnegan stepped inside, moving to the left to make room for the others.

"We'll get the next one," Erin said, making no move to join him.

To her surprise, Maggie also stayed where she was.

"'Goodbye' is a blurring of the old phrase, 'God be with ye,'" Finnegan said. "Just as the Spanish *adios* originates in the phrase, *vaya con dios*, which also means, 'go with God.' All people are so very much alike, don't you think?"

The elevator doors closed on whatever else Finnegan had to say.

"We do want to be gone, darling," Carlyle said gently.

"Not with that nut-job," Erin said. "I'd rather get in an elevator with Ted Bundy."

"Point taken," Carlyle said.

"I don't blame you," one of Evan's goons said, startling everyone, including himself. He shrugged. "That guy is seriously whacked. You hear what he did in Detroit?"

"Everyone's heard that story, lad," Carlyle said.

"The thing that gets me," the guard said, "is that those union pricks got the first swing in. They caved in his freaking skull. Way I heard it, his head had this big dent in it. They thought he was dead, so they turned their backs on him. Then what does he do? He gets up, picks up the same damn tire iron, and beats three guys' asses with it! You believe that? Like he don't even care!"

"That's the story, aye," Carlyle said.

"And now he tastes colors, or some shit," the guard went on. "And he's always saying weird stuff. He oughta be in one of those places, you know. Where the walls are soft and they don't let you have scissors."

"Perhaps you should tell Mr. O'Malley your concerns," Carlyle said.

The guard's eyes got a little wider. "Hey, I wouldn't want to be telling the old man his business," he said.

"Then perhaps you should keep your opinions to yourself in the future, lad," Carlyle said with a fatherly smile.

The elevator's arrival saved further awkwardness. This time Maggie did get in, along with Erin, Carlyle, and Rolf. Carlyle pushed the button for the lobby. The car started its downward journey.

Erin stared blankly at the elevator doors, trying to unravel what had just happened. She hoped, she prayed there was some innocent explanation for all of it. Because the alternative...

"Mr. Carlyle?"

The quiet, shy voice was so unexpected that it took Erin a moment to realize it had come from Maggie. Erin couldn't remember Maggie having ever spoken directly to Carlyle. But there she was, one wrist clasped in her opposite hand, almost managing to make eye contact with him.

"Aye, Maggie?" Carlyle said, giving her his polite attention.

"Could I talk to you for a moment?"

"Of course," he said. "Are you thinking it's to be a long conversation?"

"I... I don't know," Maggie said. She was trembling slightly. Erin knew the woman was nearly her own age, but she was so petite and withdrawn that she seemed much younger.

"How are you getting home, lass?" Carlyle asked.

"Mr. O'Malley has a car waiting for me. Out front."

"Then we'll talk in the lobby," Carlyle said.

Erin immediately wondered about surveillance. There'd be security cameras in the lobby, and Evan would have access to those cameras. But what was the alternative? They were lucky to have this opportunity to talk with Maggie without Evan beside her in the flesh. At least the cameras probably didn't have audio, so what they talked about would remain secret from the

O'Malley chieftain. Erin's own recording wire was still humming merrily away.

The elevator settled into place at the ground floor. The doors opened. Erin got out first, looking around for potential trouble. All she saw was the doorman outside the big glass front doors. Finnegan had apparently gone on his way. The lobby was a pleasant place, tastefully decorated with potted plants, a cluster of chairs and couches around a marble-topped table that matched the floor tiles, and a big gas fireplace. A fire glowed comfortingly on the hearth, in deference to the cool autumn night.

Erin made for the fireplace. The roar of the fire would help screen them from eavesdroppers, and it was certainly the coziest part of the space. Rolf trotted beside her. Behind, Carlyle politely motioned Maggie to exit the elevator ahead of him. He brought up the rear.

"Let's sit down," Erin suggested. "Rolf, *platz*."

The Shepherd was glad to settle himself on the warm hearth. He circled once and lay down just a couple of feet from the fire, wrapping his bushy tail around his snout. Erin pivoted the left-hand chair slightly so she had a view of the elevators, just in case any O'Malleys decided to come down. Then she took her seat.

Maggie perched on the forward edge of the middle chair, sitting in a hunched-over posture, shoulders curled in, hands between her knees. Carlyle sat on her right, crossing one leg over the other and laying his hands on the armrests, apparently completely calm. Erin wasn't fooled. His eyes were keen, bright, and attentive.

"Now, what's on your mind, Maggie?" Carlyle asked.

"Corky," Maggie said.

"What about him, lass?"

"Do you know where he is?"

The directness of the question might have rattled some guys, but not Carlyle. He answered it simply and truthfully.

"I don't, sorry to say."

Maggie looked directly at him for the first time. "Is he alive?" she asked.

"As far as I know, aye, he is," Carlyle said, smiling reassuringly.

"Would you tell me if he wasn't?"

"I'd not lie to you about something like that," he said. "Why would you think anything's happened to him?"

Maggie's eyes slipped away from Carlyle's again. "I just thought... maybe I'd said something wrong and upset him."

"Maggie, darling, I can't imagine you'd do anything of the sort," Carlyle said.

"It's just... the last time I saw him, we were talking, and I said, 'I'm glad you're not the way everybody says you are.'

"'How's that, love?' he said.

"'You're just... nice,' I said. 'You haven't tried to kiss me, or get me in... in bed with you, or anything.'

"'Do you want me to?' he asked. He seemed like he was surprised.

"'Of course not,' I said.

"'That's all right then, love,' he said. 'Just don't tell anyone. A lad's got to think of his reputation.'"

Erin knew Maggie, with her uncanny memory, was reciting the conversation precisely as it had occurred, word for word. She'd even done a fair approximation of Corky's Belfast accent.

Maggie swallowed. "The next day, he was gone. Was I wrong about him? Was he really just pretending to be my... my friend? Did he want something else from me?"

"Corky's a great many things," Carlyle said. "But he's not dishonest. He's a bit of a scoundrel, aye, but he'd never trick a lass into putting out for him. That's not his game, never was. If he'd wanted to sleep with you, you'd have known it. He'd have made no secret of the fact."

"But... was that why he left?" Maggie asked. Her cheeks had reddened slightly and she was very interested in her own hands. "I... it wasn't something I wanted. But I think maybe I could have... if it would have helped..."

Erin, in spite of her preoccupation with everything else that was happening, felt a pang of sympathy. "Maggie, you never have to do that if you don't want to," she said. "Not with Corky, not with anybody."

"I'm different," Maggie said miserably. "I know. I don't work right. I just... don't want things like that."

"You've nothing to be ashamed of," Carlyle said firmly.

"Nothing," Erin agreed. "Look, Maggie. Corky just had to leave town for a while. I couldn't say exactly why, but I know it had nothing to do with you. He likes you, Maggie. As a friend. He'd never hurt you."

Maggie cautiously turned toward Erin. "Does he have female friends? That he doesn't... you know..."

Erin smiled. "Yeah, he does," she said. "I should know; I'm one of them."

"It's a small club," Carlyle said. "But that simply means the membership's quite exclusive. You're a member of an elite group, Maggie, and here's what it means; Corky isn't merely spending time with you because he wants your body."

Erin suppressed an internal wince. Carlyle was doing what he did best; telling the technical truth. Corky didn't want to sleep with Maggie. But he did want something from her. He wanted Evan's ledger.

Maggie sagged back in her chair, relief written all over her face. "Thank you," she said. "I... I don't have very many friends, especially men. I didn't want to lose him over something stupid."

"However you tally your friends, I'd like you to count me among them," Carlyle said.

Maggie smiled shyly. It made an enormous difference, lighting up her mousy, plain face and making it almost pretty. "I'll do that," she said. "And... Corky will come back, won't he? Someday?"

"Oh, he'll be back, I've no doubt of it," Carlyle said. "There's plenty of mischief still to do in New York."

"So he's not in town?" Maggie said.

"I believe he's traveled out of state," Carlyle said smoothly, giving no sign of distress over the slip. "You know the lad's work. The Teamsters are all over the country. He could be anywhere."

"If you hear from him, will you tell him something from me?" Maggie asked hesitantly.

"Of course."

"Tell him I said hello, and thank him."

"For what, precisely?"

"For Puzzle."

"Puzzle?" Carlyle echoed. "I confess, lass, you've got me at a disadvantage. I've no notion what you're talking about."

"Puzzle showed up the day after I talked to him," Maggie said. "A man delivered her, along with a note. I... I thought the note might be a joke. Or maybe some sort of insult. I know I'm easy to make fun of."

"I've never laughed at you, lass," Carlyle said. "And I won't. What did the note say?"

"It said, 'So you won't be too lonely. She'll kiss you the way you ought to be kissed.'"

"What, exactly, is Puzzle?" Erin asked, though she already had a suspicion.

"She's a Golden Retriever," Maggie said. "The veterinarian says she's about nine weeks old, probably a purebred."

Erin felt her heart melt a little bit. "Corky gave you a puppy?" she exclaimed.

"I'm certain he meant no insult," Carlyle said. "In fact, I'd bet a case of fine whiskey he meant you nothing but good. What do you think of her?"

"I love her," Maggie said. "I want her around all the time. I wanted to bring her with me tonight, but she still has accidents sometimes, and I didn't want Mr. O'Malley to be angry with her, so I left her in her crate at home. I should get back to her."

"I'm thinking you should," Carlyle said. "I hope you're feeling better."

Maggie nodded. "Thank you."

"And I'll be certain to tell Corky how much the wee pup means to you."

"If you have any questions about dog care, I'd be happy to help," Erin added.

"I've read fifteen Internet articles and three books," Maggie said with her usual bizarre precision. "But if I come across anything that isn't covered, I'll ask you."

Chapter 14

Rolf hopped up into the back of the Mercedes and began putting nose-prints on the inside of the window. Carlyle, having held the door for Erin, went around to the shotgun seat. Erin slid in behind the driver's seat, closed the door, buckled her seat belt, and put her hands over her face.

"Problem, sir?" Ian asked.

"Everything's fine, lad," Carlyle said. "But we'd best be on our way."

"Roger that, sir," Ian said, putting the car in gear.

"No," Erin said. "Everything is not fine. Everything is pretty goddamn far from fine."

The technical term for the way Ian's post-traumatic stress manifested was "hypervigilance." He didn't know how to turn off his heightened awareness of his surroundings. No matter what else was going on, he was always looking for potential ambushes, enemies, firing positions, and escape routes. But Erin's words put an even sharper edge on his razor-keen alertness. He scanned the street as he drove, his eyes jumping all over the place.

"What's the situation, sir?" he asked. His voice was level and controlled, but then, it almost always was. It took a lot to rattle Ian Thompson.

"Nothing that directly concerns us, no fear," Carlyle said.

"He didn't know!" Erin burst out. "She was dealing behind his back and he didn't know! And I told him!"

"I'd a notion it was something of the sort," Carlyle said. "That's why he wanted Miss Blackburn to stay behind."

"What's he going to do to her?" she demanded.

"I expect first he's going to talk to her and find out exactly what she's been up to."

"Oh, is that all?" Vic would have been proud of the amount of sarcasm Erin managed to load into the question. "And what then, once they're done 'talking?'"

Carlyle sighed. "I imagine that's why Pritchard is also hanging about."

"Son of a *bitch!*" Erin swore. "They could be beating information out of her right now! Shit, she might even be dead! Why'd you pull me out of there? I could've stopped them!"

"And just how would you propose to do that?" Carlyle asked quietly.

"I'm a cop! I've got a shield and a gun and a K-9! I could've arrested everybody in that goddamn room! Veronica would be in a jail cell, but she'd be alive!"

"Darling, think," Carlyle said. "Even supposing you could have dealt with everyone in Evan's apartment, and that's far from certain, there'd still be the guards outside, not to mention the rest of Evan's lads. We're not ready to make our final moves yet and you know it. Once we cross that line, there's no going back."

"There's a life on the line here!"

"And you weren't the one who put it there," Carlyle said. "Veronica planted her own field and now she's reaping the harvest she sowed. You're not responsible for her."

"Of course I am! I'm responsible for everybody in this damn city! That's the Job!"

"All eight million? And just how are you intending to keep the rest of them safe if you're lying dead in an overpriced Manhattan apartment? I've made some inquiries about Gordon Pritchard, darling, and you'd do well not to underestimate him. He's a very dangerous lad."

"So was Mickey Connor," Erin growled.

"Not to mention Finnegan," Carlyle went on. "You think that story from Detroit is smoke and mirrors? It's exactly what happened. Three crooked union lads jumped him, bludgeoned him with a tire iron from behind, and half caved in his skull. The lad got back up and beat all three of them to death."

"Finnegan's crazy."

"And you think that makes him less dangerous, do you?"

Erin said nothing.

"Evan would have found out sooner or later," Carlyle said. "And it's just as well you were the one who brought it to him. He'll depend on you a wee bit more than before, and that's all to the good."

"Miss Blackburn's not a civilian," Ian said. "She's a combatant, just like the rest of us. Takes her chances."

"And that makes it okay?" Erin shot back.

Ian's shoulders moved in a fractional shrug. "Lots of things get done in war, aren't okay back in the World. We at war now?"

Erin took in a deep breath, held it, and let it out again. "I guess so," she said.

"Then you do what you've got to," Ian said. "To keep you and your people safe."

"I wish it was that simple," she said.

"It is," Ian said. "But just because it's simple doesn't make it easy."

"You got that right," Erin said. "I'd better call Phil, let him know I'm okay."

"Would you like to wait until we get home, so you've a bit of privacy?" Carlyle asked.

"Might as well do it here," she said. "You know everything that's been happening anyway. Not much point keeping secrets from you now."

Phil must have been waiting by his phone. It only barely had time to ring before he answered.

"How's it going?" he asked.

"Depends who you ask," Erin said.

"Right now I'm asking you."

"My cover's still intact," she said. "I hope it was worth it."

Phil heard something in her voice that made him pause. The Manhattan streets rolled past outside the Mercedes. Rolf watched the city, his tongue hanging out.

"What happened?" Phil asked quietly.

"I said something that got one of the others in trouble."

"Which one?"

"Veronica Blackburn."

"What did you say?"

"I told Evan O'Malley about the rumor his people were moving drugs in Little Italy."

"And he was unhappy the police knew about it?"

"No. He was unhappy it was happening."

"I see," Phil said. "So Blackburn was freelancing?"

"It looks that way. She was using disgruntled Lucarellis to handle the product, to deflect suspicion."

"I see," he said again. "How did O'Malley take the news?"

"It's hard to tell with him. But I think he was pretty pissed off."

"But not at you?"

"No. He's happy with me."

"Then it's a successful night."

She clenched her fist on her knee. "Phil, listen to me!" she snapped. "I might've just gotten a woman killed!"

"I am listening, Erin," Phil said. "And now I need you to listen to what I'm saying. We're engaged in a long-running undercover operation here. That means we're permitting crimes to continue to take place while we're preparing to dismantle the organization. The O'Malleys are racketeering. They're committing robberies. They're setting teenage girls out on street corners, renting out their bodies an hour at a time. And they're killing people. Do you think this is the first time Evan O'Malley has made a decision about killing someone since you started going after him?"

She closed her eyes. "I know it isn't," she said.

"From what you're telling me, Veronica Blackburn is suffering the consequences of her own decisions," he said. "Whatever happens is on her, not on you. Do you copy?"

"Yeah, I copy," she muttered. "Carlyle said pretty much the same thing."

"Then we might be worth paying attention to. Look, Erin. I know it's late, but if you need to meet somewhere and talk this out further..."

"No, that's okay," she said. "I can handle this."

"Are you sure?"

"Yeah. Oh, one other thing."

"What's that?"

"Corky gave Maggie Callahan a puppy."

"A what?"

"A puppy. A little Golden Retriever."

"Is that a good development?"

"I think so. She misinterpreted it as a goodbye gift, but I think we managed to talk her around. It'll be on the recording. I'll get it uploaded as soon as I get home. I've used up just about all the space on the drive, but the meeting's over, so I shouldn't need to record anything else tonight."

"I'll look for it. Good work, Erin."

"If you say so."

She hung up, not feeling much better. Maybe Phil and Carlyle were right and Veronica had it coming. But that thought wasn't as comforting as she'd thought it might be. She'd gradually learned that justice was more than making sure bad people got what they deserved. Street justice wasn't good enough. She had to be better than that, or she risked losing her own soul.

Ian turned into the parking garage across from the Barley Corner. He guided the Mercedes into its numbered space and turned off the engine.

"Thank you, lad," Carlyle said. He unfastened his seatbelt and turned in his seat to look at Erin. "Are you all right now, darling?"

Erin really did try not to lie to Carlyle, but sometimes it just slipped out. Sometimes it was the only thing she could think of to say.

"Yeah," she said.

"Thank you for your help, lad," Carlyle told Ian. "You're off for the rest of the evening, unless I'm mistaken."

"Need me for anything?" Ian asked.

Carlyle shook his head. "Enjoy the night. Will you be seeing that fine colleen of yours?"

"Affirmative," Ian said. "I'll stop by my place first, get Miri. Then I'll be at Cassie's."

"Miri still working out well for you?" Erin asked.

"She's a good dog," he said, as if that answered everything. In a way, Erin supposed it did.

Erin, Carlyle, and Rolf crossed the street. Erin saw a man at the entrance. The guy was wearing a topcoat and a watch cap. An unlit cigar dangled from his mouth. He was leaning against the wall, one foot propped against the stonework, hands in his pockets, just another blue-collar guy relaxing outside a bar.

They were almost at the front door when Erin's Patrol instincts tickled the back of her mind. It was a cool night, sure; that would explain the hands in the pockets. But why a cigar and not a cigarette? And what kind of man put a cigar in his mouth, then just lounged against the wall *without lighting it?*

The kind who didn't want to wreck his night vision by having a glowing cancer stick right in front of his nose; that was what kind. In other words, the kind of man who was standing watch. He looked familiar, but he sure as hell wasn't one of Carlyle's security guys.

Less than fifteen feet separated them. Erin had just stepped onto the sidewalk. She paused, just for an instant, and made eye contact with the man.

He looked different without the sunglasses. But she recognized Conrad Maxwell, NYPD Organized Crime Division. And he recognized her.

Maxwell pushed off from the wall and pivoted toward her. He dropped the cigar to the pavement. His eyes, very dark, caught the reflection from the lamp over the Barley Corner's front door. Little points of white glittered in them. His face was unreadable.

Erin stopped walking. So did Carlyle. Rolf, at Erin's hip, looked up at her for instructions. The dog had gone rigid, sensing his partner's sudden tension.

Erin dropped a hand to her hip, belatedly remembering that she wasn't wearing a gun at her waist. It was a silly gesture anyway. Maxwell was a cop, just like her. Wasn't he? But the way he was standing in front of her sent warning signals screaming along her nerves.

"A little jumpy, aren't you, Detective?" Maxwell said. He smiled sardonically. "Trigger-happy, you might even say."

"You'd know all about that, wouldn't you, Detective?" Erin retorted. The hairs on the back of her neck were prickling. At some level lower than conscious thought, she was completely sure another man was standing behind her. She was in a kill-zone, a perfect ambush spot. On the far side of the street, behind Maxwell, was a storefront with a big plate-glass window. That shop was dark, closed for the night, so the glass threw back a near-perfect reflection of the street. In it, Erin could see a man standing on the sidewalk just a few yards behind her. She didn't turn to look.

"I don't believe we've had the pleasure," Carlyle said. His voice was pleasant and smooth, no hint of nervousness in it. "Morton Carlyle, at your service. I'm the proprietor of this grand establishment. If you'd care to step inside and have a drink? Always proud to cater to New York's Finest."

Maxwell ignored Carlyle, keeping his attention focused on Erin. "You shot one of my guys," he said.

"Yeah," she said levelly. "I did. But he'll live. Unlike Janovich."

"What were you doing there?" Maxwell asked. "Who sent you?"

"Nobody sent me," Erin said. "I was doing my job, getting scumbags off the street."

"Bullshit," Maxwell said. "You're not a Narc. You had no business there. Old Man O'Malley sent you, didn't he?"

"What?" Erin was startled almost out of her anger. "Why the hell would you think that?"

"Gee, I dunno," Maxwell said with a sarcastic shrug of his shoulders. His hands remained inside his coat pockets, and Erin was increasingly sure one of those hands was holding a gun. "Maybe we could ask O'Malley's second-in-command. He's right here. Yeah, you don't know me, Cars, but I know all about you."

"I doubt that," Carlyle said mildly.

"What do you want?" Erin demanded.

"I want to know what O'Malley's doing muscling into Little Italy," Maxwell said. "I want to know why he sent his personal lap-dog to keep tabs on a couple of low-level pushers and botched a clean operation."

"Your operation was clean, was it?" Erin said. She wondered what would happen if she went for her ankle gun. Maxwell would probably shoot her on the spot. If he did, he'd have to kill Carlyle, too, to remove the witness. And probably Rolf into the bargain.

Maxwell snorted. "I'm asking the questions," he said. "Why are the Irish getting back into the heroin trade?"

"They're not," Carlyle said.

"I've got twenty keys of uncut smack says they are," Maxwell said. "That's three million worth of product, wholesale. What's your game? I've got a guy in the hospital because of you."

"And we've got a guy in the morgue because of you," Erin shot back. "Who sent you there?"

"What's it to you?" Maxwell replied. "It's got nothing to do with you."

"Give my regards to the Oil Man next time you see him," she said. It was a guess, but a pretty good one. Maxwell's face stiffened slightly. Then it went perfectly still.

Erin's eye caught a hint of motion in the plate-glass reflection. Someone else was standing there now, between a pair of parked cars, just behind the guy at her back. She shifted her gaze back to Maxwell. His hands were starting to slide out of his pockets.

"Don't do anything," she said loudly. "I don't want anybody getting hurt."

"Are you threatening me?" Maxwell asked. The corners of his mouth curled slightly upward.

Erin matched his smile with her own, an icy one she'd learned from Evan O'Malley. "No," she said. "I wasn't even talking to you."

Maxwell's smile faltered slightly. "What do you mean?"

She didn't speak. In the momentary silence, a metallic *snick* was audible. It was the sound of the hammer being thumbed back on a Beretta automatic pistol.

Maxwell did have a backup man. Erin had seen him, and had correctly identified him as the other Organized Crime detective, the one she'd shot in the vest. But she and Carlyle had a backup man, too. It seemed Ian Thompson hadn't gone home just yet. He was standing between the cars on the street, his pistol held in both hands, aimed directly at Maxwell's guy.

Maxwell saw Ian then. "You're pointing your gun at a New York Police Detective, buddy," he warned Ian.

"So are you, sir," Ian said, not even sparing him a glance. "Orders, ma'am?"

"These guys were just leaving," Erin said, keeping her own eyes on Maxwell. She opened her fingers and let go of Rolf's leash. If Maxwell pulled a gun, or started shooting, she'd order Rolf to attack. Maxwell would have time for one shot, maybe two. She was betting he'd miss.

Maxwell didn't like the odds anymore. His smile came back. "Be a shame to have another Department funeral," he said. "Be seeing you, Detective. Come on, Freddy."

The man behind Erin walked quickly past her, shooting her a venomous look. He and Maxwell backed away. Maxwell pulled out another cigar and a lighter. He flicked the lighter and held it to the tip of the cigar. He raised the stogie in a sardonic salute. Then they disappeared from view.

Erin let out a breath she hadn't realized she was holding. Ian joined them, his Beretta held beside his leg, pointed at the ground. Rolf, momentarily forgotten, ducked his head. He came up with the loop of his leash in his mouth. He held it toward Erin, who took it and scratched him between the ears.

"That was the lad you and yours were swapping bullets with?" Carlyle asked.

"Yeah," Erin said.

"He's dirty," Carlyle said.

"No shit," Erin said.

"Let's get off the street, sir," Ian said. "We're exposed here."

"That's a fine idea, lad," Carlyle said. "Do you think Miss Jordan can do without your company a short while longer?"

"Won't be a problem, sir," Ian said.

"I need a drink," Erin said. "And then I need to make a phone call."

Chapter 15

"Hey Vic," Erin said into her phone. "Are you awake?"

"That's the dumbest question I've ever heard," Vic's voice came back. "And that's saying something. There's layers of stupidity in it, like an onion made of morons."

"That's a little harsh," she said.

Vic was still going. "The first layer is the fact that I answered my phone. It'd be hard to do that if I was asleep. The second layer is that I'm talking to you. Now, maybe I talk in my sleep. Zofia, do I talk in my sleep?"

"I don't know," Piekarski's reply came faintly through the phone. "You think I've got nothing better to do when I'm awake than watch you snore?"

"Anyway," Vic went on, "layer three is that I'm able to explain to you what a dumb-ass question that was. And layer four, I'm in traffic right now, and we all know sleeping and driving is a lousy idea. Fifth, it's not even midnight yet. When have you ever known me to go to sleep before midnight?"

"You done?" Erin asked.

"Sixth, and last, I'm a Major Crimes detective," he said. "When do we ever get any sleep?"

"Okay, that's actually a good point," she said. "Where are you?"

"I'm on my way to meet Firelli. He got a call from his buddy Benny."

"And where's Firelli?"

"Bellevue."

Erin blinked. "The hospital? What happened to Benny?"

"He got mugged or something. Firelli wasn't clear on the details."

"I'll meet you there," she said.

"What'd you get on the O'Malleys?"

"I'll explain when I see you."

She hung up and turned to Carlyle. "Looks like my night isn't over yet," she said.

He nodded. "Take Ian with you."

"I'll be fine. Besides, he needs to see his girl."

"Darling, you nearly got in a gunfight on my front step. For tonight, we'll all feel a mite better if you've a bit of extra security."

"I'll have Rolf." But Erin was fighting a losing battle and she knew it.

A few minutes later, fortified by a shot of good whiskey, Vic's borrowed Delta Elite at her belt, Rolf at her side, Kevlar swaddling both of them, and Ian on duty, Erin emerged from the Barley Corner. Ian was in full-on bodyguard mode, checking every spot an assassin might be hiding. She thought it was a little paranoid. There was no way Maxwell would still be hanging around. But she didn't protest. In spite of her arguing, Erin knew Carlyle was right; this was no night to be running around solo.

"Won't Cassie be disappointed?" she asked, once they were in her Charger and on the way to the hospital. Ian would have preferred to drive, but Erin was more accustomed to the car and she figured Rolf had left enough of his hair in the back of Carlyle's Mercedes. The Charger had the K-9's rapid-deployment compartment and a more powerful engine under the hood. It also had Erin's AR-15 rifle, and if they got in a firefight, Departmental regulations be damned; Erin intended to put the gun in Ian's hands and see some of that Marine Scout Sniper experience in action.

"Called her while you were upstairs," Ian said. "Told her something came up at work. She's a nurse. She gets it."

Why was she thinking this way? Erin shook her head and tried to concentrate on her driving. She'd been hanging around gangsters too long. Their violent paranoia was contagious. She was a cop, damn it. She had the law on her side, along with thirty-five thousand armed men and women, plus three dozen K-9 units, she could call for backup. That was a whole lot of guns and teeth.

And there she was, still thinking in terms of firepower. She had to get out of this situation, and soon.

"You good?" Ian asked suddenly.

"Huh? What do you mean?"

"Your driving's a little stiff. Got a problem?"

"No. I'm just thinking too much."

He nodded. "Better not to," he said. "Gets you in trouble in combat."

"Thinking? Really?"

"Stay in your head too much, you lose track of what's going on outside of it. Miss things. Lose your edge."

"I'll keep that in mind."

"Don't do that. That's my point." He didn't crack a smile, or give any hint of what he was feeling. That was the thing about Ian. Until you really got to know him, his jokes tended to slide right past you.

The Bellevue Hospital emergency room was about as busy as usual. Erin and Rolf threaded their way among the various victims of health emergencies and mishaps, while Ian stayed near the entrance. Erin showed her shield to the nurse at the desk.

"I'm looking for a patient," she said. "Benito Argent."

The nurse didn't even look at her computer. "He's in protective custody," she said. "Are you expected?"

"Yeah," Erin said. "A couple of my people should already be here. A big guy with a short haircut and a broken nose, and a little blonde woman."

"They just got here a couple minutes ahead of you. I'll call up to the room. One of them can come get you."

Vic arrived at the desk a few minutes later. His thin smile when he saw Erin fell right off his face when he spotted Ian.

"What's he doing here?" Vic demanded.

Ian completely ignored him. They'd never gotten along. Vic thought Ian belonged in jail, and while Erin had never asked Ian what he thought of Vic, she'd always suspected he had no respect for the Russian whatsoever.

"He's with me," Erin said. "Forget about it. It's been a kind of weird night."

"You're telling me," Vic said. "You can come on up. But that guy's gotta stay here."

"How come?"

"Because only cops get in to see our boy Benny."

"Vic? What's going on?"

"I'll explain," he said, glancing darkly at Ian. "Later."

"It's not a problem," Ian said to Erin. "I'll wait here, watch the perimeter."

"Watch the perimeter," Vic snorted as he led the way upstairs. "Somebody ought to tell that punk he's not in Iraq anymore."

"He's always got one foot in the desert," she said. "And he's really not a bad guy. He protected my family. Remember?"

"Yeah, I know. I also remember he's killed four people in front of police witnesses and gotten away with it every damn time."

"That's because those were justifiable homicides. He was protecting cops and civilians."

"Erin, that's three separate fatal shooting incidents. Hell, when one of us gets in that many gunfights, it raises eyebrows at IAB, and we're the cops! Everybody knows we're supposed to be the good guys! He's a damn vigilante! A guy shoots that many people, it's a pattern. He's doing it because he enjoys it. He's like a serial killer who only blows away assholes."

Erin shook her head and stopped talking. She wasn't going to convince Vic, not tonight.

They found Piekarski in the hallway with a uniformed officer. Somebody had put a chair in the hall, but only one. The uniform had been enough of a gentleman to give Piekarski the chair. She was flipping through a magazine; Erin noted, with wry amusement, that it was a *Bridal Guide*. She wondered if Vic had noticed, and if so, what he thought of it.

"Hey," Erin said. "What's up with Benny?"

"Firelli's inside with him," Piekarski said. She offered Rolf her hand and rubbed his chin. "He's not hurt too bad."

"Let's go talk to him," Vic said. "Officer Friendly here can keep an eye on things."

"My name's Hawkins," the Patrol officer said. He did not, in fact, look particularly friendly.

"Thanks for the help, Hawkins," Erin said. "Sorry about my partner. He skipped sensitivity training."

Firelli was sitting next to the hospital bed. In the bed lay Benny Silvers. The CI had already looked disreputable. Now he was a mess. His head was swathed in an enormous quantity of gauze which covered one of his eyes as well as the whole upper and left parts of his skull. He had a nasty swelling on his visible cheek and his good eye was puffy.

"You said he wasn't hurt bad," Erin said to Piekarski.

Benny smiled bitterly, showing meth-rotted teeth. "I've looked worse," he said.

"You called me," Firelli said to him. "I have to say, I was a little surprised after how things shook out earlier."

"Yeah, I thought I'd lay low for a day or two, until the excitement died down," Benny said. "You can see how that worked out for me."

"This wasn't a mugging, was it," Erin said.

"Not a chance," Benny said. "There was three of 'em, dressed way too nice for street hoods. And they was looking for me. I kinda stand out, y'know?"

Erin nodded.

"That was a joke," Benny said. "On account of I can't stand up, I gotta stand out instead. Get it?"

Erin and Piekarski managed a slight smile.

"When they started in on me, I knew they was connected," Benny said. "And I don't want no trouble with guys like that."

"How did you know?" Firelli asked.

"The way they dressed, the way they talked," Benny said. "How do you know I'm a tweaker?"

"The smell, mostly," Firelli said.

Benny grinned. "Wiseguys got a smell, too," he said. "They all wear that fancy cologne, and lots of hair gel. I shoulda smelled those dopes a block away, but I was careless. I'd just gotten a hit of some really good shit, so I didn't care about things like I should. You know how it is."

"Why'd they come after you?" Erin asked.

"At first I thought it was on account of you guys, and all the trouble you caused," Benny said. "But they didn't ask no questions about cops. Nah, all they wanted was the same thing you did."

"Stallone," Erin said.

Benny pointed his finger at Erin like the barrel of a gun. "Bingo," he said. "This girl's smart *and* smokin' hot. Where'd you find her, Bobby? I shoulda been a cop. You bangin' her?"

"If I tried, she'd mail my dick to me in the hospital," Firelli said, smiling at Erin. "Besides, I'm married, Benny."

"Like that ever stopped a guy," Benny said. "Anyway, this beating was kinda my own fault. If I'd been sober, I'd have told 'em what they wanted right off the bat, or else sent 'em on a wild goose chase. But the meth was talking, so I told 'em where to stick it. Then the big one pulled out one of those little crowbars. You know, the little eight-inch jobs. He gave me a couple taps with it. Then he stuck it in my mouth and said either answers or teeth were gonna start coming out."

"Yeesh," Piekarski said.

"So what could I do?" Benny said. "I got hardly any teeth left, I like 'em where they are. I couldn't talk with a mouthful of steel, so I started nodding as hard as I could, until they took the thing out. And I told 'em what I knew, which wasn't much. Then the big guy whaled on me some more, I guess. I don't really remember. Next thing I knew, I was here and a cop was asking me a bunch of questions. I tried to tell him I was a victim, not a bad guy, but he wasn't having none of it. Probably on account of the meth. So I asked him, could I make a phone call, and he said sure, that was my right. And I called Bobby, 'cause I figured what happened earlier wasn't his fault, and he's always been a stand-up guy and he could maybe get me out of trouble."

"I appreciate it," Firelli said. "You want to try to get the guys who did this to you?"

"You crazy? I don't want nothing to do with those boys. Far as I'm concerned, if I'm lucky, they'll forget I'm alive. At least they didn't want me bad enough to put a bullet in me."

"Why'd they want Stallone?" Erin asked.

"Same reason you did, I expect," Benny said. "Find out who he's dealing to."

"They already knew the answer to that," Erin said.

"Sounds like you know more than I do," Benny said.

"Guys, let's step outside," Erin said. "Mr. Argent here needs some rest."

* * *

They found an unoccupied alcove a short distance down the hall from Benny's room. Vic positioned himself so he could make sure nobody snuck up on them. The only other person in view was Officer Hawkins, who had picked up Piekarski's discarded bridal magazine and was idly thumbing through it.

"Okay, O'Reilly," Firelli said. "You clearly have some idea what's going on. Start talking."

"The O'Malleys used to be in the heroin trade," Erin said. "But they had a war with the Lucarellis over control of the business a while ago."

"Yeah, we know," Piekarski said. "The Italians won."

"It's more complicated than that," Erin said. "They negotiated an agreement. The Oil Man got control of the drug trade in the disputed territory. In return, Evan O'Malley got his hands on all the labor racketeering in the same area. That's mostly Long Island and Little Italy."

"Okay," Firelli said. "What's that got to do with what went down at the White Stallion?"

"One of Evan's lieutenants arranged to set up shop there, dealing heroin."

"So it was the O'Malleys?" Piekarski asked. She whistled softly. "The Oil Man is gonna be pissed."

"Everyone's angry about it," Erin said. "Maybe Evan even more than Vinnie. She did it without his permission."

"She?" Piekarski repeated. "Who's this babe we're talking about?"

"Veronica Blackburn," Erin said.

"I read her file," Vic said. "Skanky bitch, right?"

"That pretty much describes her, yeah," Erin said. "But she's ambitious and desperate, too. She backed Mickey Connor when he tried to take over the O'Malleys, and you know how that turned out."

"She's lucky Evan didn't have her whacked then and there," Vic said.

"Vinnie and Evan both have some housecleaning to do," Erin said. "Veronica was using Vinnie's malcontents to front the business."

"We get what you're saying," Firelli said. "I can see how this would lead to a bunch of gangsters blowing each other away, but that's not what happened. What we got was two squads of NYPD crashing the same party and shooting one another."

"There's only one explanation that makes sense," Erin said. "Maxwell is working for the Oil Man. He's a Mafia cop."

"You sure about that?" Firelli asked.

"Pretty sure."

"How do you know?"

"He almost killed me less than an hour ago."

Erin's words were followed by fifteen seconds of unbroken silence.

"You know," Vic finally said, "some girls would've led with that."

"Then what are we waiting for?" Piekarski demanded. "Let's go get the son of a bitch! Slap the cuffs on him and haul him downtown!"

"It's not that simple," Erin said.

"Why not?" Piekarski retorted. "First he starts executing people in Manhattan, in broad daylight. He kills three guys and he gets Janovich killed. Now he's taking shots at other cops? Fuck this guy! He's a goddamn disgrace to this city, to the Job, to the frigging shield we're wearing!"

"Take it easy," Firelli said.

"Don't tell me to take it easy! You say that again and I'll kick your ass, rip that silly little mustache right off your face, you greasy wop loser!"

Firelli raised his eyebrows. "That was uncalled-for," he said. "Even for a foul-mouthed, inbred Polack bitch."

"Hey Erin," Vic said. "These two remind you of anybody?"

"Yeah, like looking in a mirror," Erin said. "You kids can fight on your downtime. And no, Piekarski, we can't slap the cuffs on Maxwell, not yet. He didn't actually draw on me. The threat was implied."

"Why don't you tell us exactly what happened?" Firelli suggested. "And leave my mustache out of this, Piekarski."

"Hey, you're the one who insists on growing the thing," Piekarski said. "What you gotta remember is, if you want to look like Clark Gable, it helps if you've got the bone structure. A little face fuzz isn't gonna hide that."

"My wife likes it," Firelli said. "And no offense, but she's a lot more likely to be touching it than you are."

"As if I'd want to."

Erin cleared her throat meaningfully. The others fell silent. She laid out what had happened outside the Barley Corner.

"Yeah, he sounds shady as hell," Firelli agreed. "But none of this constitutes proof. Maybe it's time to take it upstairs to IAB, let them handle it."

"We can't take it to Internal Affairs," Erin said. "Hell, we're under investigation ourselves. That's why we're working this whole extracurricular bullshit case in the first place."

Vic sighed. "I guess I'd better get into his financials. I was hoping we wouldn't have to."

"Hold on," Firelli said. "Why are the Lucarellis beating up on Benny? What does that get them?"

"They want Dom Silvestri," Erin said. "And not because of what he can tell them."

"It's punishment time," Vic said. "They're planning to make an example of him."

"The Oil Man loves killing traitors," Erin said.

"He wants everybody to see what happens when they deal with his competition," Firelli said, nodding. "Shit. I'd better try to find him, before they get to him."

"I'll ride with you," Piekarski said.

"Me too," Erin said.

"I'm in," Vic said.

"You're looking at bank records, remember?" Erin said.

"I hate you sometimes," he grumbled.

"There are times you don't?" she asked.

"Few and far between."

Chapter 16

"What makes you think you can find Silvestri?" Erin asked.

"I can't find him," Firelli said. "Get on Canal Street and take it east, then hang a left on Mulberry."

Erin shrugged and followed his instructions.

"I can't find him, but I know a guy who might be able to," he went on.

"What guy are you talking about?" Erin asked. "And why didn't you call him earlier?"

"I didn't call him before, because I didn't know the name of the guy we were looking for," Firelli said. "And afterward, you let Silvestri walk, so I didn't see the point in tracking him down again. The guy I know is a retired wiseguy."

"I didn't think anybody ever retired from the Life," Piekarski said. "They *get* retired, but they don't retire on their own."

Erin winced, thinking of Carlyle. He'd once made the observation that, while there were a lot of young gangsters, there were precious few older ones.

"He was kind of a mentor to me, back in the day," Firelli said. "You ever heard of Dario the Hatchet?"

"Should I have?" Erin asked.

"Probably not. Before your time. I wasn't out of high school the last time he was making moves on the street. Your dad was a cop, wasn't he?"

"Yeah."

"He might've heard the name. Or your buddy Carlyle."

"This Dario," Erin said. "Was he a Lucarelli?"

"Nope. Would you believe, he managed to go his whole career unaffiliated?"

"Sounds dangerous," Piekarski said.

"It was," Firelli said. "Dario was really good at staying out of trouble. And he had one hell of a rep."

"I assume he got that nickname for doing something horrible," Erin said.

"They say a couple hitmen came after him once," Firelli said. "He runs this movie theater, a little hole in the wall place on Hester Street. Sort of a hobby, and it gave him a legitimate front for his business. Anyway, these two punks tried to rush him in the lobby. He grabbed a fire axe off the wall and went full Jack Nicholson. You know, 'Heeeere's Johnny!'"

"Did he kill them?" Erin asked.

"Both of them survived," Firelli said. "They still had three arms and two legs between them."

"Ouch," Piekarski said. "You know, Erin, I think maybe I'll stick to ordinary narcotics busts after this. You Major Crimes folks run into too many psychos."

"Don't worry," Firelli assured her. "That was years ago. The guy's in his seventies now. If he starts chasing you with an axe, you'll have to stop running every twenty yards to let him catch up. He's harmless."

"Yeah," Erin said, deadpan. "He sounds like a totally harmless guy. Why do you think he'll know about Silvestri?"

"Dario knows people," Firelli said. "He may be retired, but he's still the guy you go to if you need someone to hook you up with freelancers. He's got great contacts. Relax, you'll like him. He's real polite."

*   *   *

Firelli's description of the theater as a hole in the wall was generous. It was tiny, a single-screen neighborhood theater of the sort that had been pretty much wiped out by modern multiplex cinemas. It had a little sign over the door, outlined by glowing light bulbs, advertising *The Third Man*.

"He doesn't get first-run films," Firelli explained as they walked up to the entrance. "He likes the classics, the old black-and-whites."

"Does he make any money at all on this joint?" Piekarski asked.

"Doesn't matter," Firelli said. "He's got enough laid by."

"Most gangsters don't save for retirement," Erin said.

"Dario's always been an optimist," Firelli said, opening the door.

They found themselves in a small room with a twentysomething olive-skinned woman in a ticket booth. She looked up at them without much interest.

"Next show starts at midnight," she said. "You might want to come back in an hour or two."

"Hey, Cece," Firelli said. "Been a while."

"Bobby?" the girl said in surprise, becoming more alert. "Bobby the Blade! Hey! How's it going?"

"Hanging in there," he said. "I'm here to talk to your grandpa. Is he around?"

"Yeah, he's watching the movie," she said. "Your wife know you're taking other girls to the movies, two at a time?"

"They're friends from work," Firelli said.

"Yeah, I'll just bet they are," Cece said. She slid three tickets across the counter. "On the house," she added.

"Thanks," Firelli said. He handed tickets to the other two and led the way into the lobby. Like the rest of the building, it was small, dark, and old. The carpet was heavily scuffed, but the rope line that cordoned off the screening room was made of thick, rich velvet and its brass posts were lovingly polished. Erin could see, under the years that lay heavy on the place, the affection and care that had gone into its upkeep.

"Ooh, popcorn," Piekarski said, angling to the side.

"Seriously?" Firelli said.

"I'm hungry," Piekarski said, fishing out her wallet. She bought a bag of popcorn and held it out to Erin, who took a handful. So did Firelli, who dropped a couple of kernels. Rolf swept them up almost before they hit the floor.

"Show's already started," said the ticket-taker, a young man who strongly resembled Cece.

"I know, Eddie," Firelli said, handing over his ticket. "I just need to see your grandpa."

"Family business, huh?" Erin said in a low voice.

"Yeah, those are Dario's grandkids, Cecelia and Eduardo," Firelli said. "They're good kids. Totally legit, as far as I know."

He eased open the door to the screening room. The room was almost completely deserted. Apparently not many New Yorkers had an appetite for late-night black-and-white classic cinema. In the third row from the back sat a white-haired old man. He was staring at the screen, his chin resting on his clasped hands.

"Excuse me," Firelli said quietly.

The old man turned, the light from the screen showing an expression of annoyance on his face. Then he recognized Firelli and his wrinkled mouth cracked into a smile. His eyes crinkled with sudden good humor.

"Bobby, my *figlio*," he said. "You come to see me! How are you, boy?"

One of the four other patrons turned in his seat and indignantly shushed him. Dario gave no indication of pulling out an axe. He just smiled indulgently and rose creakily from his chair. He picked up a cane which had been leaning against the adjacent seat.

"We don't want to bother my customers," he said more quietly. "Let's go to my office."

Dario took them through another small, dark door, up a very narrow flight of stairs. Erin worried the old man might have trouble with the steps, but he took them slowly and methodically. At the top, he hauled out a big old ring of brass keys, found the one he wanted, and unlocked the door.

He ushered them into a small, cozy room. It had a stuffy smell and poor ventilation. Rolf sneezed and shook his head.

"Sorry to pull you out of your movie," Firelli said.

"Ah, Bobby, forget about it," Dario said. He looked like a sweet old gentleman, but his accent was straight off the Long Island streets. The phrase came out as one long word, *fuggeddaboudit*. "I've seen this one a hundred times. You gonna introduce me to your friends here?"

"Zofia Piekarski and Erin O'Reilly," Firelli said.

"And Rolf," Erin added.

"You know, I never kept product around here," Dario said, looking at the dog. "Not even when I was in the trade, which was many years ago. Not that I'm talking about any particular trade, you understand."

"Rolf isn't a narcotics dog," Erin said. "He's a Patrol K-9 with explosives and search-and-rescue training."

"Of course," the old man said. He offered Erin his hand and gave it a surprisingly firm shake. "Dario D'Agostino, at your service. Seems like I've heard of you. You're not wearing a ring. Are you married?"

"Um... no," Erin said. "But I'm seeing someone."

"Of course you are," Dario said, snapping his fingers. "You're that young lady who's been hanging out with Cars Carlyle, aren't you. How is old Cars?"

"He's good," she said.

"Tell him the Hatchet Man says hello," Dario said. "And I hope he's keeping out of trouble."

"I'll do that."

"And you'd be Miss Piekarski," he went on, turning to the other woman. "I can't make up my mind which of you is prettier. But it don't matter, I expect you're spoken for, too."

"My boyfriend's six-foot three and can bench press two-fifty," Piekarski said.

Dario laughed. He had a pleasant laugh. "Don't worry, Miss Piekarski. Your virtue's safe with me. These days all I really want to do is look, anyway. I suppose you're a cop, too."

"That's right," Piekarski said. "I'm on Firelli's squad."

"And I'm a detective with Major Crimes," Erin said.

"Then you're here about something serious," Dario said. "Bobby, it's been months. You don't call, you don't visit. I've missed you, *figlio*."

"Sorry," Firelli said. "I've been busy."

"You're never too busy for family," Dario said. "Besides, I remember when I was out of town, and you came up to see me. Five times, you came. I ain't gonna forget that. You didn't have to do that. Took time off from his studies and everything. This boy," he cocked a thumb at Firelli, "he didn't forget me when I got sent upstate."

"Receiving stolen merchandise," Firelli murmured to the others. "He got three to five."

"Only served fourteen months," Dario said cheerfully. "On account of good behavior. Like I ever behaved badly in my life. And this boy, he had his mother bring me cannolis, just like my mama used to make. And how's that wife of yours, Bobby? You making her happy?"

"We're making each other happy," Firelli said.

"That's good. If you got a home you don't want to come home to, you got no home," Dario said. "My wife, God rest her soul, she gave me forty-seven happy years. She gave me three sons and two beautiful daughters, and now I've got grandkids, thank God. I'm sorry, I don't have much to offer here. I used to have a bottle of hard stuff in my desk, but my doctor, he says it's not so good for me. Now I just have a glass of wine with my supper."

"That's okay," Piekarski said, holding up the bag of popcorn. "I'm good."

"So what can I do for you, Bobby?" Dario asked. "I'm glad to see you, but we both know this ain't a social call."

"I need to find a guy," Firelli said. "Fast."

"So you can arrest him?"

"So I can protect him. He's in danger."

"We're all in danger," Dario said. "Especially guys in the Life. This guy in the Life?"

Firelli nodded.

"But he's in more danger than usual?"

Firelli nodded again.

"He a snitch?"

"No."

"Who wants to clip him?"

"Vincenzo Moreno," Erin said.

Dario whistled. "And who is this unlucky *ragazzo*?"

"Dom Silvestri," Firelli said. "I have to find him tonight, before the Oil Man's goons get to him."

"You want the Italian Stallion?" Dario said. "You're not yanking me around, are you, Bobby?"

"Of course not!" Firelli said. "Why would you think that?"

"You're a narc, Bobby. You're a good boy, always were, but you're working the other side of the street these days. That's okay, I respect that, it's all the same game, but it's the truth. Now you give me a name, and you know he's a horse trader, and you tell me you don't want him for himself?"

"Word of honor, Dario," Firelli said.

The old man nodded. "Your word's as good as gold to me, Bobby. Always was. Let me see what I can do. It'll take a little time. You got your phone on you?"

"Yeah." Firelli handed him one of his cards. "Here's my number."

"I don't need that, I never forget a number. Don't go far. I'll give you a call in thirty, forty minutes."

"Thanks," Firelli said. "I appreciate this."

Dario patted Firelli's cheek. "Forget about it, kid."

* * *

"You really do know people," Erin said. She stuck her hands in her jacket pockets. The night was getting cold. They were standing on the sidewalk outside the D'Agostino family theater, considering their next move.

"So do you," Firelli replied. "I think it's about time you leveled with us, O'Reilly."

"About what?"

"You and the Irish."

Erin had known this was coming. She looked from Firelli to Piekarski. The SNEU officers looked back. Rolf, unconcerned, sniffed the brickwork and cocked a leg.

"It's complicated," she said.

Firelli shrugged. "We're not going anywhere for a while."

Erin shook her head. "Look, guys," she said. "I'd like to tell you. But I can't."

"What, that you're sleeping with a mob boss?" Piekarski said. "That's pretty obvious."

"Carlyle's not..." Erin began. Then she stopped.

"Not a mob boss?" Firelli asked. "Or you're not sleeping with him?"

"It's complicated," she said again.

"I've got a street nickname," Firelli said. "Bobby the Blade. I earned it, but that was a long time ago. I assume you did something to earn yours, too, Junkyard O'Reilly. Care to share?"

"I didn't ask for it," Erin said.

"Of course not," Firelli agreed. "You don't get to pick your own Mob name. It doesn't work that way. Do you have one, Piekarski?"

"Hell no," Piekarski said.

"I wonder, if I went back in there and asked the Hatchet Man about Junkyard O'Reilly, what he'd tell me," Firelli said.

"You'd go to a retired street hood to run a background check on an NYPD detective?" Erin replied. "And you'd believe him?"

"If we're not going to believe him, why are we coming to him for information?" Firelli countered.

"We're your teammates, Erin," Piekarski said. "Don't we deserve to know at least as much as the street punks?"

"You want to know what they're saying about me?" Erin said angrily. "Fine, I'll tell you. Word on the street is, I'm dirty as hell. I'm Cars Carlyle's personal attack dog. As in, junkyard dog. When Mickey Connor turned on Evan O'Malley and tried to take over the family, I blew Mickey's brains out. I'm a killer, a hired gun with a shield. You know the bomb that took out that woman who was going to testify against the Lucarellis? The bomb that almost killed me? I planted that. I kill innocent women. If you so much as look at me wrong, I'll shoot you in the face. That's the word on the street. Any questions?"

"Jesus Christ," Piekarski said quietly. "I didn't mean—"

Firelli was looking at Erin steadily. He hadn't flinched. "How much of that is true?" he asked.

"Why don't you ask IAB?" Erin shot back. "Lieutenant Keane would be a good place to start. He's been checking up on me too. You can compare notes with him. Maybe he's got a couple vacancies in Internal Affairs, if you're tired of working street narcotics."

"Why are you mad at us?" Firelli asked.

"Because you think I'm one of them!" she snapped, making an angry gesture in the direction of the theater.

"Isn't that what you want people to think?" Firelli asked. "You've been cultivating an image."

Erin couldn't think of anything to say to that, so she settled for glaring at him.

"You love Carlyle," Piekarski said. "I get that. But that's not the whole thing. There's something else going on..."

Her voice trailed off. She narrowed her eyes, thinking things through.

Erin had been pissed off. Now she was alarmed. She shot a quick look up and down the street. She saw a few people, but nobody within easy listening distance. "Zofia," she began.

"It's a sting," Piekarski said in a low voice. "Holy shit, you're infiltrating the O'Malleys."

"Either that, or you're actually whacking guys for the Mob," Firelli said. "Either way, I'm impressed."

Erin sighed. "Why are you a cop, Firelli?" she asked.

"I've told you that," he said. "My best friend OD'd on some bad shit when I was a teenager and it gave me a wakeup call. I figured I could keep going down that dead-end road, or I could do something with my life. So I got my shit together and made it happen. And you know what? I love it. I love taking down bad guys. I love Logan, and Piekarski, and damn it, I loved Janovich, too. I love wearing this bright, shiny shield."

He yanked his silver shield out from under his coat and held it up on its necklace. "And I'm damned if I'm going to let anybody rub dirt on it," he finished. "Not you, not Maxwell, not anybody."

"Nobody preaches like a convert," Piekarski said. "You'd have made one lousy gangster, Firelli."

"Somebody's dirty here," Firelli said to Erin. "It's either you, or Maxwell, or maybe both. And don't insult my intelligence feeding me some bullshit line like, 'Don't you know me better than that?' You and I both know there isn't much a person won't do when the chips are down. So which is it? Do you deserve that gold shield you're wearing, or don't you?"

Erin didn't give him an inch. A hundred angry replies died on her lips. She didn't want to fight Firelli, because the two of them had something in common.

"My dad was a cop," she said. "He loved it, just like you do. He taught me to love it. All I ever wanted to be was a police officer. I love the NYPD. I'd never do anything to hurt it. I'd die to protect this crazy, dirty city, because I love New York too. And I love the two of you for being willing to lay it all on the line and have my back. I've done some things I'm not proud of, but yeah, I still deserve to carry this shield. Does that answer your goddamn question?"

She and Firelli stared at one another. He nodded once.

"I guess, if you were doing some sort of deep-cover thing with the O'Malleys, you wouldn't be allowed to tell anyone," he said.

"Hypothetically, yeah, that'd be true," Erin said.

Firelli nodded again. "Okay," he said. "Sorry. Things have just been a little strange the past couple of days. I need to know where everybody stands."

"Right beside you," Erin promised.

"I don't know about you two," Piekarski said. "But I am really feeling the love right now. Group hug?"

They looked at her.

"I was kidding," Piekarski said to Erin. "We're not real huggy in SNEU. One question, Erin."

"Just one?"

"Does Vic know about all this?"

"Yeah."

"And he didn't tell me?"

"That's two questions."

Piekarski scowled. "Smartass."

"Vic understands. And you need to understand, what he did or didn't tell you has nothing to do with you, and whether he trusts you."

Piekarski rolled her eyes. "Yeah, yeah, I know. Operational security. This isn't some soap opera where the girl flips out because her guy kept a secret from her. I tell you what. I could really go for some coffee right now, and a raspberry Danish. You know any good late-night cafes around here, Firelli?"

"Yeah, I know a place just around the corner," he said. "We can hang there until Dario calls me."

Chapter 17

They were halfway through their second cup of coffee when Firelli's phone rang. He scooped it off the table and put it to his ear.

"Firelli," he said. "Yeah? You sure? Thanks. Listen, you're doing both of us a favor. I won't forget it. Yeah, I'll drop by for dinner. Sandy and me both. Yeah, we'd love to. Okay, I'll do that. You watch yours, too."

He put the phone away. "Saddle up, team," he said. "We're going to Brooklyn."

"Silvestri?" Erin asked as they got to their feet. Rolf scrambled up, tail wagging.

"Dario says he's at the Atlantic Basin," Firelli said. "Near the boat yard."

"How good is this info?" Piekarski asked.

"He's sure Silvestri was there a couple hours ago. That's as good as we're going to get."

"I'll call Vic, have him meet us there," Erin said.

Vic was, predictably, overjoyed to get away from his computer. "On my way," was all he said when Erin told him what was happening.

"Do we want any uniforms for backup?" Piekarski asked as they drove south.

"Not a good idea," Erin said. "We're still playing this quiet. Anybody we call might have ties to Maxwell for all we know. We don't want him hearing about Silvestri from us."

"Then it'd get back to the Lucarellis," Firelli agreed. "Just the four of us, then."

"Five," Erin corrected, glancing at Rolf in the rearview mirror.

"Five," he said. "Sorry, Rolf."

Rolf let his tongue hang out in a doggy grin. He didn't care what was said, as long as he got to ride along.

It was after ten when Erin pulled onto Bowne Street, just east of Atlantic Basin. It was an industrial loading area, all concrete and corrugated metal. On the left were a couple of six-story office buildings belonging to the New York Dock Company, while the right-hand side of the street was one long loading dock and parking lot.

"Nice place," Piekarski observed dryly.

Erin nodded. Her jaw was tight. She remembered the last time she'd gone after someone on the New York docks. That had ended in a vicious gunfight with a gang of Neo-Nazi terrorists.

"There's Vic," Piekarski said.

Vic's Taurus was parked on the left. He was leaning against the rear bumper, trying unsuccessfully to look nonchalant. There was something about Vic that radiated danger. He was the sort of guy that, if he hadn't been a cop, would have set off all Erin's Patrol instincts.

She slowed and rolled down her window. "See anything?" she asked.

"Just a bunch of off-duty cops looking for trouble," he said. "I only got here a couple minutes ago. I've got no idea what's going on."

She parked next to him and the officers spilled out of the Charger. This late at night, the loading area was deserted. They were the only people in sight.

"So where's our buddy Sylvester?" Vic asked.

"My guy said he's in there," Firelli said, pointing to the loading dock across the street. "Or he was."

"That's not very specific," Vic said. "That building's a quarter mile long."

"Silvestri's dealing out of a front," Firelli said. "Some party-supply rental company."

"Let's get looking," Erin said. "And be discreet. If we spook him, he'll run for it. Everybody got their vests?"

"Yeah," Vic said. "But I wasn't expecting a firefight. Should I grab my rifle?"

"Let's keep it low-profile," Erin said. "Remember, Silvestri isn't our enemy. We think the Lucarellis are gunning for him, but we don't have anything that says he's violent."

"What're we gonna do with him?" Vic asked. "Assuming we find him."

"We tell him the truth," Erin said. "Vinnie the Oil Man wants him dead, and his best chance is to make a deal with us and go into WitSec."

"Because Witness Protection is such a safe place if Vinnie Moreno wants to kill you," Vic said, deadpan.

"I'm open to other suggestions," Erin said sharply.

"We'll figure something out," Firelli said. "The Mafia isn't all-powerful. We can get to the bastards."

"Here's the place," Piekarski said. She pointed to a corrugated steel sliding door. "Any idea what's inside?"

"I think it's just a warehouse," Firelli said. "Most likely full of tents, folding chairs, tables..."

"...heroin, guns..." Vic added.

"Maybe," Erin agreed. "And there could be other guys here, not just Silvestri. Let's be careful. I think we should send two around to the front, keep two back here in case he makes a break for it."

"I'll go in," Vic said immediately.

"So will I," Piekarski said, moving closer to Vic.

"I'd better stay here," Erin said. "Rolf can catch him if he's stupid enough to run. But if you don't find him, give me a call and we can sweep the building."

"Radio check," Firelli said, clicking the handset he'd clipped to his vest.

"Got you, loud and clear," Piekarski said into her own radio. "Let's do this."

*　　*　　*

Erin, Firelli, and Rolf took up position beside a semi-trailer in the parking lot. Erin drew her borrowed pistol. The Delta Elite was heavy and unfamiliar in her hands. She wished for her trusty old Glock.

"That's a lot of gun you got there," Firelli said. He had a Department-issued Glock in hand.

"It's Vic's," she said.

"Makes sense it'd be his, not yours."

"Because he's got bigger hands?"

"Because you don't need to compensate for anything."

Erin snickered. "Sorry if I made you mad earlier," she said.

Firelli stopped smiling. "Not your fault," he said. "I guess it's Jan, mostly. After he got hit, when I went home, Sandy... she was pretty upset, too. You know what she does?"

"She works a suicide hotline," Erin said. "Logan told me at the hospital, when you got tagged a while back."

He nodded. "So she's used to dealing with some pretty dark shit. Me getting shot was hard on her, though. I told her it was a fluke, that the Job really isn't that dangerous. But then with what happened to Jan... she wants me to quit."

"Turn in your shield?"

"Yeah."

"And do what?"

"I guess I could always go back to petty street crime."

"Oh, yeah," Erin said. "That's much safer."

"It'll be okay. She knows this is important to me. I just... I want to do this right. But I've got to be careful. It's not justice I want for Jan. It's payback. And I know that's wrong, but it's all I've got. Maxwell and his guys are taking contracts for the Mob. So they're going down. No matter what, I'm going to get them for what they did to my squad."

"I get it," Erin said.

"And that's why I went off on you," he said. "Because it seemed like maybe you were in the same boat with them."

"I'm nothing like Maxwell."

"That's good," Firelli said. "Because if you were, we'd have words." He patted his left hip. To her surprise, Erin saw he had a black leather sheath buckled to his belt. He was wearing a nasty-looking knife in addition to his handgun.

"I didn't see that earlier," she said. "That's sure not Department-issue."

"Been wearing it under my coat," he said. "It's that old fish knife I told you about. Damascus steel. You ever notice people get more nervous around knives than guns? What sense does that make? I know I'm not going to use it. I just thought I'd better have it handy, just in case."

"It's a primal thing," Erin said. "Knives are like teeth. K-9s have a similar effect." She patted Rolf's head. He leaned against her leg and panted happily.

"Piekarski here." The voice crackled over Firelli's radio.

"Go ahead," Firelli said.

"Front door's locked. No answer when we knocked. Can we make entry?"

Erin did some quick thinking. "We've got a credible threat against Silvestri's life," she said. "And a good tip he's here. Go for it."

"Good enough for me," Piekarski said. "Vic? Try your key."

The splintering of the doorframe under the impact of Vic's boot was clearly audible over the radio.

"They're inside," Erin said softly. She and Firelli got set. If anything was going to happen, it was coming soon.

The loading area was eerily quiet. She, Firelli, and Rolf were silent and motionless. The air was cold and slightly misty. A ship's foghorn sounded mournfully. A single car crawled past, slowly turning into a parking space a short distance away. Erin felt goosebumps on her forearms under her jacket. She shifted her hand on the Delta Elite, trying to get used to the checkered grip. She wished she'd taken the time to go out to the range and fire off a few clips to familiarize herself.

Piekarski's voice came over the radio again. "Doesn't look like anyone's here."

"Just a bunch of party supplies," Vic said in the background. "Hold on a sec. I got... wait! Hey! Stop! NYPD!"

"One man running," Piekarski said. "In pursuit!" Erin could hear pounding footsteps and the sound of a door slamming.

"We just want to talk, dumbass!" Vic shouted, loudly enough to be heard without the aid of the radio.

Erin tensed. She exchanged glances with Firelli. He nodded.

With a rattle of corrugated metal, the loading-dock door slid open a couple of feet. A man dropped and rolled under it, coming up running. He was less than twenty feet from Erin, Firelli, and Rolf.

"Silvestri!" Erin shouted.

The man faltered and turned his head. He lost his footing and stumbled.

It saved his life. Even as he fell, a volley of gunshots rang out. Bullets ricocheted off the warehouse wall. The muzzle flashes lit up the fog.

"Shooters, left!" Firelli yelled.

Erin didn't have a line of fire. The trailer they'd been using for cover was between them and the gunmen. It sounded like two shooters, using handguns.

Rolf barked excitedly. He was ready to get into the fight.

"*Bleib!*" Erin said over her shoulder as she hurried toward the front of the trailer, Firelli beside her. Rolf obediently stayed put, tail wagging, front paws bouncing a couple inches off the ground, every muscle poised for action.

Silvestri scrambled for cover. More gunshots rang out. A bullet whined and skipped off the concrete. Another slammed into his thigh. He went down screaming, clutching his leg.

Firelli leaned around the trailer. "NYPD!" he shouted. "Drop your weapons!"

The only answer was a pair of bullets that punched into the trailer less than a foot from his face. Firelli snapped off two shots in return.

Erin crouched down. The trailer had a couple feet of ground clearance. She tapped Firelli's shoulder and pointed to herself, then to the underside of the trailer. He nodded. Then he fired three more times, rapidly, into the foggy night.

"*Fuss!*" she ordered Rolf. She ducked low and scooted under the trailer, angling left to stay out of Firelli's line of fire. The Shepherd came with her, sticking close by her hip.

"We're coming out! Don't shoot us!" Piekarski called over the radio. Erin ignored her and tried to block out the continuing gunfire. All she had to do was outflank the gunmen. Then she and Rolf could take them from the side.

She came up on the other side of the trailer, gun leveled, looking for a target. She saw nothing but fog and another trailer. Then a gun fired and she saw the flash and the man holding the pistol.

"*Fass!*" she hissed. Rolf hurled himself forward, paws flying over the asphalt.

The gunman caught the motion out of the corner of his eye. He was quick, but no human reflexes were a match for a German Shepherd. He was trying to bring his gun around, but Rolf was already airborne. The dog struck the man teeth-first, his ninety-pound bulk flinging both of them sideways into the concrete loading dock with a meaty thud. Rolf's jaws crunched down on the guy's arm. The shooter cried out in shock, the sound cut off as he bounced off the corner of the dock, the impact driving the wind out of him.

Erin sprinted toward them. The man was trying to fight the dog, but he was getting nowhere. Rolf had an unshakable grip. The K-9 growled joyfully, tail lashing the air. He was doing what he'd been put on Earth to do and loving every second of it.

But there had been two shooters. Erin didn't see the second man. He was kneeling, aiming around the other trailer. All she saw was the sudden flash as he fired, then another one. Rolf yelped and tumbled over on his side on top of the man he'd been biting.

Erin spun on her heel, raising her own gun. She made eye contact for an instant with Conrad Maxwell. He was almost close enough to spit on. He was pivoting away from his first target, aiming at her. She saw the barrel of his gun, smoke curling from the black hole in the tip, and she fired.

The Delta Elite jumped in her hand with a much heavier recoil than she was used to. Maxwell's pistol flared and she felt the impact right in her center of mass, just under the rib cage. It was like taking a swing from a sledgehammer. The breath left her in a sobbing gasp, but she fired two more times on reflex. The ground tilted crazily, though she wasn't aware of any sensation of falling. Then her cheek scraped blacktop. Red pain flared in her face.

With the pain came a surge of fear and anger. *Rolf*, she thought but didn't say. She rolled over, planted a hand on the pavement, and came back up. She didn't see Maxwell anymore. Maybe he'd gone down. She took two running steps, then stumbled as a wave of dizziness washed over her. Belatedly, she realized she'd been shot. She hadn't taken a breath since. She gulped in a tremendous lungful of air. It was cold, but it still burned going down.

Right in front of her, a pair of figures were struggling on the ground. One was a man, trying to drag himself free of his opponent. The other was Rolf. The Shepherd was lying on his side, but he was scrabbling and raking at the man with his claws and still holding on by the teeth. He was snarling nonstop and his tail wasn't wagging any more.

Two more figures rushed around the trailer toward Erin. She tried to take aim at them, but the pain in her abdomen bent her almost double. It was just as well; a moment later she recognized Vic and Piekarski.

"Maxwell," she gasped, waving her pistol in the direction she'd last seen him.

Vic hurried that way, disappearing into the fog. Piekarski came to Erin's side.

"You okay?" Piekarski asked.

Erin nodded. "Rolf," she managed to say. "He's been shot."

"You've been shot too!" Piekarski protested. "Firelli! Call in a 10-13! We need a bus!"

"No!" Erin snapped. "Not yet! Can't... let IAB... know yet."

She staggered toward her K-9. Rolf had twisted himself around onto his belly and gotten his paws under him. His target was still trying to get away, but dragging ninety pounds of pissed-off dog by the jaws was a losing proposition.

Erin's breath was coming back now. A hit to the gut was scary if it knocked the wind out of you, but the breathlessness didn't last long. Her vest must have taken the bullet, or she'd have been bleeding out by now. She took two more breaths to steady herself. Then she aimed the Delta Elite at the man's head.

"Stop fighting my dog, asshole," she said. "Or I'll blow your damn brains out."

It was the way she said it more than the words themselves. She wasn't bluffing and he knew it. He stopped fighting, sagging back into a half-sitting position against the loading dock.

"Get him off my arm," he muttered. "I did what you asked."

Rolf, still growling, showed no signs of letting go.

"Light," Erin said. "I need light! Now!"

Firelli had joined them. He pulled out a little pocket flashlight and shone it on the man's face.

"Detective Lombardo," Erin said, unsurprised. She glared at Maxwell's partner. "You're under arrest."

"What for?" he spat. "You just spoiled another stakeout, bitch. You'll lose your shield for this."

"Attempted murder," Erin said. "Of Dom Silvestri, not to mention the rest of us. Including my dog."

"I identified myself!" Firelli said angrily. "And you shot at us! You crazy bastard!"

"Erin," Piekarski said urgently. "Your dog's bleeding."

"So what?" Lombardo retorted. "*I'm* bleeding! He's biting me!"

"Shut up," Erin snapped. "Rolf, *pust!*"

Rolf immediately relaxed his jaws. He shifted his growl into a lower register but kept it going, like an engine revving in neutral. He backed away from his quarry, limping slightly and turned his eyes on Erin. Then his tail started wagging again.

While Firelli and Piekarski covered Lombardo, Erin took Firelli's light and examined Rolf. Her heart was hammering. Rolf was awake and alert, but that didn't mean a thing. There were plenty of injuries that would kill a dog, just not right away.

On Rolf's shoulder, just below his vest, his coat was sticky and matted with blood. She probed the injury as gently as she could. The dog flinched slightly, but his face remained stoic, denying the existence of such a thing as pain.

"Oh, kiddo," Erin said softly. "What did that asshole do to you?"

Rolf wagged his tail harder and licked her face. He'd done his job; now it was time for his reward. He understood she was upset, but he really thought she ought to be giving him his rubber ball. That was the way these things were supposed to go.

A car engine roared. Tires squealed. Someone fired a pistol several times as the sound of the car rapidly diminished into the distance.

"Vic!" Piekarski called. "Are you okay?"

There was a brief silence. Then they heard Vic cursing. If he was hurt, it must not be too bad, Erin thought; to swear like that required good breath support and the full use of his mental faculties. A moment later he came back into view, still swearing. He appeared unhurt.

"I need the aid kit from my car," Erin said, tossing him her keys. "Now!"

"I'll check on Silvestri," Piekarski said. "You got this jerk?"

"I've got him," Firelli said grimly. He wrenched Lombardo's arms around behind his back, drawing a cry of pain, and cuffed him. "How bad is your K-9 hit?"

"I don't know," Erin said. "I better get him to the vet." Rolf was so stoic, it was hard to tell. She didn't think the bone was broken, and he wasn't bleeding enough for an artery to have been cut, but she wasn't sure of anything else. At least he wasn't dying right there on the spot.

"Copy that," Firelli said. "Christ, these bastards tried to kill us."

"We didn't want anything to do with you," Lombardo protested. "We didn't even know you were here!"

"Yeah, you just came to kill Silvestri for that douchebag Moreno," Firelli growled. "You're just a Mafia hitman minding his own damn business. Who told you where to find him?"

Lombardo looked daggers at him and said nothing.

Vic came at a run, holding the Charger's first-aid kit. He handed it to Erin, who grabbed the disinfectant and a roll of gauze. Before she started tending to Rolf's injury, she fished out his beloved Kong ball.

"*Sei brav*," she told him, delivering the toy to his waiting mouth. "*Sei brav*, kiddo. You are such a good boy."

Rolf's eyes went soft and the rumble in his chest stopped. He chomped the toy, making it give out a slobbery squeak. He didn't even seem to notice as Erin began cleaning and wrapping his wounded shoulder.

"I've got Silvestri over here," Piekarski called. "He's hit in the leg. Not too bad, I think."

"Like hell it's not bad," Silvestri said through clenched teeth. "I've been shot! You ever been shot? It hurts like a son of a bitch!"

"You'll live," Piekarski said. "But we better get you to a hospital."

"We can't keep this quiet, O'Reilly," Firelli said.

"You're right," Erin said. "Let's get Silvestri and Rolf their medical attention. Then I'd better call Lieutenant Keane. Maxwell got away, but he was definitely here. He shot me."

"Jesus," Vic said. "Let me take a look."

"If you think I'm taking my shirt off for you, you're crazy," she said. "Forget about it. He hit the vest. I'm fine."

"Bullshit," Vic said. "You can still break a rib that way. You need to get checked out."

"What about Maxwell?"

"He got to his car and booked it," Vic said angrily. "I put a few holes in the bodywork, but I don't think I tagged him. Somebody did, though. There was a blood trail."

"Good," Erin said. "I'd hate to think I could've missed at that range, even with this silly hand-cannon of yours." She was trying to speak lightly, but she kept looking anxiously at Rolf, who was obliviously gnawing away.

Piekarski approached the group. "Silvestri can't walk," she said. "But I don't think he'll die. I still say we should call an ambulance."

Vic laid a hand on Erin's shoulder. "Get to the vet," he said. "And then go to the hospital. That's an order."

"Vic, I outrank you. You can't give me orders."

"Damn. I was hoping you'd forgotten."

"I can't get sidelined now. Maxwell's in the wind."

"We'll have all the guys we need to take him down once IAB gets involved."

"Assuming they believe us!" she shot back. "Whatever they do, it won't be fast enough. Keane will need to report to his boss, and that guy will report to his, and so on, all the way up to the PC. Then the PC will think about the optics and the politics of cops shooting cops, and who knows how long he'll take to make up his mind! And in the meantime, Maxwell goes off and does God knows what."

"There's a way we can all come out of this as winners," Lombardo said.

"Shut up," Vic said.

"No, let him talk," Erin said. "What do you mean?"

"O'Reilly knows what I'm talking about," Lombardo said. "Look, we do this the Department's way, we all lose. Everybody looks bad: you, me, the NYPD. But if you want to handle this like reasonable people, you can talk to the Oil Man. He's a businessman. Just listen to what he's got to say."

"You believe this friggin' guy?" Firelli said. His hands were clenched into fists and he looked ready to murder Lombardo on the spot.

Erin's brain was running in overdrive. What was the right thing to do, to protect her cover and to take down the bad guys? What if she had to choose one or the other?

"Guys," she said quietly. "Let's talk for a second. Over here."

She motioned them a short distance away from Lombardo, out of immediate earshot.

"Erin, you're not seriously saying we should make a deal with the Oil Man," Piekarski said.

"Of course not," Erin said. "I'm saying we should talk to him, and listen to him."

"And then we all lose our pensions and end up doing five-to-ten upstate," Firelli said. "No thanks. I'm not for sale."

"I know that," Erin said in a low voice. "None of us are. But they don't know that. Vinnie thinks I'm already bought. Let's use that."

"How?" Vic asked suspiciously.

"I'll get him to give me Maxwell," she said with a grim smile.

"What makes you think he'll do that?" Firelli asked. "Maxwell's one of his."

"And he's Vinnie the Oil Man," Erin said. "He'd sell out his own mom if it helped pad his profits."

"How's it going to look to IAB?" Firelli asked.

"Let me worry about Internal Affairs," she said.

Chapter 18

"You've got a very lucky dog," the veterinarian said.

"I'm the lucky one," Erin said. She ruffled Rolf's fur. The K-9 lay on the examining table on his side, his injured shoulder toward the ceiling. He was panting and his ears were slightly back. These subtle indicators were the only hints he was in any discomfort.

"The bullet entered here," the vet went on, indicating a fresh bandage on Rolf's shoulder just in front of the joint. "It missed the bone and traveled through the muscle, exiting here. It didn't hit any major blood vessels. The damage is purely to the muscle tissue."

"So he'll recover?" Erin asked, trying to keep the anxiety out of her voice and failing.

"Completely," he assured her. "Just be sure to keep both holes clean. I've trimmed the hair around them. There's some risk of infection, but if that hasn't shown up in a week, he should be fine. You'll want to put him in a cone, of course."

Rolf gave Erin a mournful look.

"What about the other shot?" Erin had found a second bullet lodged in Rolf's vest over his ribs.

"The vest did its job," the vet said. "Stopped it cold. Looking at his medical history, I see he's had broken ribs in the past."

"Yeah, a few months ago."

"Fortunately, those appear to have healed completely, and the only thing I see on him now is some bruising. He's one tough pooch."

"He is that," Erin said.

"But you really should try to keep him from suffering any further significant injuries," the vet said. "This sort of cumulative wear and tear is awfully hard on an animal. He's what, six?"

"Yeah."

"At this rate you'll be lucky to get another three years out of him. I know he's a working animal, but you should really consider taking him off the street for a while. Maybe for good."

Erin's heart lurched. "I can't ask him to do that," she said. "It'd break his heart. He lives for his work."

"He may live for it, but it'll eventually kill him if he keeps this up," the vet said. "That's my professional opinion."

"You know retirement kills cops, don't you?" Erin said.

"I've read that paper," the vet said dryly. "That study back in 2013 about the Buffalo Police Department. Officers who live to age fifty have a little less than eight years left, on average. That's a lot lower than your typical American. But it's one study and hardly conclusive. Do you mean to suggest police dogs are the same way?"

"I don't know about K-9s in general," Erin said. "But I know my dog. He'll ride with me as long as he can stand on his own feet."

"Just be sure you're doing what's best for him, not just for yourself," the vet said. "I've written a prescription for some painkillers and antibiotics. They'll have them for you up front. And here's a treat for your good boy."

Rolf accepted the dog biscuit and crunched it. Then he licked the crumbs from the examining table and watched the vet in case another was forthcoming. He didn't know what all the fuss was about.

*   *   *

Erin called Vic as soon as she got Rolf out into the veterinary clinic's parking lot. Rolf was walking slowly, but not with much of a limp. He wanted her to know if there were any more bad guys, he was ready and willing to come back for another round.

"How's the mutt?" Vic asked.

"He'll be fine. What about Silvestri and Lombardo?"

"I told Silvestri we might have to take him out back and shoot him."

"What? Why?"

"Because that's what they do to stallions who get busted legs."

"What did you really do with him?"

"You're not laughing."

"It wasn't funny."

"Silvestri didn't laugh either. I think the problem's in my delivery. We've got him at Bellevue under a John Doe. One of the other docs took a look at him; I guess your brother was busy. I think it was that guy who took care of you when Connor tuned you up."

"Doctor Nussbaum?"

"Yeah, that's the one. Says Silvestri ought to be okay. Hit him in the meat, nothing important."

"Did Silvestri say anything?"

"Just words my mom told me not to use. Says he doesn't know anything and he's got no idea why the Mob is gunning for him."

"He's lying."

"Of course he's lying. That's what perps do when they talk to detectives. Well, everybody does it, but perps more than most. Now he's cuffed to his bed and I've got my old pal Chunky looking after him."

"That's good." Chunky was a former squadmate of Vic's by the name of Campbell. "And Lombardo?"

"Piekarski and Firelli have him. They weren't sure the Five was safe, and they sure as hell weren't taking him to his home precinct. That left the Eightball, and after what happened to that one guy in Holding, I didn't think that was such a hot idea. So they took him to Firelli's place."

Erin was appalled. "His home? That isn't secure!"

"I know, I know," Vic said. "But what else could they do? It was that or turn him over to IAB, and you said to hold off on that. Anyways, Firelli's wife is at work. She works nights, if you recall. And they haven't got any kids yet, so it's just our people and Lombardo, no pain-in-the-ass civilians. He'll keep for a few hours. Nobody but us knows he's there. Now tell me about you."

"Nothing to tell," Erin said. "I'm taking Rolf home. Then I'm going to see the Oil Man."

"I'll back you up."

"I don't need backup. Vinnie thinks I work for him, remember?"

"And I don't trust the slimy bastard. Cops are getting killed over this."

"I'm not going to be one of them."

"Damn right. Because I'll be watching your six."

"Vic, this is going to be a delicate negotiation."

"I can be delicate. I'll keep my pinkies extended when I punch his face in."

"See, that right there is why you can't come."

"I was joking."

"You're still not funny. I need you to check on that injured cop, Melvin Plank."

"You mean the one I shot? Thanks for reminding me. I never shot a cop before, not even a dirty one, and I'm not feeling real good about it. Why?"

"Because if I can't get Vinnie to play ball, and if Lombardo keeps his mouth shut, Plank may be our best way to get to Maxwell."

"Are you nuts? They'll never let me in to see him. To repeat, he's the guy I shot."

"You're at Bellevue now, aren't you?"

"Yeah."

"He's literally in the same building with you. Just find out what you can."

"Okay, I'll see what I can do. But watch your back. I hear Vinnie's got a bad habit of sticking knives in people who're supposed to be on his own team."

* * *

Erin slipped into the Barley Corner the back way, doing her very best to avoid notice. She knew she and Rolf looked like they'd been through it. The last thing she needed was to attract the eyes and gossip of Carlyle's clientele. She kept her face turned away from the main room as she punched in the access code and got through the door and up the stairs.

In the apartment, she peeled off the Velcro straps on her vest and laid it on the bed. The Kevlar weave showed two torn spots. Maxwell had done his best to punch her ticket, but the body armor had stopped both nine-millimeter rounds. The bullets were still lodged in the tough fabric, halfway through, their tips smashed flat by the force of the impact. She'd be needing a new vest.

She unbuttoned her blouse and stood in front of Carlyle's mirror, the one he used to get his necktie knot just so. She saw a dark, swollen spot just under her rib cage. It was going to be one hell of a bruise. Since the impact had been so low, she didn't have to worry about broken ribs. She didn't think she had any internal bleeding, but her buddies were right; she really ought to get checked out by a doctor.

"Later," she muttered. Her cheek was bloody where she'd scraped it on the asphalt, but that was just cosmetic. Still, it wouldn't do to meet Vinnie with blood running down her face. He could sense weakness the way a wolf knew to pick off the stragglers from a herd of deer. She had to be hard as nails, and pissed off for good measure. That shouldn't be too difficult. All she had to do was look at Rolf and see the shaved patches of hair and the bandages. Then the anger came bubbling right to the top.

She was in the bathroom, dabbing disinfectant on her face, when she heard the door open and feet on the stairs. A moment later, Carlyle appeared in the bathroom doorway.

"Ian told you I was back?" she guessed.

"The lad told me you'd come in with the look of a lass who'd been in a wee scuffle," he confirmed. "He doesn't miss much. Were you planning on telling me?"

"I get in fights all the time," she said.

His eyes traveled down her blouse, which still hung open, and she could feel him examining the developing bruise. "Something's telling me there's more to this than a ruckus with a few lads in a pub," he said.

"I'm handling it," she said grimly.

"Is that what I think it is?"

"Forget about it. The vest took most of the impacts."

"You were shot?" His eyes hardened. "By whom?"

"This is police business. I said I'm handling it." She buttoned her blouse with quick, angry fingers.

"Is there something I've done to upset you?" Carlyle asked quietly.

"No!" she snapped. Then she registered his face. She saw a hint of pain there, but mostly she just saw love and concern.

"I'll help as I can," he said. "But if this is something you're needing to do alone, I understand."

"No," she said more gently. She put out a hand and touched his shoulder. "I'm sorry. It's been... Jesus, Rolf almost got killed tonight. By another cop!"

"I saw the lad on my way in," Carlyle said. "I'm hoping he's not hurt too badly."

"It looks worse than it is," she said. "But that prick Maxwell nearly got him and me both. I'm taking his ass down, as hard as I have to. Don't wait up for me."

"Anything I can do?"

She shook her head. "Pray, I guess."

"Where will you be?"

"Lucky's Restaurant."

He blinked. "That's a Lucarelli front."

"I know. That's why I'm going there."

"Erin, given what's been happening, you'll not be safe there. Think, darling. Vinnie may not know Miss Blackburn was operating independently."

"He's not going to kill an NYPD detective in his restaurant."

"Are you certain of that?"

"Pretty sure, yeah."

He measured her with a long, searching look. "I'll not be talking you out of this, will I," he said.

"No. Sorry."

"Then at least listen to me on this. Don't go anywhere private with Vinnie, nor any of his people. Stay in the open, in public."

"I'll try."

"And take Ian with you."

She shook her head. "I'll look stronger if I go by myself. You know how important image is."

"I don't like it. At least let the lad drive you."

"And do what? Avenge my death if they whack me?"

"You said he wasn't going to kill you."

"In which case I won't need Ian. Seriously, it's okay. Trust me."

He leaned in and kissed her lightly, careful of her injured cheek. "I do trust you, darling. But I love you, too. So I worry."

*   *   *

It was late, but Lucky's was a place that was always open, no matter the hour. It always seemed to contain the same scattered bunch of old Italian guys, men too old to work and too young to die. It was dimly lit, furnished in a style the tourist guides probably called "Old World charm," but that Erin found dark and depressing.

She noted the way three much younger men reacted when she walked in. All three sprang to their feet, hands going inside their coats. Her own hand twitched and she wanted to reach for her own gun, but she made herself stand perfectly still. She looked from thug to thug, staring them down one after another.

"Holy shit," one of them murmured. "That's Junkyard O'Reilly."

"What do we do?" another asked.

Erin ignored them. They were small fry and she was after bigger fish. Disregarding twelve years of police experience, she walked straight past them toward the back of the restaurant. This left three armed, dangerous criminals with a clean line on her unprotected back, but her best armor was confidence. She didn't think they'd fire the first shots, not against a cop. In any case, they'd already told her what she needed to know. They wouldn't have been this jumpy if there hadn't been a boss in the restaurant.

She found the old Italian gentleman right where she'd expected to, at the back corner table. He smiled when he saw her.

"Detective O'Reilly," he said, getting creakily to his feet and spreading his hands in a gesture of greeting. "I wasn't expecting to see you tonight."

"Evening, Mr. Vitelli," she said. "I was hoping to find you here."

"It's wonderful to see you again," Valentino Vitelli said. "Come, come. Sit down!"

Two of the young men had trailed Erin to the table. One of them gave Vitelli a questioning look.

"Boss?" he said.

"Go on, get out of here," Vitelli said with a dismissive wave.

"But, boss..."

"I said get out of here. Worry about something else. I'm too old to be a babysitter and I don't need a chaperone."

The bodyguards withdrew, but they weren't happy about it. Erin slid into a seat opposite Vitelli.

"Forget about them," Vitelli said. "They're just nervous on account of that nasty business at the White Stallion. I heard you was involved in that. I hope you wasn't hurt or nothing."

He was looking at the scab on her cheek. Erin resisted the urge to touch it. "I'm fine," she said. "I actually came here looking for the Oil Man. Would you happen to know where he is?"

Vitelli nodded. "I think he might want to talk to you, too. I've got an idea. How about I give him a call and get him down here? Then you and he can have a nice sit-down."

"That's a great idea," Erin said.

"I'll just be a second," Vitelli said, getting up for the second time. "Make yourself comfortable. You hungry?"

"A little, yeah." She hadn't realized it, but her stomach was rumbling in spite of the pain in her abdomen. Adrenaline burned a lot of calories.

"Then I'll ask the waitress to get you some pancakes and coffee," Vitelli said. "You remember the pancakes, right? I don't know what it is about breakfast at night, but it's the best. Never too early to eat breakfast. You just sit tight. I won't be long."

Erin tried to settle herself in her seat and wait patiently. It wasn't easy. In spite of Vitelli's warm welcome, she knew if she made the wrong move, she was seconds from death. She could feel the tension in the air. The guys at the door were on high alert. Something was happening, or about to happen. She reminded herself that they thought she was one of them.

Yeah, she told herself. *And so were the Manzano brothers and Luca Frazetti. Not to mention Mattie Madonna and all the other guys the Oil Man's had whacked.*

It was a long ten minutes until Vitelli came back.

Chapter 19

"Erin O'Reilly. I must say, you're a braver woman than most."

The voice was smooth and silky, like high-quality olive oil. Erin turned in her seat and saw Vincenzo Moreno walking toward her, Valentino Vitelli two steps behind him. Two new bodyguards trailed Vinnie, staring at Erin with unfriendly eyes. It was after one in the morning, but the Oil Man was impeccably dressed in an old-style three-piece suit. His hair was perfectly slicked back, not a strand out of place.

"I guess you were in the neighborhood," Erin said. "Thanks for taking the time out of your busy schedule."

"Of course." Vinnie offered his hand. Erin stood up and shook with him. His hand was clean and well-manicured, his grip firm.

"I hope I'm not keeping you from anything important," she said.

Vinnie's smile was coldly charming. "I'll always find time for you." The way he said it came across more like a threat than a courtesy. "I hope Mr. Vitelli has seen to your refreshment."

"I'm good, thanks." Erin sat down, as did Vinnie and Vitelli. Vinnie's goons took up position two tables away and continued eyeballing Erin.

Vinnie folded his hands on the tabletop. "So you're the one O'Malley sent to straighten things out. I suppose it makes sense. You've worked with my people not so long ago. Did he think that would buy you some goodwill?"

"Evan didn't send me, Mr. Moreno," Erin said. "I'm here on my own."

One elegant black eyebrow rose a fraction of an inch. "Really? Then you're even braver than I thought."

"I'm sure you'll sort out your troubles with Evan," she said. "I expect you'll hear from him soon. But that's not why I want to talk to you."

"But suppose it's what I want to talk about?" Vinnie replied.

"If you want to talk, I'll listen," she said. "But you need to understand, I don't have the authority to negotiate any sort of settlement."

"Oh, I wouldn't worry about that," he said. "It would be something more along the lines of a message for Mr. O'Malley."

Erin's skin crawled. She forced herself to keep looking steadily at Vinnie, not showing any sign of fear. She had a pretty good idea what sort of message Vinnie might have in mind. Nothing underlined a point in the underworld quite like bullets and bodies.

Carlyle had been right to worry. If she said the wrong thing, or if Vinnie was determined to send a particular message to the O'Malleys, she wasn't going to walk away from this table.

She wondered, if she went for her gun, how many of them she could take with her. She decided, if the guns came out, she'd get Vinnie first. It would be some small satisfaction if the last thing she did on Earth was blast the cold, psychopathic smile off that smooth, handsome face.

"We had an agreement," Vinnie said. "You understand the importance of a man's word, Miss O'Reilly. When a man breaks his promises, there need to be consequences."

"I completely agree, Mr. Moreno," she said. "However, in this case, Mr. O'Malley wasn't the one who broke his promise."

"Oh? Would you care to elaborate?"

"There was an internal misunderstanding. He's taking steps to rectify the situation."

"I thought you weren't his representative."

"I'm speaking unofficially."

"Who was responsible for the fiasco at the White Stallion?" Vinnie asked abruptly.

"There's plenty of responsibility to go around," Erin said. "The Manzano brothers, for starters. Luca Frazetti. Conrad Maxwell, Freddy Lombardo, and Melvin Plank."

"I don't think I'm familiar with all those names," Vinnie said.

"And you," Erin finished, meeting his dark eyes.

"Me? I'm sure I have no idea what you're talking about."

"You're the one who brought the NYPD into this," Erin said. "Maxwell was your guy. He handled it the way you wanted him to."

"Maxwell," Vinnie repeated. "I'm sorry. Doesn't ring a bell."

"Look," Erin said. "Are we going to talk, or are we just going to bullshit each other?"

"We're professionals, you and I," Vinnie said calmly. "I suggest we act like them."

"*Parla come mangi,*" Vitelli said. "She wants to talk like an Italian, Vincenzo. Simple food, simple talk, plain speaking."

"And she understands why I'm not going to do that," Vinnie replied. "As long as we're quoting proverbs, I'm sure you're familiar with this one: three men may keep a secret..."

"...If two of them are dead," Vitelli finished.

"Maxwell shot me earlier tonight," Erin said.

Vinnie showed no surprise. "He must have done a very poor job of it," he said.

"He's gone completely off the chain," Erin said. "He's shooting up everybody he runs into. Now he's trying to kill cops. I've been able to keep a lid on it for now, but that lid's coming off soon, and when it does, Maxwell's going to bring all kinds of heat down. You don't want to be standing anywhere near him when that happens."

"Very interesting, I'm sure," Vinnie said. "Particularly for any friends of this Maxwell, whoever he is. What that has to do with me, I'm sure I don't know."

"You know your business," Erin said. "But the longer Maxwell is running around doing damage, the worse things are going to get when he goes down."

"And is that why you're here? To give me some sort of warning?"

Erin kept looking into his eyes. "I'm here to get Maxwell."

Vinnie met her stare and matched it. They looked at one another for five seconds, ten, fifteen. Neither blinked. Then he smiled. And he laughed.

The sound startled Erin. It was so real, so apparently heartfelt, that it was completely out of place bubbling up out of Vinnie Moreno's heartless chest.

"Erin O'Reilly!" he exclaimed. "I wish my men had half the balls you do! You should have been a Sicilian!"

Erin gave him the coldest smile she could. "I'll take that as a compliment."

"As you should. And just how am I supposed to help you get this Maxwell?"

"You're going to tell me where he is."

Vinnie stopped laughing. "Why would I do that?" he asked, sounding genuinely curious.

"Maxwell is useless to you," Erin said. "It helped you for a while, having your own guy in the Organized Crime division, but he's overplayed his hand. Whatever else happens, I guarantee less than twenty-four hours from now, his shield might as well be made of tinfoil. Every cop in New York will be looking for him. The NYPD takes care of its own, but he's been going after other cops. He'll be radioactive. He's damaged goods; I'm not."

"You're saying I should invest in the future?"

She nodded.

"And you're that future?"

"Run the numbers," she said. "What do you think?"

"I notice your dog isn't with you tonight," he said.

"Rolf caught one in the fight with Maxwell. He'll be fine."

"He shot your dog?" Vinnie shook his head slowly. "I almost feel sorry for him."

"I doubt you've ever felt sorry for anyone in your life."

"I like you, Miss O'Reilly," he said. "You're a straight shooter, but devious when the situation requires it. And you're right. From the sound of it, this Maxwell fellow sounds like he's no use to anybody. I hear things. It's possible I might be of some assistance to you in locating him. What can you tell me?"

"He was last seen driving a Chevy Impala, dark blue or black." Vic had given her the description of Maxwell's getaway car. Unfortunately, what with the dark, the fog, and the gunfire, he hadn't caught the license plate. "It's got a few bullet holes in the trunk and probably the back windshield."

"That's a fairly conspicuous vehicle," Vinnie said. "I'd think your people would be able to track it more easily than mine."

"Maxwell himself has at least one hole in him, too," she said. "Forty-five caliber."

"I noticed you're wearing a weapon of that caliber, instead of your customary sidearm," Vinnie said. "Would that be the pistol that made the hole in question?"

"It would," she said grimly.

"And if a man were to go to a hospital with such an injury, the doctors would be legally required to report it, even if the wounded man was a police officer," Vinnie said.

"That's right. But I'm guessing Maxwell may know some people who would provide a more discreet brand of medical assistance."

"And you're thinking I might know some of the same people?"

She nodded.

"I might at that." Vinnie smiled. "However, if I did, those people would be very useful to myself and my associates. I wouldn't want them to be scooped up by the police for practicing medicine in a legal gray area."

It wasn't a legal gray area; it was flat-out illegal to treat gunshot wounds without reporting them. Under New York Penal Code 265.25, it was a class A misdemeanor. That was pretty small potatoes as far as criminal charges went, but it could still send a doctor to jail for a year. It could also lead to suspension or revocation of the doc's medical license. Vinnie doubtless knew this as well as Erin did.

"What if I gave you my word that they wouldn't be charged, or even arrested, for involvement in this incident?" she asked.

"I'd take you at your word," Vinnie said. "You're a woman of honor."

"Then you've got it," Erin said. "You've also got my word that anyone who cooperates with my team and me in tracking Maxwell down will have nothing to fear from us for anything they've done for him. But I'm going to promise one more thing. If

I find out anyone is hiding him, or helping him escape, I'll treat them the same as him. Am I making myself clear?"

"Clear as a sunny day in Sicily," Vinnie said. "Have you ever been there?"

"No."

"You should go. It's a beautiful island. You'd be very welcome. I can make the arrangements if you're interested. All expenses paid, of course."

"Thanks for the offer." Erin remembered the last time she'd gone out of the country on a gangster's dime. That trip had ended in a hospital emergency room, with one person dead and another fighting for life. She'd travel to warm, sunny Sicily on Vinnie's money when hell froze over and not one minute before.

"I'll need to make some inquiries," Vinnie said. "I believe I have your telephone number. One of my people will call you."

"Thank you," she said. "I appreciate it."

"I'm sure you do," Vinnie said. *Now you owe me a favor* was his unsaid subtext.

"I guess we're done here," she said, sliding out of her seat. Vinnie's goons twitched slightly. Vinnie gave them a look and they subsided.

"I won't forget this," she promised Vinnie. Dealing with the Mob had made her an expert in double meanings.

"Give my compliments to Mr. Carlyle," Vitelli said, stepping back into the conversation just as it was ending.

"And give mine to your son," Erin replied with a sweet smile she hoped didn't look as artificial as it was. "How are his legal proceedings going?"

"The State is moving ahead with a trial," Vitelli said, shaking his head. "I don't know why. They haven't got a case after that terrible accident with their star witness. But the DA still thinks he can make it stick. But they gotta know they have a weak case. He'll be okay."

"I'm sure it'll all get sorted out," Erin said.

She walked out of Lucky's feeling the aptness of the name more than ever before. She could feel the eyes of Mafia hitmen on her as she stepped onto the sidewalk. If Vinnie had wanted her dead, she had no doubt she'd be dead. But she'd convinced him of her value. More to the point, she'd convinced him she was more valuable than Maxwell.

She'd also recorded every word of the conversation on her hidden wire, though as usual, Vinnie hadn't said anything that could directly incriminate him. He wasn't called the Oil Man for nothing; he was the slipperiest son of a bitch in the five boroughs.

She'd done everything she could here. Now it was time to circle back to the rest of her ad hoc team. The clock on the Charger's dashboard read ten past two. Any reasonable person would be in bed and asleep.

There were thirty-five thousand men and women in the NYPD. Not many of them could be accurately described as reasonable, under that definition. Erin put the car in gear and drove away from the Mafia restaurant. According to the NYPD database, Firelli and his wife lived on Long Island. Like many a New Yorker, he commuted rather than pay the sky-high rent for a Manhattan apartment.

"Back to Brooklyn," she sighed. You could take an O'Reilly off Long Island, but something was always pulling her back. If she had a nickel for every time she crossed the East River, she thought, she might be able to buy one of the bridges.

Chapter 20

Firelli lived in a brick duplex on 43rd Street in Borough Park. Erin saw his T-Bird parked in the bay out front, next to a little brick flower-box. The house was three stories, with a little balcony on the second floor and a basement unit that was probably rented out. A short flight of steps led up to the main floor and down to a sunken door that accessed the basement. The curtains were drawn, and they were good blackout jobs, but Erin could see a glimmer of light on the second story through a small gap.

She climbed out of the Charger and slowly made her way up the stairs. She buzzed the doorbell, glad in the knowledge Firelli's wife was at work and wouldn't get jolted out of bed.

The lock rattled for a long moment. Apparently the mechanism was a little finicky. After an awkward few seconds, Firelli opened the door. His sidearm was in his hand.

"Whoa, take it easy," Erin said, holding up her hands. "It's just me."

"Okay, come on in," he said. He lowered the gun, but didn't holster it until the door was locked behind her.

"A little jumpy, are we?" Erin said, taking in the surroundings. There was a dining room to her left, dominated by a big old oak table. Behind that, she could see another door that presumably led to the kitchen. But Firelli was leading the way up a staircase that ran along the right-hand wall.

"Yeah, I guess I am," Firelli said. "I don't usually bring my work home with me. We didn't know what else to do with the guy."

"Where've you got him?" she asked.

"Spare bedroom on the third floor, cuffed to the radiator," he said matter-of-factly.

"The radiator solid?"

"Cast iron, original with the house," he said. "Lombardo wants to break free, he'll have to rip it clean out of the floor, and good luck with that. It probably weighs three hundred pounds."

They found Piekarski in the living room on the second floor. It was furnished with an interesting mix of secondhand furniture that looked worn but comfortable. Piekarski was sitting at one end of an old leather couch, her feet curled up under her. She looked very tired, but when Erin and Firelli walked in, she perked up a little.

"Hey, Erin," she said. "How's Rolf?"

"He'll be fine. Just a graze, really. He's at home, sulking."

"What about you?"

"Bruises. God bless Kevlar."

"Amen," Piekarski and Firelli said in unison.

"Did Lombardo say anything?" Erin asked.

"Besides threatening to get us all fired and thrown in jail?" Piekarski said. "Not a thing."

"We really do need to figure out what we're going to do with him," Firelli said. "And whatever it is, it has to go through IAB. We're walking right on the line of kidnapping an NYPD detective right now, and I, for one, don't want to go to prison for this."

"Has he asked to leave?" Erin asked.

"Yeah, and he demanded a hospital," Piekarski said.

"That's not great," Erin said. They were required by law to provide necessary medical attention to anyone in custody. They also had to either release or officially arrest anyone who wanted out.

"I Mirandized him," Firelli said. "I know you arrested him already, but you didn't read him his rights."

"I was a little distracted. I'd just been shot."

"Can it, O'Reilly," Firelli said with a smile. "Nobody likes a whiner."

"What about a doctor?" Erin asked.

"I took a look at him," Piekarski said. "He's fine. Rolf chewed on him a little, but it's just tissue damage, nothing deep. I disinfected the arm and slapped some gauze on it. He's got nothing to complain about."

"He'll keep until morning, I guess," Erin said. "We don't need to charge him right away. We need to start thinking what we're going to tell IAB."

"Tell them the truth," Piekarski suggested. "We were following up some narcotics leads and one of the dealers we were looking at got attacked. When we intervened, the bad guys started shooting at us. We nabbed one of them and he turned out to be one of the Organized Crime detectives who started this whole thing in the first place."

"We're all supposed to be on administrative leave," Erin reminded her.

Piekarski shrugged. "So we get a rip for doing extra police work. I can live with that. Logan won't be too pissed."

"He'd rather have that than the opposite problem," Firelli agreed.

"But what if Lombardo walks?" Erin asked.

"He tried to kill us," Firelli said. "We may not be able to make the thing with Janovich stick, but we've still got him shooting at police officers. Not to mention he opened up on Silvestri without any warning, from behind. We saw him do it. The guy's a murderer. No way does he walk."

Erin nodded. "But a lot of this is our word against his," she said. "I told Vinnie that Maxwell and his guys were done, but I'm not so sure."

"You had a meeting with Vinnie Moreno?" Piekarski asked.

"Yeah."

"How'd that go?"

"He considered having me killed, but decided not to, and we parted as friends."

Firelli whistled. "You're crazy, you know that?"

"Yeah, I get that a lot. Say, you got a coffee machine in this house?"

Firelli grinned. "Are you kidding? This household's got two people who work nights, one of whom is a cop. If our furnace, our fridge, and our coffeemaker all broke down, we'd fix the coffee machine first. It's in the kitchen and there's already a pot made up. We knew this would be an all-nighter."

The kitchen was the newest-looking part of the house. The countertops were polished faux marble and the linoleum was clean and unscratched. All the appliances looked brand new.

"Nice," Erin said.

"Yeah, we just had it done last month," Firelli said proudly. "The old stove was a piece of crap, just an accident waiting to happen. We got this sweet new gas job installed. Sandy loves it."

"It's a cozy house," she said, taking the cup of coffee he held out to her. The cup was dark blue with big yellow letters spelling NYPD. "Reminds me of the one I grew up in."

"How many in your family?" Firelli asked.

"Four kids," she said. "Three brothers plus me. Two older, one younger. Dad always wanted Junior to become a cop like him, but he decided to be a doctor instead. Somebody had to carry on the family tradition, so here I am."

"I bet he's proud of you," Firelli said. "I know we've got a lot of space for just Sandy and me, but we're planning to have kids one of these days. I want six, she wants two. Maybe we'll compromise on four."

"And maybe you'll just have to take what the good Lord gives you," she said.

"Hell, I'd be happy with one," he said. "As long as it's the right one. It's not like you can send 'em back for a refund. But we figure—"

Erin held up a hand to silence him. Firelli froze. He'd heard it too. There was a rattle at the front door. Somebody was messing with the lock.

She set the coffee down on the counter and drew the Delta Elite. A sidelong glance at Firelli confirmed he'd pulled his own piece. He nodded to her. They moved quickly and quietly out of the kitchen and through the dining room, splitting up and slipping around the table, aiming their guns at the door. The lock jiggled and clicked open. The door began to swing inward.

"Freeze, NYPD!" Erin barked.

"Show me your hands!" Firelli said, his words overlapping hers.

They stared into the astonished face of a woman, a pretty brunette with shoulder-length, wavy hair framing a pair of wire-rimmed glasses. She was holding a ring of keys in one hand and a plastic cup half-full of what looked to be a fruit smoothie in the other.

"Rob?" the woman said, more surprised than frightened. "What on Earth are you doing?"

"Sandy?" Firelli said. "What are you doing here?" His hand fell to his side and he very nearly dropped his gun. It dangled forgotten from his fingertips.

Erin hastily tucked her pistol back in its holster. As first impressions went, holding someone at gunpoint was about as bad as it got. At least everyone was fully clothed. "Sorry, ma'am," she said.

"I thought you were at work," Sandy said to Firelli. "Who's this? What's going on?"

"It's complicated," Firelli said. "Can you close the door, please?"

Sandy swung the door shut. "I assume you're one of Rob's coworkers," she said to Erin.

"Detective Erin O'Reilly," Erin said, extending her hand. "I've been working with him and a few others on an important case."

"Sandy Firelli," the woman said, taking her hand. "I think I've heard about you. Wasn't there a thing a while ago with some terrorists?"

"Yeah," Erin said. "It wasn't that big a deal."

"Zofia Piekarski is upstairs," Firelli said. "And don't go in the spare bedroom."

"Why not?" Sandy asked.

"We've got a perp chained to the radiator," Erin said.

Sandy laughed. "No, seriously," she said.

Neither of the other two joined in the laughter.

"Oh my goodness," Sandy said. "You were serious."

"Like I said," Firelli said. "It's complicated. And I promise, I'll explain. But what are you doing home? You're supposed to be at work."

"They had to upgrade our phone network," Sandy said. "And some genius figured two in the morning was a great time to schedule the update, which would have been true if we were a corporate office that keeps nine-to-five hours. But we're a twenty-four-hour hotline, and we actually do a lot of important work at this time of night." She sighed. "Be that as it may, all the phones went down. A hotline without phones isn't much use, so they sent us all home."

"Classic bureaucracy," Erin said.

"Tell me about it," Sandy said. "Have you been here all night?"

"Piekarski and I have," Firelli said. "O'Reilly just got here."

"Are you hungry?" Sandy asked. "I could whip up a little late-night snack."

"I had some ricotta pancakes just a little while ago," Erin said. "And your husband got me some coffee, so I'm good."

"I could use a sandwich," Firelli said. "But I can get it. It's no problem."

"Nonsense," Sandy said. "You're still working, I'm not. I'll get it. You didn't eat the pastrami yet, did you?"

"No, it's still in the fridge," Firelli said.

"Will Zofia want one, you think?"

"Absolutely," Firelli said. "She's been really hungry lately. I don't want to be rude, but I think she's putting on some weight."

"That's what you think, is it?" Sandy replied with a twinkle in her eye. "Now that's just like a man."

"Wait a second," Firelli said. "You don't mean..."

Erin maintained a rigid poker face.

"You go on up," Sandy said. "I'll bring you a couple of sandwiches in a few minutes. It's very nice to meet you, Erin. Welcome to our humble home."

"It's a really nice house, Ms. Firelli," Erin said. "Thank you for your hospitality. Let me just grab my coffee out of the kitchen and I'll get out of your way."

* * *

"What was that commotion downstairs?" Piekarski asked.

"My wife came home early," Firelli said.

"And found you with two pretty girls and a guy handcuffed in the bedroom?" Piekarski said. "Not a good look."

"Just for that, I'm going to eat the sandwich my wife is making for you," Firelli said. "My sweet, loving wife, who trusts me and is a good person who would never believe the worst about me."

"I'm just screwing with you," Piekarski said. "What kind of sandwich?"

"Pastrami, Swiss, lettuce, tomato, and mayo. My favorite."

"I agree," Piekarski said immediately. "Your wife is a wonderful human being and clearly has no reason to distrust your wholesome and non-worrisome habit of handcuffing strangers in the spare bedroom."

"That's better," Firelli said.

"So I figure we'll just sit tight until morning," Erin said. "Then we'll take Lombardo to the Eightball. I don't trust Lieutenant Keane a hundred percent, but I do trust Kira Jones. I'll just make sure she and Captain Holliday are in the room when we tell our story. They're both solid."

"Then we put out a BOLO on Maxwell?" Piekarski said.

"And run his ass the hell down," Erin agreed. "Maybe Lombardo will flip once we charge him. I think he still doesn't get it. He's expecting to walk away clean. When that doesn't happen, I think maybe he'll crack. The DA might offer him a plea deal to give us Maxwell."

"We still need to catch Maxwell," Firelli said gloomily.

"We'll get him," Erin said. "He's hurt and he's on his own. He can't go to the cops, and if he goes to the Lucarellis, I'll hear about it. He's got no options left but to run, and he can't run forever."

On cue, her phone buzzed. She pulled it out and was unsurprised to see an unknown number on the screen. Holding up a finger to shush the other two, she brought the phone to her ear. She'd installed an app that automatically recorded every conversation on it, figuring it was better to have to delete a bunch of irrelevant audio files than to miss something important. These days, if a gangster said something incriminating over a phone line, he deserved to get caught.

"O'Reilly," she said, expecting some tough-sounding stranger to deliver Vinnie's message.

"The guy you're looking for went to a clinic in Brooklyn," Valentino Vitelli said.

"It's you!" Erin blurted out.

"Is that a problem?" the old man replied. "I thought you might appreciate the personal touch. And I really am grateful for what you did to help my boy. I figure you and me, we're practically family now."

"That's sweet," she said. "What clinic? What time?"

"It don't matter which one," Vitelli said. "On account of he ain't there no more. He checked out half an hour ago. Didn't say where he was going, and the guys there didn't ask. But he was pretty dinged up. Had a bullet in his shoulder and lost a chunk of one of his ears. Right one, I think. Too bad that shot wasn't a couple inches to the side, would've made everyone's night a lot easier."

"You got that right," she said. "But he walked out under his own power?"

"Drove off. Different car than the one you said, so he must've switched rides. It was unmarked, but my guy says it was a cop car. He saw one of them spotlights you got. So you look it up in your motor pool, you should know what he's driving."

"Okay," Erin said. "When you say he was pretty dinged up, how bad was it? Could he use the arm?"

"They gave him a sling, to keep the weight off it, but it wasn't broke or nothing. But I tell you, I got shot once, when I was just a kid, and it ain't no picnic. I couldn't use my arm for nothing for almost a month. You run into this guy again, he won't put up too much fight, I'm thinking."

"So he was in Brooklyn half an hour ago? What part?"

"Flatbush. Near Coney Island Avenue. That's as much as I can tell you."

"Okay, thanks," she said. "You've been a big help."

"Forget about it. Stop by again, you ever want more pancakes. Oh, one other thing."

"What's that?"

"I heard he was looking up stuff. You know how you got those computers in your cop cars?"

"Yeah?" Erin felt a crawling sensation in her gut. "What about them?"

"You guys don't trust each other," Vitelli said. "You know your bosses can see what you're looking up on those things?"

"That's not unusual," she said, a little nettled. How dare a Mafia boss lecture her about trust and privacy? "Corporations are the same way about their workers. Those computers belong to the city."

"Well, I just thought you might want to know, he was looking up stuff about other cops."

"Which ones?" Erin asked sharply.

"I don't know the names," Vitelli said. "But it was the other guys from that narco squad. You know, the one that got one of its guys clipped."

"What information was he looking up?" Erin became aware she was gripping her phone very tightly. Piekarski and Firelli were staring at her, their faces showing confusion and growing concern.

"Personal stuff," Vitelli said. "You know, phone numbers, addresses, family members, all that sort of thing. But don't worry, he wasn't looking for nothing on you. He knows better than to mess with you and your people, he knows what happened last time somebody tried that."

Erin scarcely heard his last sentence. Numbly, when he stopped talking, she said, "Anything else you can tell me?"

"No, that's it. Sorry it ain't more. You take care."

"You too," she said automatically. There was a beep in her ear as Vitelli hung up.

"What's up?" Piekarski asked. "Jesus, Erin, you look like you're about to throw up."

"We have to move," Erin said. "Right now."

"What?" Piekarski asked.

"Who do you have listed in the NYPD personnel database?" Erin demanded. "Family. Next of kin."

"My mom," Piekarski said, bewildered. "In Queens. But—"

"Call her," Erin interrupted. "Wake her up. Get her away from home."

"But—" Piekarski began again.

"Do it!" Firelli snapped. "All your family in New York. And call Logan. Make sure he's okay, get him to do the same thing. Come on, O'Reilly. With me."

He'd come to the same conclusion Erin had. For Erin, it was the memory of what had so nearly happened to her sister-in-law earlier that year. For Firelli, it was years of experience on both sides of the law.

"You'd better call your people, too," Firelli told Erin. He was moving across the living room toward the stairs as he said it.

"In a minute," Erin said. "I think they're okay." She was thinking something else, and the look on Firelli's face mirrored her thoughts. It didn't take long to make a couple of sandwiches, probably no more than five minutes. Sandy Firelli had gone into the kitchen more like ten minutes ago.

The light over the front door had been turned off. Erin paused at the foot of the stairs. The ground floor of the Firelli house was almost pitch-black. Firelli, two steps ahead of her, was moving toward the kitchen. He put out a hand, just a shape in the dark, groping for the light switch.

"Wait!" Erin whispered sharply. She'd caught a whiff of something, and her time with Rolf had taught her to pay attention to her nose.

Firelli froze. "What?" he whispered back.

"Gas," she said. Natural gas was itself odorless, but gas leaks were so dangerous that a foul-smelling additive was mixed in with the stuff before it was piped out into circulation.

Both officers knew they couldn't risk turning on the lights. Completing an electrical circuit might make a spark, and if the gas smell was strong enough to pick up, it might be sufficiently concentrated to cause an explosion.

"Flashlight?" Erin whispered.

Firelli had already sidestepped to the front closet. He fumbled in the dark for an agonizing moment. Erin tried to breathe shallowly. They needed to evacuate and ventilate the house right away, but they also needed to make sure Sandy was all right. The most likely place for a gas leak was the kitchen, so if Mrs. Firelli was there, she'd probably already gotten a heavy dose. That stuff didn't need to catch fire to be lethal; inhaling it was plenty bad. It could cause disorientation, nausea, unconsciousness, and death.

There was a click and the bright cone of light from an LED flashlight sprang into existence. Then Firelli, knowing seconds counted, was rushing toward the kitchen. Erin pounded along behind him. Her gun was in her hands now, though she had no memory of drawing it.

"Sandy!" Firelli called, bursting through the kitchen door.

"Stop right there!" a man snapped.

Firelli froze. Erin stopped short so she wouldn't run into him. The kitchen was dark, but in the light of Firelli's flashlight she could see Conrad Maxwell.

Chapter 21

Maxwell looked like warmed-over shit. The harsh blue LED light made his complexion waxy and ghoulish. His hair was plastered to his forehead. Sweat was running down his face. His right ear was bandaged and there was indeed a piece of it missing. Vitelli had said he'd been given a sling, but he wasn't wearing it now. His black leather jacket had a hole high up on the left, where the bullet had caught him, and was stiff and crusted with dried blood. His left arm hung at an awkward angle. He was down on one knee on the Firellis' nice, new linoleum.

But his right hand was holding a wicked-looking butcher's knife, and that knife was pressed against Sandy Firelli's throat. Sandy was lying on the floor. Her eyes were closed and she looked very pale. The smell of natural gas was heavy and rancid in the room.

"Drop the knife!" Erin ordered, leveling the Delta Elite.

"Ah ah ah," Maxwell said. His voice was tight and breathy. He was obviously in significant pain. "Smell the air. You fire and we all go up."

"He's right," Firelli said. His voice was surprisingly calm and quiet. "Sandy? You okay?"

She didn't answer.

"I think she hit her head on the counter," Maxwell said. "She probably needs a doctor. But don't we all?"

"You sure do," Erin said. In spite of what the others had said, she kept her gun pointed at Maxwell. "Put down the knife and we'll get you to a hospital."

"What are you doing here?" Firelli asked. "What do you want?"

"You stupid bastards just couldn't leave it alone," Maxwell said. He coughed, either from the pain or the gas that permeated the air. The hand holding the knife quivered, drawing a thin, bright line of blood across Sandy's pale throat. "You couldn't just walk away. Now you've got Freddy, and the whole thing falls apart if I don't take care of this."

"It doesn't have to," Erin said. "I talked to Vinnie the Oil Man earlier tonight. We can work this out together. Your buddy Lombardo suggested it, and I'm game if you are."

As she spoke, she drifted into the kitchen and started angling toward the stove. She thought she might at least be able to plug the leak or turn off a valve. The air was heavy and pungent with gas. She was starting to feel a little light-headed.

"Bullshit," Maxwell said. "Too many people know. Too many straight-arrow cops like this asshole here. I checked his record. He's been a total boy scout. Never takes a payoff, never skims when his team makes seizures. His whole damn squad is like that. Cleanest narcs in the business. Un-freaking-believable. Time was, everybody in Narcotics was on the take."

"Those were the good old days, huh?" Erin said.

"I don't think you looked deep enough into my history," Firelli said. His voice was still calm, light, almost conversational.

"Oh yeah?" Maxwell said. "What was I supposed to find?"

"I wasn't always a cop," Firelli said. "I wasn't always a boy scout. And if you don't stop holding that knife on my wife, I'm going to kill you."

"Back off!" Maxwell snarled. "I don't give a shit about you and I don't care what you've got to say. You're in my way. I'm walking out and I'm taking this sweet little number with me for insurance. Once I'm over the state line, I'll turn her loose. Maybe."

"You're dreaming, Maxwell," Erin said. "There's no way we're letting you walk out of here. Firelli's right. You leave in handcuffs or in a body bag. Those are your choices."

"You can't shoot me unless you want to kill everybody in this house," Maxwell sneered. "She wasn't even supposed to be here. It should've just been you, asleep in bed. Nobody would've known it wasn't an accident. But now I've got to run for it. You want me, you've got to be prepared to burn right alongside me. That's the only way I'm staying here."

"Don't worry," Firelli said. "I'm not going to shoot you. And neither is she. Put the gun away, O'Reilly."

"No way," Erin said.

"I've got this," Firelli said. "Everything's cool, Maxwell. Look, here's my gun. I'm putting it down."

He laid his Glock on the kitchen counter. He held out the flashlight to Erin, without taking his eyes off Maxwell.

Erin, still holding the gun in her right hand, reached out to take the flashlight. She had some idea what Firelli was planning and hoped they'd be up for it. The gas was really getting to her. She had a pounding headache and felt like she was going to throw up. It was getting hard to focus.

"Watch where you're pointing that thing," Firelli said. "And holster your piece, please." Then he turned toward her, just for a second, and winked. Then he pivoted back toward Maxwell. But as he turned, his right hand was screened from Maxwell's view by his own body. That hand went to his belt. His knife came out of its sheath with the faintest whisper of well-oiled leather.

"Nobody's getting shot," Erin said. "See? Now let's get you to a doctor."

"You're staying right where you are," Maxwell said. "Until I'm gone. This is how it's going to go—"

"Light!" Firelli barked.

Erin, praying she understood, pointed the flashlight directly into Maxwell's face, aiming for his eyes. And everything happened very fast.

Maxwell flinched and turned his head away, and for just a second his uninjured arm, the one holding the knife, came up to shield his face. He started to stand up. Firelli lunged, stabbing at Maxwell. Erin angled in from the right, hooking around to flank the other two.

Sandy's legs were splayed out on the floor. Erin's foot caught the unconscious woman's ankle and she stumbled. The flashlight beam lurched crazily. Maxwell cried out and managed to get his arm in the way of Firelli's thrust. The knife glanced off Maxwell's forearm and sliced across his cheek as he scrambled back to get out of Firelli's reach. Maxwell's feet tangled and he went down on his ass. He scrambled back to his knees.

Firelli couldn't see Sandy in the dark, so he wasted a critical second stepping over her, feeling for his footing. Maxwell swept the butcher's knife across in a low arc, trying to take out Firelli's leg. Firelli jumped blindly and flung out a foot. He kicked Maxwell in the chest, sending the other man reeling back against the fridge.

Erin came up and closed from Maxwell's left. The flashlight was a flimsy thing, plastic-framed, not one of the big, sturdy D-cell ones cops carried on duty. It would make a crummy club. She pulled Vic's pistol again. She had no intention of firing it, but it was a large, hefty handgun. She reversed her grip, grabbing it by the barrel as a makeshift hammer.

Maxwell jabbed at Firelli, who sidestepped and delivered a backhand cut. Firelli's knife drew blood across Maxwell's knuckles. The dirty cop hissed in pain but didn't drop the knife. Instead, he dove down and forward, trying to close with Firelli. Erin took a swing. The Delta Elite crashed down on Maxwell's back, narrowly missing his skull. Maxwell grunted. Firelli caught him with one arm. His other arm was hidden from view by Maxwell's body.

The two men stood that way for what seemed a really long time, but was probably just a second or two. Erin wound up to deliver another blow. But Maxwell sagged against Firelli. He coughed. Something dark sprayed out of his mouth, spattering Sandy Firelli's brand-new, pristine countertop and the half-made sandwiches on it.

Firelli pushed. Maxwell tumbled away from him on rubbery legs and went down, collapsing in a floppy half-sitting posture against the refrigerator. Erin turned the flashlight's beam on him. About halfway up his chest, just to one side of center, the handle of Firelli's knife was sticking out of him. The entire blade was jammed between his ribs. Maxwell's eyes went down to the knife, then up to meet Erin's. His face showed a sort of dull surprise, not even any real pain. Erin supposed the pain would come later, if he lived.

Firelli wasn't even looking at Maxwell anymore. He was already bending down, looping his arms around his wife's limp body in a fireman's carry. He groaned, strained, and stood up. He was a small man, only a little larger than Sandy, but he forced himself to stagger toward the back door.

Erin sucked in a breath and got a lungful of gas. Her head spun and for a second she thought she'd pass out. She tried to brace herself. There'd be plenty of time to keel over in a minute. "Piekarski!" she shouted. "Gas leak! Get out!"

Firelli was at the back door, fumbling with the latch. Erin took a shaky step toward Maxwell. He was a murderous asshole, but she couldn't just leave him here to die. She knelt beside him.

He coughed again, sending a fine mist of blood into the air. Firelli must have punctured his lung. But in spite of the damage, Maxwell managed a weak, sardonic laugh. His right hand came out of his pants pocket with something small and shiny in it.

"Want a light?" he chuckled. He flipped the thing open.

Erin's head was thick and fuzzy. What was going through it wasn't exactly conscious thought. Twelve years' police experience told her that whatever a perp had in his hands was likely to hurt you. Operating purely on reflex, she slammed the butt of her borrowed pistol onto his wrist, crushing it against the linoleum. His fingers flew open and the little metal thing skittered across the floor. Vaguely, she recognized a cigarette lighter.

Maxwell coughed again and began to choke, going into convulsions. Erin shoved the gun into its holster, dropped the flashlight, and seized the man under the arms. She dragged him across the kitchen floor and out the back door, stumbling and tumbling out into the night.

The cool, fresh autumn air washed across her face and into her body like the breath of life, sweeping away the fog of natural gas and leaving dizzy nausea in its wake. There were three concrete steps leading down into the Firellis' little postage-stamp of a backyard. Erin hauled Maxwell down the stairs. Then she fell over and went to her knees, retching weakly. A few feet away, Firelli was on all fours, vomiting onto the grass. Sandy was lying next to him, very pale, unmoving.

"Erin? Firelli?" Piekarski's voice came from the front of the house. She sounded confused and scared. "Where are you?"

"Back... back yard," Erin choked out.

A moment later, Piekarski hurried down the narrow passage between the Firellis' house and their next-door neighbors. She had Lombardo with her, hands cuffed behind him, and was pushing him in front of her. She gave him a final shove and yanked out her phone.

"Dispatch, this is Officer Piekarski," she said. "Shield eight three three niner. I've got a natural gas leak at my location and multiple casualties. I need at least two buses and FDNY forthwith."

"Sandy," Firelli said weakly. He knelt over his wife and ran a hand across the back of his mouth, wiping away the trail of bile. "Sandy!"

Sandy's eyelids fluttered. "Rob?" she whispered.

Firelli wrapped his arms around her and held her close. A sob of relief burst out of him.

Erin turned her attention to Maxwell. The man lay where she'd dumped him, Firelli's knife grotesquely protruding from his chest. She knew the best thing was to leave the blade in the wound. Pulling it out would only cause more damage and might make him bleed out.

"Maxwell," she said. "Don't you dare die on me, you sick son of a bitch. You've got too much to answer for."

But Conrad Maxwell was answering to a higher authority than the New York Police Department. His eyes were half open, but the light had gone out of them. Firelli's knife might have missed his heart, but that heart was no longer beating.

In the middle distance came the familiar howl of police sirens. The first responders would be there in a matter of moments. Erin started trying to think what the hell she was going to tell them.

Chapter 22

"Two dead cops," Captain Holliday said. "Both of them killed by other cops. Another one in the hospital, plus one in a holding cell. Off-duty officers taking the law into their own hands, shooting it out with other officers and getting in knife fights. One civilian casualty, along with a known drug trafficker who claims he was shot from behind, without warning."

Erin and Vic did the smartest thing they could, which was to keep their mouths shut. They were in Holliday's office, standing in front of his desk at stiff attention, not daring to look either at the Captain or at one another. Lieutenants Keane and Webb, Kira Jones, and a lawyer from the Police Union were squeezed against the wall opposite the door.

The window, between Keane and the lawyer, showed a pink glow over the Manhattan skyline, the sun starting to reach down into the concrete canyons of the city. Erin felt like she'd been awake for days.

"Am I forgetting anything important, Lieutenant?" Holliday asked, glancing at Keane.

"We have an unreported contact with the head of an organized crime family," Keane said. He appeared well-rested, every stitch of his expensive suit in perfect order. Erin wasn't sure he actually grew facial hair; she'd never seen so much as a hint of stubble on his cheeks. Maybe he used lasers to remove it.

Holliday nodded. Erin risked a sidelong look at the Captain. He was maintaining an impressive poker face. Holliday already knew about Erin's contact with the Oil Man. In fact, he'd signed off on the elaborate ploy to fake the car bombing that had gotten her into the Lucarellis' good graces. They had not informed Keane of the plot, which was extremely risky. Under proper protocol, they should have told the local Internal Affairs commander of any such scheme. But then, proper protocol had gone out the window when they'd agreed to set off a powerful explosive device in front of a New York hotel.

"I'll expect a full report of that meeting," Holliday said. "Let's see what else we have here."

"Unauthorized penetration of the Internal Affairs database," Keane said. "One of these two downloaded the personnel files on Detectives Maxwell, Lombardo, and Plank."

"Really?" Holliday asked, raising his eyebrows. "I didn't think they had access."

"They don't," Keane said. "How did you do it, Detectives?"

"We didn't, sir," Erin and Vic said in near-perfect unison.

"Then they leveraged someone who did have access," Keane said.

"That sounds like you're suggesting one of your own people was involved, Lieutenant," Holliday said. "Perhaps you should investigate that angle before making additional accusations."

"It's not important at the moment," Keane said. "But I'll look into it."

"As far as using computers for unauthorized business, sir," Erin broke in, "Maxwell's the one who misused a Department computer."

"Explain," Holliday said.

"He didn't know where Firelli lived," she said. "The only way he'd know would be to look it up in the system."

"She makes a good point," Holliday said. "There's a very good reason we don't publicly post the home addresses of our officers. But we're jumping into this story in the middle. I want a full and complete explanation, Detectives."

"We really should hear the other two officers' statements as well," Keane said.

"Officers Piekarski and Firelli are not under my command," Holliday reminded him. "Nor are they under your supervision. That matter has been referred to Captain Markos at the Five. Now, Detective O'Reilly, we're waiting."

Erin took a deep breath. "Sir, Detective Neshenko and I accepted an invitation from Sergeant Logan's SNEU squad to accompany them on what we believed to be a routine drug bust."

"Why?" Keane asked.

"We were bored," Vic said. "Wanted some action."

"You were hoping to get in a gunfight?" Keane asked.

"You ever been in a gunfight, sir?" Vic retorted.

"I'm asking the questions, Detective Third Grade," Keane said coldly.

"This is pertinent," Vic said.

"No, he hasn't," Holliday said. "Relax, Lieutenant, it's in your service jacket. Now, Neshenko, how is this pertinent?"

"If he'd been in one, he'd know better than to ask a dumbass question like that," Vic said, then added, "sir."

"You've been in numerous lethal confrontations," Keane said. "How, exactly, is it a dumbass question to suggest you might enjoy it?"

"Gunfights are no fun, sir," Vic said. "I don't mind smacking a few guys' heads, sure. But I've seen people die and I've killed them myself, and I don't want to kill any more."

"Yet you exchanged fire with Detective Maxwell last night," Keane observed.

"Didn't want to," Vic said. "But once he started shooting, I sure as hell wanted to make him stop."

"Please continue, Detective O'Reilly," Holliday said. "And Lieutenant, I think it might be better if we kept interruptions to a minimum."

"Officer Firelli had gotten a tip about a big shipment of heroin," Erin went on. "The tip came from a CI on the street who goes by the nickname Silvers. The heroin was being delivered to a club called the White Stallion, which was being used as a front for a new narcotics operation in Little Italy.

"We arrived on scene simultaneously with the delivery vehicle and Detective Maxwell's squad, who had received similar information from a similar source. The deliverymen were Gianni and Carlo Manzano, and they were dropping off the shipment into the care of Luca Frazetti. All three men were disaffected members of the Lucarelli family.

"We attempted to take them into custody, but one of Maxwell's people shouted, 'Gun!' and started shooting. That set off a three-way firefight. We didn't know who Maxwell and his guys were. For all we knew, they were a rival gang. In the exchange of gunfire, Detective Plank was badly wounded and the Manzanos and Frazetti were killed, as was Officer Janovich of SNEU."

"One moment," Keane said. "Excuse me, but did nobody identify themselves as NYPD officers?"

"The SNEU squad did," Erin said. "Maxwell's unit did not."

Keane nodded. "Continue."

"After the shooting, Neshenko and I initiated a side investigation," Erin said. "We were assisted in this by Officers Piekarski and Firelli."

"Not Logan?" Keane asked.

"Logan didn't know anything about it," Vic said. "Leave him out of this."

"In the course of our investigation, we learned the following," Erin said. "The dealers at the White Stallion were working for a splinter element of the O'Malley Mob, in violation of a turf-sharing agreement between the Lucarellis and the O'Malleys. We believe the Lucarellis retaliated by sending Maxwell and his guys to take care of the interlopers."

"You believe?" Keane asked quietly.

"We have no direct proof of that," Erin said. "Maxwell admitted as much to Firelli and me in Firelli's kitchen, but we don't have a recording of the conversation." She wished she'd tried to squeeze a little more data onto her hidden recorder, but everything had happened too fast.

"And Maxwell himself is conveniently deceased," Keane added.

"Since the drug deal had been brokered by Dominic Silvestri," Erin continued, "we believed his life was also in danger from the Lucarellis. We accordingly tracked him to a building on the Brooklyn waterfront he was known to use as a stash house. However, it appears that Maxwell's information sources were equally good. He arrived shortly after we did, together with Detective Lombardo. They ambushed Silvestri and wounded him, but Officer Firelli and I intervened. They opened fire on us, even after Firelli ID'd us as NYPD. Lombardo was taken into custody and Maxwell was injured. So was my K-9."

"What's your K-9's status?" Holliday asked.

"It's not a serious wound," Erin said. "He's expected to make a full recovery."

"I'm glad to hear it," Holliday said. "He's a good dog and an asset to the force."

Erin nodded. "Maxwell fled," she said. "But the game was up. He assumed Lombardo would talk. His last shot was to try to take out the people who'd been chasing him and hope it would be enough to derail the case we were building against him. So he downloaded our addresses through the NYPD's personnel database. I assume he was planning to take care of all of us. Firelli's place was the closest to where he was, so he decided to hit Firelli first.

"He didn't know Piekarski and I were there, along with his buddy Lombardo. Firelli's wife was supposed to be out of the house, but she left work early. Maxwell surprised her in the kitchen and knocked her out. Then he tore open the gas line to the stove. His plan was to stage a fatal gas leak and make it look like an accident. But Firelli and I interrupted him. He refused to surrender. There was a struggle, during which Firelli stabbed Maxwell. We evacuated the residence and called for backup. Maxwell died before the EMTs arrived."

"I'm curious," Keane said. "Why did you detain Detective Lombardo at the Firelli residence instead of taking him to the nearest station?"

Erin squared her shoulders and looked him in the eye. "That was my call, sir," she said.

"I'm sure it was, as the ranking detective," Keane said. "But taking responsibility is not the same as explaining."

"He's a member of a corrupt unit that's been operating within the NYPD, probably for years, without discovery," she said. "We were trying to determine whether other officers might have been compromised before putting him under their care."

"So that's it?" Holliday said.

"That's what happened, sir," Erin said.

"And you didn't think to inform Internal Affairs of your extracurricular investigation?" Keane asked. "Even while worrying about pervasive institutional rot?"

"We considered it," Erin said.

"How... *considerate* of you," Keane said. He didn't crack a smile. "Need I remind you, Detectives, that this sort of situation is precisely why we have an Internal Affairs department in the first place?"

"No, sir," Erin said stonily.

"And we have only your opinion that Detective Maxwell was compromised?"

"I wouldn't say that," Vic said.

"You have something to add, Neshenko?" Keane said with dangerous softness.

"I was looking through Maxwell's financials last night," Vic said. "And I found some discrepancies."

"What sort of discrepancies?"

"Well, sir, I'm just a dumb meathead," Vic said. "But it looked to me like he was shifting a lot of cash around. Just a few thousand at a time, moving it into accounts in the names of his sister, his brother, and his dad."

"That's hardly conclusive," Keane said.

"Yeah, that's what I thought," Vic said. "Until I double-checked his next-of-kin listing and found out he's an orphan and an only child."

There was a short, meaningful silence.

"But then, you IAB guys would probably already know about something like that," Vic said.

There was another, longer silence.

"I mean, that seems like the sort of thing that would raise some red flags," he added.

"You've made your point, Detective," Keane said.

"So, you'll be looking into Maxwell, Plank, and Lombardo?" Erin asked.

"IAB does not discuss the subjects of its investigations with other officers," Keane said. "For obvious reasons. This meeting is concluded."

"What?" Holliday demanded. "Hold on a second. This meeting isn't over until I'm satisfied, and I am very far from satisfied."

"This is an Internal Affairs investigation, and as such, I have jurisdiction in the Eighth Precinct," Keane said. "Detective Jones will collect your written reports, Detectives. Good day, all of you."

He left the office almost before Erin had realized he was going. She tried not to look as startled as she felt.

"I suppose that's the end of this for the present," Holliday said. "I'm sure IAB will have more questions for you. In the meantime..."

"Don't leave town, sir?" Vic suggested.

Holliday smiled thinly. "Something like that. You're on modified assignment. Again."

"We didn't kill anybody," Vic protested.

"Did you, or did you not shoot Detective Melvin Plank?"

"He didn't die," Vic said sulkily.

"And Detective O'Reilly assisted Officer Firelli in the struggle which resulted in the death of Detective Maxwell," Holliday said. "If you genuinely believe either of you shouldn't be on modified assignment, I'd be fascinated to hear your reasons."

No reasons were forthcoming.

"Dismissed," Holliday said.

Kira Jones followed the Major Crimes detectives out of Holliday's office. She obviously had things on her mind, and Erin wanted to talk to her, but she didn't want to risk her saying anything in the open office. Erin held up a finger and touched it quickly to her own lips. Kira frowned, but nodded her understanding.

"I shouldn't have drunk so much coffee," Erin said loudly. "I'll be right back."

She headed for the restroom and didn't look over her shoulder, trusting Kira to take the hint. Sure enough, Kira walked into the room about twenty seconds behind Erin. The IAB detective flipped the lock on the outer door.

"If you think your office is bugged, how do you know the bathroom is clean?" Kira asked.

"I don't," Erin said. "I don't know if the Charger is clean, either. Hell, for all I know, Rolf's got a bug in his collar."

"You really believe that? Erin, what in God's name is going on?"

"Kira, I need you to listen to me," Erin said. "And listen carefully. I didn't tell Keane and Holliday everything."

"What? Why not?" Kira's eyes were very wide.

"Because I don't know who to trust."

"But you trust me?"

"Yeah. I do."

Kira swallowed. "Thanks. I think."

"Vinnie Moreno thinks I'm a gun for hire," Erin said, speaking quickly and quietly. "You know the bombing at the JFK Hilton? He thinks that was me."

"And Carlyle," Kira said, nodding. "That makes sense. Holy shit, Erin. *Was* that you?"

"I didn't kill that witness," Erin said, sticking to the technical truth of the matter. "But what matters is what Vinnie believes. I got him to throw me Maxwell. This is sensitive, deep-cover shit, Kira. You can't tell anybody this. *Anybody.* Not Keane, not the PC, not whatever God you believe in. You got that?"

Kira nodded unhappily.

"Here's the thing," Erin said. "One of Vinnie's guys told me Maxwell was looking up addresses in the personnel system."

"Yeah, I know. You said that in the Captain's office."

"How did Vinnie know that?" Erin shot back.

"That wouldn't be hard," Kira said. "All he'd have to do is get someone with access to the personnel database."

"No," Erin said. "That would get him the information. How'd he know Maxwell was looking up the stuff?"

"He'd have to have access to the NYPD's monitoring setup," Kira said. "Which means... shit."

"It means he's got someone in IAB," Erin said quietly.

"But you're sure that someone isn't me, or you wouldn't be telling me this."

"We worked together for months," Erin said. "We were in gunfights. I know you've got my back. Besides, you helped us with Maxwell and his guys. You wouldn't have done that if you were playing for Vinnie's team. You went out on a limb for us."

"And this is my reward," Kira said bitterly. "Fantastic. Why are you telling me this?"

"We had a guy who died in custody a little while back," Erin said. "Remember? That perp who hanged himself in the holding cell?"

"Yeah, I remember," Kira said. "But that was a suicide."

"Not according to Dr. Levine," Erin said. "She was ready to rule it a homicide."

"But that would have to mean someone in my office was behind it," Kira said.

"Exactly."

Kira bit her lip and looked at her feet. "I thought when I transferred out of Major Crimes, I'd be done with this crazy shit," she said. "What are you asking me to do?"

"Your job," Erin said. "Somebody upstairs is working for the bad guys. You need to find out who. You can do things I can't.

You've got full access to personnel records. You've got a great head for running financials. You know every line of the damn Patrol Guide. You were made to do this."

"You're asking me to spy on Internal Affairs," Kira said. "From the inside."

Erin nodded. "You get to be the one who watches the watchmen," she said.

"No, I'm watching the guys who watch the watchmen," Kira corrected. "This is nuts. I'm going to get caught. And when Keane catches me, he'll burn my ass. My career will be over. I'll be lucky if I end up throwing drunks out of Yankee Stadium."

"It's risky," Erin agreed. "I know it's a big ask."

"Big? It's enormous. What's your endgame on this?"

"How do you mean?"

"Suppose I find a dirty IAB cop. Suppose I get proof. Then what?"

"Then we take it all the way to the top. To Holliday, and then to the PC himself."

"You say that like it'll be easy." But Kira said it more firmly, with her jaw set, and Erin knew she'd do it.

"I'm sorry, for what it's worth," Erin said.

"Sorry and five bucks will get you a cup of coffee," Kira said. "I'm going to regret this. What the hell, I'm in. I'll need everything you can tell me about every incident that's suspicious."

"I'll get you everything I can."

"And we can't use my office computer. If there's a mole, they might have a backdoor into the system. Probably best not to use electronic communications at all."

"Meeting in person is risky too," Erin said.

"We'll set up a dead drop," Kira said. "Like in spy movies, you know? Duct-tape the files under park benches, that sort of thing?"

"Admit it, you're going to enjoy this a little," Erin said. "Come on, it'll be fun."

"Fun is loud music, bright lights, dancing, and funky-colored drinks with swizzle sticks and little umbrellas," Kira said. "This is work. It's not supposed to be fun."

"Rolf would disagree," Erin said. "But we'd better get back out there, before Vic and Webb start getting suspicious."

"They'll just assume we're talking about them," Kira said. "You ever heard of the Bechdel Test?"

"Is that something from the Patrol Guide?"

"It's a movie thing. A movie passes the test when two women have a conversation and it's not about a man. It's surprisingly rare. That's why men always assume they're what we talk about."

"Did we pass the test?"

"Until a minute ago, yeah."

"Damn." Erin looked at Kira. Both of them smiled.

"I've missed you Major Crimes idiots," Kira said. "Even Vic."

"Yeah, I know what you mean. Tell you what, I'll leave what I've got on the leak under your car, driver's side, taped to the undercarriage."

"Oh, good. Now if people see me, they'll think I've pissed off the Mob and I'm checking for bombs."

"I check for bombs every day. Rolf helps."

"Really?"

"Yeah."

Kira shook her head. "I wouldn't trade places with you," she said. "Not for a million bucks and a Ferrari. Because the Ferrari would get blown up."

Erin put out her hand. Kira took it. Then, without really planning it, they pulled in close for a hug.

"Be careful," Erin said softly.

"Copy that," Kira replied. "Back at you."

Chapter 23

There was a saying in the military that being a soldier was ninety-nine percent boredom and one percent sheer terror. Erin figured being a detective was similar; one percent action, ninety-nine percent paperwork. There were the ubiquitous DD-5s, to start with. Then there were arrest reports, use-of-force reports, logging of evidence, and much more.

The sun was coming up when she and Vic started climbing the mountain of bureaucratic paper. By the time the summit was in sight, it was almost lunchtime. Vic had made six trips to the downstairs vending machines, returning with a can of Mountain Dew the first five. On his last trip he came back cursing and squeezing a can of Cherry Coke so hard Erin was surprised it didn't explode in his fist. Erin herself subsisted on a slightly stale donut from the break room, two Diet Cokes, and about a quart of gourmet coffee from the fancy machine Carlyle had given the Department.

"What do you think, Vic?" she asked. "What's going to give out first? Your heart from that caffeine, my kidneys from this coffee, or Webb's lungs from the smoking?"

"Good question," he replied. "We could start a pool on it."

Webb himself had left a little after seven, answering a call to investigate a body that had turned up in the early-morning hours. Erin and Vic would have loved to accompany him, but as Holliday had reminded them, they were on desk duty until IAB formally cleared them.

"Sorry about your gun," Erin said.

"Forget about it," Vic said. "I'll get it back from Evidence as soon as they clear us. It's not like I don't have others. How'd you like it?"

"It's shitty for target practice, but it makes a good substitute for a nightstick," she said. "I hope I didn't bend the barrel when I clocked Maxwell with it."

"If you're hitting them with the gun, you're doing it wrong. You do know you can pull the trigger and bullets come out, right?"

"The place was full of natural gas, Vic. If I'd shot him, you'd have needed a Shop-Vac to pick up the pieces. Anyway, the grip's too big for my hand. I expect you don't have any problem with those big chunks of meat you've got hanging off your wrists."

"Don't knock the .45," Vic said. "That's the bullet that won World War II."

"I thought the atom bomb won World War II."

"Now who's talking about bigger bullets?" Vic scowled at his computer. "I wish the Lieutenant had let us come along. I'd rather look at a corpse than another goddamn report."

"There'll be other bodies," Erin said.

"You got that right. This friggin' city. But I had to miss all the fun down in Brooklyn and I have to pay for it anyway. You got in a fight without me. All while I was sitting on my thumb at the hospital, wasting time trying to see Plank."

"They didn't let you in, did they?"

"Wouldn't have mattered if they had. The son of a bitch was intubated, on account of me being too good a shot and putting a hole clean through his lung. I got a quick look at him through the door before the unis on duty shooed me off. Guy had a tube right down his throat, a plug up his nose, plus God only knows what else hooked up to him. I'm glad he turned out to be a bad guy. I'd feel pretty lousy if I'd done that to a good cop."

"You didn't know he was a cop when you shot him," she reminded him. "None of us did."

"Yeah, well, we should've known. It's bad enough we have to fight criminals. How you think this is gonna play in the locker room?"

"We didn't start this," Erin said.

"No, we just finished it," Vic agreed. "But the guy who wins the fight is the one who comes out of it looking like the bad guy. Didn't you ever get in playground fights when you were a kid?"

Erin shrugged. "Half the Department thinks I'm a hero, the other half thinks I'm dirty," she said. "You'll get used to it."

The elevator dinged and the doors slid open, revealing Lieutenant Webb. He looked like he'd been up too early, which was true, and like he needed a cigarette, which was probably also true. He walked slowly into the break room and emerged a minute later with a cup of coffee.

"I hope you're done with your reports," he said.

"Yes, sir," Erin said.

"And I hope next time I won't have to find out what my squad's been up to by reading up on them after the fact."

"Yes, sir."

"Who was the dead guy?" Vic asked.

"Just your typical New York street death," Webb sighed. "They wanted Major Crimes to take a look, but this one's going to the Homicide boys. Maybe they'll clear it, but I wouldn't hold my breath."

"What was it?" Erin asked.

"It wasn't a guy, for starters," Webb said. He took a long sip of coffee. A little shiver ran through his body and he held the cup away from his face and blew on it to cool it. "And it was ugly. That's why they wanted me. They thought maybe it was a serial killer, like the Boston Strangler or something."

"How do you know it wasn't?" Erin asked.

"You always think it's a serial killer," Webb said sourly.

"Twice," Erin said. "I only thought that twice, and I was right both times."

"Technically, you were right once," Vic said. "The second one, that creepy kid, wasn't a serial killer. He'd only killed one person. Granted, he was probably gonna kill more, but if you stop him at one, it's not a series."

"I'm too tired to argue about this," Erin said.

"I don't know for sure," Webb said. "But hookers get killed all the time, and it's usually not part of a series. This one probably got done in by one of her customers, or maybe her pimp. It could've been a sex murder, I guess, but it might even have been an accident."

"How do you mean?" Erin asked.

"Some guys get into the whole choking thing," Webb said. "Maybe the john got carried away. She put up a fight, though; her fingernails were all torn up and two of them were ripped clean out. That's on top of one hell of a beating. They might get DNA scrapes from under the nails that are left, which will help if we ever get the right guy, I guess, if he's in the system. If he is, Homicide will hear about it in six months or so and scoop him up."

"Did you get an ID on the victim?" Erin asked.

"O'Reilly, this isn't our case," Webb said wearily. "And even if it was, you wouldn't be working it."

"Sir, I've been up all night and I've just spent about six hours filling out forms," she said. "Humor me. Please?"

"She wasn't carrying ID," Webb said. "But we had her prints on file. Long rap sheet, all the usuals: solicitation, lewdness, disorderly conduct, resisting arrest. Nothing too bad."

"This girl have a name?"

"Not really a girl," Webb said. "She was forty-two, according to her file. I guess she had a pretty good run. Usually streetwalkers don't last that long in the Life. Veronica Blackburn, assuming that's her real name."

"That's weird," Vic said. "I think I've heard that name somewhere. Can't quite place it. Maybe I busted her back when I was working Patrol. It would've been a while ago, but you said she'd been on the streets longer than most... Erin? You okay?"

Erin made it to the bathroom, but only barely. She lurched into the nearest stall and dropped to her knees, bruising her kneecaps on the hard tiles. Then the donut came up, washed out of her stomach on a tide of coffee. The sour acidic taste filled her mouth and climbed into the back of her nasal passages. She gripped the rim of the toilet bowl and emptied her guts. At some point she realized she was crying. She didn't care. All she could think of was the desperation and terror she'd seen in Veronica's face.

She thought of Carlyle and the quiet, calm way he'd said, "Good night, Miss Blackburn." She'd suspected it might end this way, but he'd *known*. He'd known and he hadn't lifted a finger to protect Veronica. But Erin hadn't done a damn thing, either.

She stopped retching. She had was nothing left to bring up. Mechanically, she reached out and flushed the toilet. Then she got up and stumbled to the sink. She rinsed out her mouth, gargled, and spat a mouthful of water into the basin. She could still taste the acid in her throat. It burned. A part of her welcomed the feeling. She didn't look in the mirror. She might not have been able to bear what she would have seen.

Vic was waiting outside when she opened the bathroom door. He looked worried, which was an expression that never looked quite right on his face; like a guy trying to wear a suit a couple inches too tight in the shoulders.

"You don't look so good," he said. "Jesus, you're white as a ghost."

"I'm going home," she said dully.

"Hey, you sure the docs checked you out after the gas and that fight?" he said. "Shit, you breathed in a bunch of fumes, and that was after you stopped two bullets. Maybe you'd better go to the hospital, just in case."

He was talking to her back. She'd already turned to the elevator and punched the button four or five times. Normally she would have taken the stairs, but that would have required going past the front desk, and she didn't want to run into the desk sergeant or whatever other cops might be hanging around.

The elevator finally slid open for her. She got in and hit the button for the basement garage. The doors started to close again. She leaned against the back wall of the car and let out a shaky breath.

A big, burly arm thrust through the gap between the doors. They obediently opened and Vic got in. Then the doors closed once more and the car started to descend.

"I remembered," he said quietly.

"Vic, not right now," she said. She swiped at her eyes with the back of her sleeve.

"Veronica Blackburn was with the O'Malleys," he said. "You knew her."

"A little, yeah."

"Was she a friend?"

She stared at him, blinking to clear her vision. "What? No!"

"I'd get that," he said. "You make friends on that kind of job. That's how it started with Carlyle, right? It's okay to like these people, as long as you remember who you are and who they are."

"No, we weren't friends," Erin said. "We didn't get along. She was a bitch, if you want to know. Oh, and she was sleeping with Mickey Connor."

Vic made a face. "Sheesh!" he said. "I guess there's no accounting for taste. No wonder you tossed your cookies."

Erin shook her head. "I can't explain. Not now. It's... I know what happened to her."

"Of course you do," he said. "Webb just told us."

The elevator slowed to a stop. The doors opened on the basement hallway.

"You mean, you know who killed her," he said. "And you know why."

Erin nodded.

"Good," he said. "You can call up the guys in Homicide. They'll love getting a lead. Maybe they can do their DNA-matching thing and get the guy in a day or two."

"It's not that simple," she said. The elevator, its patience exhausted, started to close again. Vic put out a hand and held the door open without looking at it.

"It's gonna compromise you," he said. "So you can't move on it. Not yet."

"Something like that," she said.

"Don't worry," he said. "That just means it's postponed a little. You can still stick it to the sons of bitches in the end, and that's the important thing, right? You'll get the bastards who did it."

"Vic," she whispered. "I think maybe it's my fault."

"What are you talking about? You didn't kill her. You were with Piekarski and Firelli, right?"

"I didn't strangle her," Erin said. "But she's dead because of me. Because of us."

Then he got it. "Holy shit," he breathed. "She's the O'Malley connection. The one who was running drugs out of the White Stallion."

"Yeah."

"Tell me you didn't rat her out to the Oil Man. Christ, Erin, you know what kind of guy he is!"

"No. I didn't say a word about her to him." She felt the bile rise in her throat again and fought to keep it down. "And I didn't mean to do it. I thought Evan already knew. I thought he was behind the whole thing."

"Oh, man," Vic said. "You talked to O'Malley about it and he blew his stack. That's... that's some heavy shit."

"Yeah."

"You need help with any of it?"

She shook her head. "No, I'll handle it. I just didn't know what this was going to cost when I got started."

"Look, Erin, this Blackburn chick made her choices," Vic said. "What happened to her is on her, not on you."

"I'm not talking about what happened to her. I'm talking about what's happening to me."

They looked at one another for a long moment. Vic's jaw tightened.

"We've got to get you out of there," he said.

"Soon," she promised.

"Soon enough?" he asked. "It'd damned well better be, or I'm going to personally kick the ass of every jerk named O'Malley in New York, and maybe Jersey while I'm at it."

She gave him a watery smile. "Do you have any idea how many O'Malleys live in New York, Vic?"

He shrugged. "I've got a good pair of boots."

"That's actually kind of sweet of you to offer," she said. "A lot of guys send sympathy flowers. You loan me a gun and offer to beat guys up for me."

"Hey, you want flowers? I can hook you up. My dad was a florist, remember?"

"I'd forgotten."

"Erin, if you need anything," he said awkwardly, avoiding eye contact, "I've got your back. You know that, right?"

"I know," she said. "But right now, what I need is to get home, take a shower, and sleep for two days straight."

"Copy that," he said. He stood back from the door. "Take care of yourself. Our squad's too shorthanded as it is."

Chapter 24

Rolf was waiting for Erin at the top of the apartment stairs. He was wearing a collapsible padded cone around his neck and an expression of wounded dignity. He'd done everything she'd asked him to, the look said. He'd grabbed hold of one of the bad guys and hadn't let go, not even when he'd been shot, and this was how she repaid him? By sticking him in a cone and leaving him behind?

As she slowly climbed the stairs, Rolf's tail started sweeping the floor behind him, almost in spite of himself. With each step, the tail moved faster. He cocked his head at her, his ears tilting way off to one side. By the time she got to the top, his entire back end was wiggling.

"Hey there, kiddo," she said, laying a hand on his head.

Rolf nosed at the hand. He could tell something was wrong. Maybe she'd been hurt, too. He licked her hand and nosed it again.

Erin ruffled his fur. She bent down and kissed his forehead. He licked her face.

"In here, darling," Carlyle called from his office.

Erin didn't want to talk to him. She wanted to crawl into bed, curl into a ball, and try to forget the world existed. Either that, or maybe drink until she passed out. But Sean O'Reilly hadn't raised his daughter to hide from her troubles. She dragged herself down the hall to Carlyle's office instead. Rolf jumped up and trotted beside her, eager to show he was ready to get back into the action, trying to lift her up with his own energy.

"You've had a long night, by the looks of you," he said, getting up and coming around his desk. He was smiling, but as he got closer and saw the expression in her eyes, the smile fell off his face. "Mother of Mary, darling. What's happened?"

"Veronica Blackburn's dead," Erin said. The words came out flat and lifeless.

Carlyle stopped short. "Aye, darling," he said quietly. "That doesn't surprise me."

"You already knew," she said.

He shook his head. "I've had no word of it, if that's what you're saying."

"You knew the moment we left Evan's," she said. "I could've saved her, damn it!"

"Erin, think what you're saying," he said. "Just how would you have done that?"

"I had a gun. And Rolf." Her eyes were filling with frustrated tears.

"That's so," he said. "And you'd have had to kill everyone else in that flat, except myself and perhaps Maggie. That's Evan, the Snake, and Paddy Ryan, for starters. And I'm thinking I know something about our lad PR that you don't. He may be a shite bartender, but he's killed five lads I know of. He's an expert marksman and a black belt in jujitsu."

"Jujitsu?" she repeated, thinking of Paddy Ryan's pleasant, talkative face. "You're kidding."

"Nay, darling. Why do you think Evan keeps him close? You were carrying a six-shot revolver, aye? That's two bullets apiece. Not much margin for error, even with Rolf and me doing what we could, and that's not even taking into account the guards outside, plus the lads downstairs. You could have called the other coppers, aye, but how long would they take to arrive? And you'd be killing five or six lads, most of whom had nothing whatever to do with what happened to poor Miss Blackburn."

"Pritchard killed her," she said. "Strangled her. He tortured her first."

"That's likely true," Carlyle said. "Evan would want to know the extent of the damage to his organization before disposing of her."

"And you're okay with this?" The tears were getting out of control now, spilling down her cheeks, leaving hot, angry trails.

"I'm not okay with any of it," he said, coming closer. He put his hands on her shoulders. She wanted to shrug him off, but she didn't. Her flesh trembled with tension under his touch. "That's why we're putting an end to it. To all of it. In a matter of months, maybe weeks, we'll have the whole rotten lot of them behind bars."

"How many people have to die before then?" she shot back. "And I'm supposed to just sit there and watch it happen?"

"Is that what you were doing last night? Sitting around watching?"

"No! You wouldn't believe the night I've had. I've been shot, gassed, and talked the Oil Man out of having me killed. I arrested one bad cop and watched another one die. I just convinced one of my friends to do something that'll cost her job if she gets caught, I'm in trouble with Internal Affairs... There's more. Want me to go on?"

"Will it help you?"

She leaned forward, resting her head against his shoulder. "No."

He put his arms around her, keeping the embrace loose, not trying to restrain her. "Who else has been killed, darling?" he asked softly.

"Conrad Maxwell. The dirty detective from the Twelve."

"What happened?"

"He tried to gas Firelli's house down in Brooklyn and kill Firelli and his wife. Firelli and I got into it with him in the kitchen, and Firelli stabbed him. We couldn't shoot him because of the natural gas." She laughed shakily. "Firelli did warn him. He said if Maxwell didn't get away from his wife, he'd kill him, and that's exactly what he did."

"Sounds to me like the scunner had it coming," Carlyle said.

"So what? Veronica had it coming. Pritchard and Evan have it coming. You've got it coming. I've got it coming. Hell, everybody's got it coming. Is that supposed to make me feel better? Is this about justice?"

"It was never about justice, darling. Justice doesn't exist."

"I guess I've wasted my career, then," she said bitterly.

"It's about protecting what we love," he said. "That's a fair sight better than justice."

"That's why I'm going through this shit? For love?" She pulled back to arm's length and gave him a wry look.

"Isn't it?" he replied. "It's why I'm doing it. And in case you've forgotten, one of the things you love is this bloody city. That's why you won't stand for these bastards tearing it apart."

"And that's why Firelli was willing to kill Maxwell," Erin said. "To protect his wife. Why couldn't Maxwell have just made a run for it? Why did Evan have to kill Veronica?"

"Are you asking me why we need coppers, darling? Because the answer to that is very simple. We need lasses like yourself because there'll always be lads who believe in their own version of justice."

"Street justice, you mean?"

"Nothing like that. I mean there'll be folk like Veronica, who were dealt a bad hand by life, and who feel it's only fair to take whatever they can, however they can, to get even. Have you ever noticed, darling, it's toddlers and criminals who always cry about life being unfair? What's that, if not a sense of injustice? And that's why I don't trust justice as an ideal. It's more liable to be twisted than most any other cause I can think of, save perhaps religion."

"But you go to church," she said.

"That's on account of my sins," he said. "And the whole point of divine grace is that we don't get what we deserve. But do you see what I'm saying about justice? Give up on it, Erin. It's a bloody will o' the wisp. It'll lead you off the straight path into the swamp. It's only love will light your proper path."

"You should've been a poet, not a gangster," she said.

"I'm Irish," he said. "I've a wee bit of the poet in my blood, as have you."

"I thought that was just whiskey," she said.

"A bit of that, too," he said, smiling.

"I'm trying to save you," she said. "You know that, right?"

"Aye," he said. He was still smiling, but his eyes were soft. "And I'm grateful."

"Are you going to save me, too?"

The smile was gone. "If it takes the last drop of blood in my body," he said. "Or the last drop of whiskey in my pub."

It was Erin's turn to smile. "Let's hope it doesn't come to that," she said.

He held her and she let him. It felt good; better than she deserved. She kept thinking of Veronica's face. It might have been easier to bear if she'd liked the other woman, because then she wouldn't have the nagging feeling of doubt, the worry that she'd let Veronica die because she'd hated her. She thought of Maxwell, dying with Firelli's knife in his chest, and Janovich, dying to a stray, one-in-a-million bullet.

Erin made a silent promise to herself. No matter what happened, no matter whose life was in her hands next, she'd do her best to keep them alive. Not for their sake, but for her own. She'd still carry a gun, and use it if she had to, but only as what it was meant to be; the absolute last resort, the best bad choice.

Erin O'Reilly didn't think she was a hero, but she was never going to become a villain.

Here's a sneak peek from Book 20: White Lightning

Coming 6/26/2023

"I hate judges," Vic Neshenko said.

"I think you should tell Ferris that when we ask for the warrant," Erin O'Reilly replied. She squinted against the glare of the oncoming headlights on the Expressway. She spotted a momentary gap in the traffic and slipped her Charger sideways into the space, drawing an irritated honk from a New Yorker who felt she'd cut him off.

"I hate New York traffic, too," Vic said. "Doesn't that idiot know we're cops?"

"We're unmarked," she reminded him. The Charger was painted solid black and its flasher bar was low-profile, as befitting a detective's ride.

"And that was a legal lane change," he went on. "You had plenty of room. Hell, I could've parked a Suburban in that hole. I hate Staten Island."

"Maybe it'd be quicker to list the things you don't hate," she suggested.

Vic said nothing. Behind the driver's seat, in his special compartment, Rolf panted audibly. The German Shepherd loved car rides.

"Can't think of anything?" Erin asked after a moment.

"What? No, I'm already done," Vic said.

"You didn't say anything."

"Exactly."

Erin shook her head. "I shouldn't keep you up past your bedtime," she said. "You get grumpy."

"What are you talking about? It's not even ten o'clock. If it was late, we wouldn't be doing this. Anyway, you're the one who didn't want to wait until tomorrow. We could've done this nice and civilized, gone to see Ferris in his office."

"And let our guy knock over another café? No thanks," Erin said. "We were lucky nobody got killed last time. Next time might be different. This guy's a fatality waiting to happen."

"I'm just saying, it's a long drive," Vic grumbled.

"Would you have preferred the ferry? It goes straight to Saint George."

"No, I would not have preferred the ferry. I—"

"Hate ferries," Erin finished for him. "Why?"

"I get seasick."

"Really?"

"Well, I did once."

"Only once?"

"It's the sort of thing you remember. I've stayed off ferries since then."

Erin got off the Staten Island Expressway and headed north. "Quit bitching," she said. "We're this close to making an arrest. No time to waste."

"If Ferris had his fax machine turned on, we wouldn't have even needed to make the trip," Vic said, continuing to bitch. "I can't believe we're still using fax machines. Might as well saddle a horse and gallop the damn warrant over to him. He'd probably prefer that. I bet he switched it off on purpose."

"Could be a mechanical malfunction," Erin said. "Like you said, it's an old piece of technology."

"Yeah, but old stuff *works*," he said. "It's the new crap that breaks down all the time. That's why you still see fridges from 1965 or whenever, but the brand-new ones go on the fritz after a year or two. Hell, take Ferris himself. How long's he been riding the bench?"

"I have no idea," Erin said. "Forty or fifty years, I think."

"And it's not like he was fresh out of law school when they put a robe on him," Vic said. "Now he's gotta be eighty or ninety."

"At least," she agreed. "How close are we?"

Vic looked at the directions on his phone. "Almost there," he said. "You want Fort Hill Park. Take a left on Victory Boulevard, then hang a right on Daniel Low Terrace and take it to Fort Place. Man, this guy lives at the ass-end of nowhere."

"It's the closest part of Staten Island to Manhattan," she said. "And if we'd taken the ferry, like I said, we could've taken the shortest route and we'd already be there. I hope it was worth it to your stomach."

"I don't even care," he grumbled. "Let's just get this done and get back to civilization."

"You've got the paperwork, don't you?" Erin said.

"I've got the damn paperwork. Warrant to search the apartment of one Dylan White, suspected of multiple armed robberies. Want to see it?"

"I'm driving. Show it to Rolf."

"He can't read."

"So what? He'll pretend to care."

They finally pulled up to Judge Ferris's house. As Vic had complained, it was remarkably remote, set back on a little road in a small patch of woods. The house had a vaulted roof with a shape that reminded Erin of a converted barn. It was a big place for an old man living alone, but hardly a mansion. She parked in the driveway, behind a blue Prius.

"That seem right?" Vic wondered aloud as they climbed out of the Charger. "Ferris never struck me as a Toyota man."

"He's not," Erin said, pointing at a big, black Buick further up the driveway. "That must be his. I guess he's got company."

"High-class call girl," Vic predicted.

Erin rolled her eyes. "Because they all drive Priuses."

Light glowed behind the shades on the ground floor. Erin buzzed the doorbell, hoping they weren't interrupting anything important. She didn't believe Vic's theory for a second; Ferris might live alone, but he'd never have engaged a hooker even when he'd been young enough to make full use of one.

After a few moments, just as she was thinking about hitting the buzzer again, she heard the bolt slide back. Then the door opened to reveal Judge Ferris's white-haired face. His lips cracked into a smile.

"Good evening, Detectives," he said. "I wasn't expecting visitors."

"We tried calling, Your Honor," Erin said.

"Yes, of course," Ferris said. "I had a problem with my telephone line. A repairman for the telephone company was out just a little while ago, tinkering with things, but he wasn't able to fix it. He'll be back in a day or two."

"That explains the fax screwup," Vic said.

"Oh, yes, it would," Ferris said. "You've got a warrant for me to sign, I imagine. Something urgent, or you wouldn't be calling at my home so late on a weeknight."

"That's right," Erin said. "We're working a string of café robberies, and—"

"Where are my manners?" Ferris asked himself aloud. "Come in and sit down. You can spare a few minutes before the drive back, and I can offer you a little refreshment. Please, I insist."

He stepped back and, to Erin's surprise, slid something long and black into his umbrella stand.

"Judge Ferris?" she said, cautiously stepping over the threshold. "Did you just put a shotgun in with your umbrellas?"

"Mossberg International Silver Reserve Two," Ferris said proudly. "Twelve-gauge over-under hunting shotgun, one of the best on the market."

"Nice," Vic said, impressed. He knew just about everything about every firearm known to man. "Slug or buckshot?"

"Buck," Ferris said. "My eyesight isn't what it used to be, so I need to dispense the law with a generous spread."

"Do you always answer the door that way?" Erin asked.

"Usually," he said. "I am rather secluded here, and a judge with my length of service does, of necessity, leave a great many enemies in his wake. I've served long enough that some of the men I put away on life sentences have been paroled by now."

"Yeah, but they're old men, too," Vic said. "You really think anyone's gonna come gunning for you?"

"If I can still handle a long gun, so can they," Ferris said cheerfully. "Come into my parlor. I'm sorry it took so long to answer the door. Roy Bean would normally have alerted me to your presence. But he seems to have taken a slight turn. He's been sleeping soundly all evening. He seems quite comfortable, or I would have taken him to the veterinarian by now. How is your dog, Detective O'Reilly?"

"Rolf's good," Erin said. "I left him in the car. I didn't think we'd be long."

They entered the parlor, which was lit by a pair of lamps and a cheerful fire in the old stone fireplace. Erin stopped short.

A woman was sitting in one of Ferris's big leather armchairs in front of the fire.

"Oh," Erin said. "Excuse me, ma'am."

The woman got to her feet. She was a slender Latina who looked to be a few years older than Erin. Her hair was still pure black, without a hint of gray, but the fine lines at the corners of her eyes showed that she'd been around long enough to have seen some things. Her hair was cut in a professional style and her clothes were those of a well-to-do, well-educated woman. Her movements were practiced and confident. In her left hand was a glass containing a small quantity of clear liquid.

"Good evening," the woman said. "I don't believe we've met."

"Erin O'Reilly," Erin said, offering her hand. "I'm a detective with Major Crimes. This is my partner, Vic Neshenko."

"Judge Miranda Rodriguez," the woman said, shaking hands. She had a cool, firm grip.

"Pleased to meet you, Your Honor," Erin said. Another judge; that explained it. Ferris was hosting a colleague.

"Now, what can I get you?" Ferris asked.

"What do you recommend?" Erin asked. "I can't get too hammered; I need to drive back to Manhattan tonight."

"Howard was just sharing the fruits of his hobby with me," Rodriguez said, holding up the glass in her hand. "You should give it a try."

"What is it?" Vic asked. "Looks like vodka."

"White lightning," Ferris said with a chuckle. "Moonshine, just like my father made during the Depression. He ran a speakeasy, did you know that? Made his own bootleg liquor in the cellar."

"You've got a homemade still set up?" Erin asked, interested.

"Of course!" Ferris said. "I inherited my father's apparatus. An old man's hobby more than a source of revenue these days, I daresay, but I'm quite happy with the results. I'll pour you some. Half a moment."

He disappeared into the kitchen. Rodriguez smiled at the detectives. "It's really very good," she said. "It has a smoky sort of flavor. He ages it in wooden casks, just the way you're supposed to. Now, if you'll just excuse me a moment?"

"Of course," Erin said. Rodriguez walked down a short hallway, presumably to the restroom.

Ferris came out of the kitchen, holding a pair of glasses. He held them out to Erin and Vic.

"Enjoy," he said. "It's the original family recipe. You can imagine you're walking the beat back in the Thirties, trying to get the cuffs on Lucky Luciano and Albert Anastasia and all the rest of the original Mafiosi."

"I don't think I've met Judge Rodriguez before," Erin said.

"You wouldn't have," Ferris said. "She presides over corporate cases, primarily, not the sort of thing you folks in Major Crimes would encounter. But she's very good."

Erin caught the glint of pride in the old man's eye. "Have you known her a long time?" she asked.

"She clerked for me when she was out of law school," he said. "I suppose you could say I've been her mentor. A very bright young woman, one of the best lawyers I've ever known. A legal mind like—"

The lights flickered. A cry came from the hallway. It was a short exclamation, of surprise or possibly pain, abruptly cut off. Then there was a meaty thud, a sound that brought Erin's police instincts to sudden, screaming life.

Before she fully realized what she was doing, Erin was running for the hallway. Vic was only a step behind her. Ferris, bewildered, stood in the middle of his den, blinking at them.

A strange smell filled the air; a wild, sharp odor. Miranda Rodriguez lay on the carpeted floor, one hand outstretched, legs crumpled beneath her. The woman's eyes were wide, staring straight up at the ceiling. She lay absolutely still.

Ready for more?

Join the Clickworks Press email list
for the latest on new releases, upcoming books and
series, behind-the-scenes details, events, and more.

Be the first to know about new releases in the Erin
O'Reilly Mysteries by signing up at
clickworkspress.com/join/erin

About the Author

Steven Henry learned how to read almost before he learned how to walk. Ever since he began reading stories, he wanted to put his own on the page. He lives a very quiet and ordinary life in Minnesota with his wife and dog.

Also by Steven Henry

Fathers

A Modern Christmas Story

When you strip away everything else, what's left is the truth

Life taught Joe Davidson not to believe in miracles. A blue-collar woodworker, Joe is trying to build a future. His father drank himself to death and his mother succumbed to cancer, leaving a broken, struggling family. He and his brother and sisters are faced with failed marriages, growing pains, and lingering trauma.

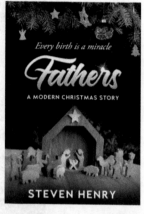

Then a chance meeting at his local diner brings Mary Elizabeth Reynolds into his life. Suddenly, Joe finds himself reaching for something more, a dream of happiness. The wood-worker and the poor girl from a trailer park connect and fall in love, and for a little while, everything is right with their world.

But suddenly Joe is confronted with a situation he never imagined. What do you do if your fiancée is expecting a child you know isn't yours? Torn between betrayal and love, trying to do the right thing when nothing seems right anymore, Joe has to strip life down to its truth and learn that, in spite of the pain, love can be the greatest miracle of all.

Learn more at clickworkspress.com/fathers.

Ember of Dreams

The Clarion Chronicles, Book One

When magic awakens a long-forgotten folk, a noble lady, a young apprentice, and a solitary blacksmith band together to prevent war and seek understanding between humans and elves.

Lady Kristyn Tremayne – An otherwise unremarkable young lady's open heart and inquisitive mind reveal a hidden world of magic.

Robert Blackford – A humble harp maker's apprentice dreams of being a hero.

Master Gabriel Zane – A master blacksmith's pursuit of perfection leads him to craft an enchanted sword, drawing him out of his isolation and far from his cozy home.

Lord Luthor Carnarvon – A lonely nobleman with a dark past has won the heart of Kristyn's mother, but at what cost?

Readers love *Ember of Dreams*

"The more I got to know the characters, the more I liked them. The female lead in particular is a treat to accompany on her journey from ordinary to extraordinary."

"The author's deep understanding of his protagonists' motivations and keen eye for psychological detail make Robert and his companions a likable and memorable cast."

Learn more at tinyurl.com/emberofdreams.

More great titles from Clickworks Press

www.clickworkspress.com

The Altered Wake
Megan Morgan

Amid growing unrest, a family secret and an ancient laboratory unleash long-hidden superhuman abilities. Now newly-promoted Sentinel Cameron Kardell must chase down a rogue superhuman who holds the key to the powers' origin: the greatest threat Cotarion has seen in centuries – and Cam's best friend.

"Incredible. Starts out gripping and keeps getting better."

Learn more at clickworkspress.com/sentinel1.

Hubris Towers: The Complete First Season
Ben Y. Faroe & Bill Hoard

Comedy of manners meets comedy of errors in a new series for fans of Fawlty Towers and P. G. Wodehouse.

"So funny and endearing"

"Had me laughing so hard that I had to put it down to catch my breath"

"Astoundingly, outrageously funny!"

Learn more at clickworkspress.com/hts01.

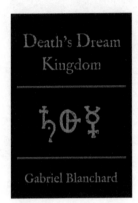

Death's Dream Kingdom
Gabriel Blanchard

A young woman of Victorian London has been transformed into a vampire. Can she survive the world of the immortal dead— or perhaps, escape it?

"The wit and humor are as Victorian as the setting... a winsomely vulnerable and tremendously crafted work of art."

"A dramatic, engaging novel which explores themes of death, love, damnation, and redemption."

Learn more at clickworkspress.com/ddk.

Share the love!

Join our microlending team at
kiva.org/team/clickworkspress.

Keep in touch!

Join the Clickworks Press email list
and get freebies, production updates, special deals,
behind-the-scenes sneak peeks, and more.

Sign up today at clickworkspress.com/join.